D0205704

It was in a proverbial locked room that Wolfe Quinlan died. They found him in his study, the only key in his pocket, and a suit of medieval armor over him, its sharp broadsword thrust through his ribs.

He had been a man who loved life and took what he wanted from it, a man with many enemies. On the night of his death, Wolfe Quinlan had angered everyone in his life—his abused wife, his alienated children, the mistress he refused to see, the business partner he had cuckolded, his not-too-honest lawyer, the mad priest whose "devil worship" cult Wolfe had violently disavowed.

Under Blackie Ryan's mild questioning, each will tell his or her story—and in these tales of twisted passions the priest will seek the clue to Wolfe Quinlan's death.

**Find it he must . . .
if no one else is to die.**

Also by Andrew M. Greeley

Nonfiction

The Making of the Popes 1978
The Politics of Intrigue in the Vatican

Fiction

The Cardinal Sins
The Magic Cup

THE PASSOVER TRILOGY
Thy Brother's Wife
Ascent into Hell
Lord of the Dance

TIME BETWEEN THE STARS
Virgin and Martyr
Angels of September

HAPPY ARE THE MEEK

A BLACKIE RYAN STORY

Andrew M. Greeley

WARNER BOOKS

A Warner Communications Company

For Nat and Judith

Monsignor John Blackwood Ryan, Ph.D., is far too wise and far too gentle to be like any existing rector of Holy Name Cathedral. Cardinal Sean Cronin has too much integrity and courage to be like any existing Archbishop of Chicago. All the other characters in the book, Ryan clan or not, are imaginary, fictitious, made-up, and otherwise products of my fantasy. Anyone thinking otherwise is wrong, that's all.

WARNER BOOKS EDITION

Cover illustration by Sean MacManus
Cover design by Jackie Merri Meyer
Floor plan by Heidi Hornaday

Warner Books, Inc.
666 Fifth Avenue
New York, N.Y. 10103

W A Warner Communications Company

Printed in the United States of America

First Printing: September, 1985

10 9 8 7 6 5

——THE BEATITUDES——

This series of stories, featuring Reverend Monsignor John Blackwood Ryan S.T.L., Ph.D., will be based on the Beatitudes from Jesus's Sermon on the Mount. A variant form is found in Luke's so-called Sermon on the Plain, which is accompanied by parallel Woes. I choose Matthew's version, which is probably later and derivative, because it is so much better known.

The Sermon on the Mount is not, according to the scripture scholars, an actual sermon Jesus preached but rather a compendium of His sayings and teachings edited by the author of St. Matthew's Gospel, almost certainly from a preexisting source compendium.

The Beatitudes represent, if not in exact words, an important component of the teachings of Jesus, but they should not be interpreted as a new list of rules. Jesus came to teach that rules are of little use in our relationship with God. We do not constrain God's love by keeping rules, since that love is a freely given starting point of our relationship (a passionate love affair) with God. We may keep rules because all communities need rules to stay together and because as ethical beings we should behave ethically, but that, according to Jesus, is a minor part of our relationship with God.

Nonetheless, some Christians, early on, went back to the rule game. Often religion came to be pictured as a sort of contract: we keep rules, and God keeps His promise to us—much like giving a professor back in our tests the material we have transferred from his notebook to our notebook.

In such a framework the Beatitudes were converted into new rules, much tougher than those revealed on Sinai. All right, some Christians said, ours is a much tougher religion. Since Catholicism had the toughest rules, it was the best of the Christian religions, the Marines of Christianity.

Jesus and the Father, one might imagine, are not amused.

In fact, the Beatitudes are descriptive, not normative. They are a portrait of the Christian life as it becomes possible for those who believe in the Love of God as disclosed by Jesus. If we trust in God, we are then able to take the risks the Beatitudes imply, never living them perfectly, of course, but growing and developing in their radiant goodness and experiencing the happiness of life that comes from such goodness.

Monsignor Ryan's explanation of "meekness" in the course of my story is that commonly taught by scripture scholars at the present time. Note that the principal characters of the story begin, however tentatively, to embrace the practice of such meekness only after they have experienced through one another a touch of God's passionate and implacable love.

AMG
Grand Beach
The End of Summer, 1984

Why comes temptation, but for man to meet,
And master and make crouch beneath his foot,
and so be pedestaled in triumph?

—Robert Browning
The Ring and the Book

Glimmerings are what the soul's composed of
Fogged up challenges, far-conscience glitters
and hang-dog, half truth earnests of true love
And a whole late-flooding thaw of ancestors.

—Seamus Heaney
"Old Pewter"

What is all this love for if we go out into the dark?

—M. R. James

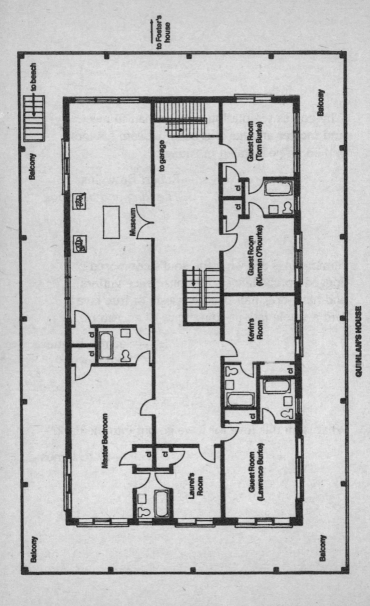

1

BLACKIE

Call me Blackie.

"The problem, Monsignor"—Lawrence Frances Xavier Burke ignored my instruction; his smooth, reasonable voice purred on, as if he were trying to explain to me a complex tax shelter—"is that Mrs. Quinlan has evidence that her husband's ghost haunts the house. Because he was denied Christian burial, you see."

"Ah."

In fact, my first sentence is misleading. It conjures up Melville and the Black Prince and Chester Morris playing Boston Blackie on late night (very late) cable films and the Black Knight and the Black Horde. Or perhaps Black Bart or maybe even the Black Death. Or even Chicago's historic Black Horse Troop.

"He was denied Christian burial because he was part of a devil-worship cult."

Cardinal Sean Cronin, from whom I take my orders, had observed before Burke arrived for his appointment that the Quinlan problem was right down my alley. I believe, in fact, he added with an unacceptable glint of amusement in his Celtic warrior's brown eyes, that as far as he could recall I'd never tangled with a classic locked-room puzzle before.

"Indeed," I said to Larry Burke.

Actually, I am the most innocuous and least romantic of men. You could enter an elevator I was riding and not even notice I was there. Indeed, often I am the little man who wasn't there. Occasionally even I manage to be not there again today. My siblings' offspring claim that I deliberately cultivate the appearance of G. K. Chesterton's Father Brown. One of their parents, my sister, Mary Kate (the distinguished psychoanalyst, of whom you've doubtless heard), comes closer to the truth when she says, "The Punk [a normally affectionate diminutive to which she is addicted] was born with the persona and cultivated the personality to fit it."

"You should approach the Diocese of Gary about an exorcism," I said cautiously. My Lord Cronin, Cardinal Archbishop of Chicago and the personage who had sent Lawrence F. X. Burke to my office, does not hold with the occult. Therefore he sends any stray manifestations of it to me so that I may, to use his neologism, "deoccult" it. "See to it, Blackie," he will say, his Doc Holliday brown eyes flashing dangerously. "And for the love of heaven keep it out of the press."

You'd be surprised at how many bleeding statues stop bleeding in my office in Holy Name Cathedral Rectory.

"Mrs. Quinlan does not want an exorcism, Monsignor. She wants a Christian burial and Masses said for her husband's soul."

Suzie (never Susan or Suzanne, nor Sue, for that matter) Wade Quinlan is one of the memorable fluffheads of our era. Not totally unattractive, mind you, until she opens her mouth. Pink cotton candy at a circus.

"And what do you want, Mr. Burke?"

His thin lips had tightened and his hard blue eyes turned harder at the mention of her name, making his square solid face look hungry. Not love, not by a long shot, but desire, lust as powerful as his massive body and his equally massive mind. An obsession of the sort to which strong-minded, high-principled men are prone. Particularly when their sex life has languished. An anchorite walking through a red-light district after twenty years in the desert.

How could anyone feel lust like that for Suzie Wade? Well, you don't have to talk in bed, I suppose.

"I want the Church's help in straightening out the mess in the Quinlan family's life. That does not seem such an unreasonable request, does it, Monsignor?"

Larry Burke looked like an aging, but well-maintained tackle from the days when you could play that position in the NFL at two hundred pounds. Broad shoulders, massive chest, thick arms, all fitted into a tailor-made dark blue suit; bushy, prematurely white hair contrasting with dark skin that hinted of an Armada survivor; low forehead, solid jaw—he might have been a leftover Irish hit man for the Outfit or a security agent at an elite hotel or a vice-president in the Teamsters union. Only a quick, infectious, precinct-captain smile saved him from looking like a thug.

In fact, he had never played football. Moreover, he worked with his brain, not his muscles. He was reputed to be one of the best investment managers in Chicago and a man of impeccable integrity, almost too much integrity, according to my sources. "Larry Burke's so damned honest that you'd think he was a Protestant."

"From their investment manager?" I flicked a pile of dust from my desk, striking a feeble blow in the losing battle of cosmos against chaos that rages in my office.

His huge paws, appropriate for a bartender or a bouncer in an old Irish saloon in Bridgeport, tightened around each other.

"The clergy don't have a monopoly on altruism, Monsignor." His grin, quick, diffident, and genial, saved him from the manner of the boss of a gang of prison guards. "Someone has to take care of them. I happen to be there."

"Why not come to your pastor directly instead of going through the Cardinal?"

I knew the answer to that question, of course. But I wanted to hear him say it.

"I haven't been around at Mass all that much since my son and I moved into the Water Tower"—he continued to grin—"and where I grew up you always approached someone indirectly."

"Ah. Through a Cardinal when one is available."

He shrugged his shoulders. The man was not without charm. A change for Suzie No Brain. Perhaps I was being too harsh. Wolfe Tone Quinlan was reputed to be a nice young man a long time ago. Long before he was found with a medieval broadsword sticking out of his stomach.

"Why not?"

"Angry at God, Mr. Burke?"

His grin faded. "What does that have to do with the Quinlan case, Monsignor?" His eyes flashed dangerously.

I did not need my sister's training in psychotherapy to judge that Lawrence F. X. Burke was an emotional mess, a mixture of altruism, guilt, and lust. Expiate and bed the woman at the same time.

And then get into the same problem all over again.

I sighed my carefully cultivated West of Ireland sigh. "I am, after all, your pastor."

His shoulders sagged; the vigorous man in his early fifties instantly became a battered and empty hulk. "Yes, Father Blackie." His sigh was authentic. "I'm angry at God. I can't give that up."

Doubtless Fly Weight Suzie was also angry at God in her own babbling fashion. And, it seemed to me, with considerably more reason. A pair of angry, guilt-ridden naifs. Two of the meek, though not in the sense St. Matthew uses the word, blundering toward self-immolation.

As my mother, Kate Collins Ryan (God be good to her!) would have said, the Lord made them and the devil matched them.

"My own theology"—I piled up the old baptismal books on my desk because that seemed to be the sort of thing Monsignors ought to do—"does not require that

God be blamed. Like George Burns in that splendid film, God tries. In any case, consider the situation: You are preoccupied with the problems in the Quinlan household. You encounter My Lord Cronin, perhaps on one of those boards on which you both sit to conspire to do good and explain your problem. He is not exactly delighted at the prospect of digging up the late Wolfe Tone Quinlan's body and reburying it in consecrated ground to put that worthy's shade to rest, but he tells you that it sounds like a case for the aforementioned Monsignor Ryan."

Larry Burke had turned a sheepish pink. Hard-headed, high-minded guardian of other people's funds, he was nonetheless capable of boyish charm. Suzie probably hadn't seen much of that from her husband for a long time before his interaction with the broadsword. "I suppose I should have come directly to you."

(My Lord Cronin actually found the matter mildly amusing. "I can see the glint in your eyes already," he chortled over his Jameson's, straight up—from my supply, of course.)

"Should a west side Irishman of your generation do anything directly," I said to Larry Burke, folding my hands piously, as Monsignors used to do in the old days, "it would be necessary to check with the Lincoln Park Zoo to determine whether leopards are indeed changing their spots this week. But the point at issue, Larry, which you seem to have missed, is what's in this for the poor man's Father Brown?"

"I could make a contribution..." He reached inside his jacket for his checkbook.

I rolled my pathetically near-sighted eyes in my typical gesture of despair at the folly of humankind.

"I see your point." He abandoned the checkbook. "You help the Quinlans and I return to Church?"

I spread my hands on the desk. "An interesting proposition..."

"I don't have to stop being angry at God?"

"A matter between you and Her in which I would not dream of being involved."

"And that doesn't mean I must go to confession?"

"Of course not." I did not tell him that the most he could accomplish between sweaty sheets with my former fellow parishioner La Suzie, should he finally manage to achieve such a position, was a minor venial sin.

"You have a deal, Monsignor." He extended his vast right hand.

Nor did I tell him that all I had done was to offer an excuse for a return to Church, which the better part of him deeply desired anyway.

We monsignors have our ways.

"You realize that you run the risk of opening up the question of whether Mr. Quinlan was murdered?" I asked lightly as I walked with him to the lobby of our gloomy rectory.

"I don't see why," he bridled. "The coroner's verdict was accidental death. The police were pulled off the case last week."

Wolfe Quinlan had died on July 4. It was now August 7. A three-week investigation. Enough time to do all the routine work and conclude that you'd come to a dead end. There had to be cops somewhere—Long Beach, LaPorte, Michigan City, Chicago—who were not satisfied. But homicide units were notoriously overworked. You spend your time on what you can do.

"Are you satisfied with that?" I held open the door for him, tempting him with the bright clarity of Wabash Avenue.

"No, not altogether." He shook his head in discouragement. "There's something wrong in that family, Monsignor. Terribly wrong."

There was no obvious reason why a man who might have been the author of what was wrong would want to reopen the case.

Unless he was convinced that it would not stay closed and wanted to shift suspicion in another direction—toward a paramour with whom he was not satisfied, for example.

Properly pushed, Larry Burke might very well shove a sword into a rival's gut.

Then have second thoughts when the woman proved not to be worth all the fuss.

I explained to him how I normally work. The various involved susp—uh, people come to my office or my parlor and tell me their stories. I piece together what they say and what I hear them saying between the lines and flesh out their story, much as did Robert Browning in *The Ring and the Book,* adding some description of my own to their perhaps overly restrained account. Sometimes I speculate on paper as to what might have happened in parts of the story that none of the witnesses have told me—in italicized sections with which my sister Nancy Ryan O'Connor, the SF writer (who deplores my poverty of imagination), collaborates.

Then I draw a conclusion. Perhaps.

When necessary to tie up a story, I may reconstruct, in italicized scenes, events that unfold in the course of the investigation to which I was not actually privy.

I administer, badly, I admit, a large and variegated parish. I cannot be expected to depart from it, even for haunted houses. (Well, I might make an exception for a haunted house.) When a problem absolutely requires travel, I engage in it, though reluctantly. Many years ago Nick Curran and I went on what seemed to be a wild-goose chase to Mobile, Alabama. This past summer I ventured to Ireland in a bootless pursuit of my suddenly manic cousin Brendan Ryan. My principles, therefore, do not exclude travel. They merely inhibit it.

No man without a wife should be constrained to pack a bag for travel.

Larry Burke suggested I read the press clippings on the allegedly accidental death of Wolfe Tone Quinlan— I had been in Ireland with Brendan in early July when the case exploded—and then interview him, perhaps tomorrow.

As he walked briskly south toward his cave high above the LaSalle Street canyon, I concluded that he had yet to possess himself of poor addle-brained Suzie. Admirable if needless restraint. From the first day of her existence the woman had been trained for submission.

Back in my office, I searched for the telephone, discovered it under yesterday's mail, and punched the Cardinal's number.

"Cronin," he said, sounding like an overpaid anchorman on the five o'clock news.

"Consider the plight of womankind," I said, continuing my thought about Suzie.

"An invitation that appears in half my mail." He did not seem enthusiastic about my suggestion.

"They are designed to be compellingly attractive to us, if only so as to strengthen the bond between male and female. Our species is blessed, as are most higher primates, with a sufficient dimorphism to make them on the average not as strong as us. Moreover, it is arguable that they are less aggressive on the average than we are..."

"Nicer too," he interjected.

"In addition"—I ignored the irrelevant, though incontestable interruption—"since they are further designed to bear and nurse offspring, they are even more at a physical disadvantage with regard to us. Hence, if one is to believe that admirable French sociologist Michel Foucault, God be good to him..."

"Does God admit sociologists?"

"...men have oppressed women in every society the world has ever known, a situation that is thoroughly unsatisfactory from a woman's viewpoint and, if the truth is told, less than rewarding for a man too."

"Ah," he said, mocking me.

"For while it may be advantageous and amusing to push them around and collect them like jewels or cattle, they are only fully rewarding when they are treated like equals."

"A woman was worth four head of cattle in ancient Ireland."

"A high market price compared to that in other ancient countries. In any case, you know the rape, wife-beating, forced incest, and child abuse statistics. All of this has gone on too long, my lord, it must stop."

"The Quinlan woman was battered by her husband?"

"As sure as the sun rises in the morning. To be human is to walk through life under the dismal shadow of terror. For women the shadow is both darker and closer. Even in our so-called civilized world, it lurks behind them, always threatening, like a dark, evil bird; a stranger, a friend, a madman, a father, even a husband, can hurt and humiliate them as a matter of male right. A stroll fifty yards down the beach at night may become a walk into hell. A few serial rapists who get special kicks out of last-minute decisions whether to kill their victims can terrorize all the women in a city. Your Polish friend in Rome does not help when he says they can't be priests."

I had warmed to my subject. Fluffhead or not, Republican or not, Suzie Wade was from the Neighorhood. She was one of our own, a pretty eighth-grade girl who had crowned the Blessed Mother when I was in fifth grade. How dare some son of a bitch beat her up?

"I knew there was a point to that lecture; this man Burke will push her around too?"

"Maybe."

"Don't let him." I could imagine his eyes flaring with anger.

"What if she wants to be pushed around?"

"Regardless. As you said, it must stop."

"Yes, my lord."

Thus do I inform him that I will take the case he has forced upon me. I also made a mental note to use the same lecture with Lawrence F. X. Burke when he returned. It would be useful to create a little dissonance in his attitudes toward the delectable Suzie. Perhaps he might be given pause if he wondered whether his obsession with her was the result of her in effect begging for someone else to force her to submit.

"You say the woman is an airhead?"

"*Fluffhead* was my word."

"Regardless. Don't let her be hurt anymore. See to it, Blackie."

I sighed in obedience. Mostly feigned obedience. I will admit that the locked-room puzzle did have some minor attraction for my curiosity.

It would have, in fact, required several angry archangels to keep me away from it.

Neither the Cardinal nor Lawrence F. X. Burke nor I realized how much Suzie Quinlan had endured the immemorially unjust cruelty to womankind.

Or how much more she would have to endure.

2

BLACKIE

In the basement of the Reilly Gallery, Mike Casey, one of what often seems to be an infinite number of Ryan cousins, was studiously copying on canvas a Polaroid picture of a *supermercado* in Pilsen. Annie, his new wife, voted last year one of the fifteen most beautiful "older women" in Chicago (with ample justification, I might add), refilled my cup of apple cinnamon tea.

Like most women, Annie finds my bumbling, near-sighted incompetence "cute." She is also amused by my admiration of her charm. Most women I admire (and there are many) are hardly aware of it. Annie is not to be deceived and immoderately enjoys being mildly flirtatious with her pastor. Not that I mind, heaven knows. One of the rewards of growing older (just past forty) is that you become aware of how many more beautiful women there are in the world than you had noticed at twenty. Annie is more than a decade older than I am and she still unnerves me. Perhaps, I thought ruefully, so would Suzie Wade Quinlan, whom I had not seen in many years.

I doubted it. If you are a celibate and do not plan to go

to bed with a woman, her conversation takes on a certain importance. If Suzie Wade could put together three consecutive sentences, it would surprise me.

"You have Larry Burke cold." He dabbed more vermilion on the supermarket, miraculously, it seemed to me, transforming it into something sad and yet archetypal. "Smart, a bit of a hard head, straight arrow, strict on everyone including himself. He was a couple of years behind me at St. Ursula."

"A possible killer?"

Mike's brush paused in mid-air. "In a good cause, sure."

Mike is a lean, tall man with thin silver hair, looking more like an abbot of a Benedictine monastery than a retired deputy superintendent of police. He is the author of two very sensible books on detective procedure and once turned down the job of police commissioner in New York City, excellent qualifications, as Annie remarked, for him to be my occasional Watson and Lestrade combined.

He was forced out of the Chicago Police Department because of racial politics (what's the point in winning an election unless you can make one of your own head of the cops, regardless of how good the acting superintendent may be?). He makes a lot more money with his painting and still affects most of the big decisions in the police department as a "consultant" ("What do we do now, Mike?").

"Ah."

"Do you think he disemboweled Wolfe Quinlan?"

"Not necessarily. And Father Armande and the Church of the Angels of Light?"

"Thought you'd ask that." Mike wiped paint off his fingers, dutifully accepted a cup of herbal from his wife, and opened a notebook. "Father Armande really is a priest. From New England. His name, however, is not Armande de St. Cyr but Louis Connery and he was ejected from his own diocese about ten years ago because the bishop didn't like the stipends he was charging for working miracles."

"Indeed."

"His church is in Hyde Park. Find me something crazy and it will be close to the University of Chicago, saving your reverence, Doctor Monsignor." He winked wickedly. "An old home on Fifty-seventh Street, east of Dorchester, fixed up with altars and torch holders and pentagrams and secret rooms. Mostly a rehash of the work of Alastair Crowley, of which I'm sure you're familiar."

"I am. Alas, those who join it have probably never heard of the good Mr. Crowley."

"Good is your word, not mine. Anyway, he has attracted a fair crowd of misfits, all of them rich. Many 'spontaneously' give the 'Church' their money, like Wolfe Quinlan tried to do. Two older donors, both women"—he glanced at me with a frown—"died suddenly. Of natural causes, as far as we know. Both suburbanites, so out of our jurisdiction at the time of death. Nevertheless, especially after the Quinlan death, the Department has been keeping a close watch on him. There is a hint that one of the women might have been poisoned, a Mrs. Carson Long. Her maid disappeared after the funeral and both the Wilmette and Chicago departments are looking for her."

"Bad business."

"Terrible," the lovely Annie agreed.

"Do you think he did Quinlan in?" Mike closed his notebook.

"There are twenty people who saw him at the Church of the Angels of Light the night someone stuck the blade in Quinlan's gut. One of their all-night vigils."

"Could they have been hypnotized or doped?" Annie plugged the electric tea kettle back in.

"Not the University of Chicago cop who was parked outside in a squad, keeping an eye on the proceedings so that nothing would happen to the students who belong to the church."

"So he could only have filleted Quinlan if he could bilocate?" Mike asked.

"Which he claims he can do. Do your colleagues think he is sincere?"

"Was Crowley? Of course, my former colleagues have never heard of Alastair Crowley. But the man from the fraud squad I talked to said that Father Armande isn't a complete fake."

"Delightful. Yes, of course, Annie. When all else fails there is always apple cinnamon tea."

"You want to help them, don't you, Monsignor, I mean Blackie?"

Even though she was now a member of our family, the sometime Anne Marie O'Brien had a hard time forcing herself to call her pastor by his right name.

I took off my glasses and endeavored to polish them with the sleeve of my clerical shirt. "They are both vincibly innocent," I insisted. "One a fluffhead, the other a scrup. They have blundered through life convinced that if you do the right thing, nothing wrong will happen. How can you help the pseudomeek?"

"Won't the meek inherit the earth?" She removed my glasses gently from my fingers and began to polish them with a tissue.

"Not that kind of meek. Saint Matthew meant those who are in harmony with the processes of life, not those who try to suppress the processes with sweetness or compulsive responsibility. The French translate the word *débonnaire*. I suppose teenagers like The Cat or Packy Jack would say 'cool.' Debonair or cool Suzie Quinlan and Larry Burke are not."

The Cat is my sister Nancy O'Connor's daughter, lifeguard this summer at Grand Beach. The name is possibly a contraction of Kathleen or maybe Catherine. Even though I baptized the child sixteen years ago, I'm not sure what her name was, since she has always been The Cat.

"How do you know she's a fluffhead?" Annie produced a spray bottle from somewhere and gave my glasses their first good cleaning of the week. I resolved that I must drop by every week.

"She was ahead of me in school at St. Prax's. The year behind Eileen."

"Eileen thinks she's a fluffhead?" She placed the

glasses back on my head.

"Eileen says she's a poor dear woman. It means the same thing."

"Even God can't help them?" She smiled that superior smile that Irish women produce when they know they're right—which is 99 percent of the time.

I grunted without conviction and adjusted the temples of my glasses. That, of course, was the point. Larry Burke and Suzie Quinlan had been set from the beginning of their lives on a course of blundering from disaster to disaster. In all likelihood they would continue to blunder.

But God, the fellow pilgrim who suffers with us, to quote Professor Whitehead, might be preparing a fast pitch. And it looked like I had bumbled into being the catcher. The Jody Davis of their lives to reflect on the Cubs again.

Or maybe only the umpire.

Hope only makes sense when the situation is hopeless.

"Sister Hilaire"—Mike was dabbing at his painting again—"his assistant—read *mistress*—never was a nun; some experience in Providence as a madam, however. It's a bad scene, Blackie. Be careful. They're even more dangerous when they really believe the stuff they preach."

"That's true of all clergy." Annie kissed my forehead as I prepared to leave. "Isn't it?"

"Indeed."

Outside a blue sky hung benignly over the Magnificent Mile, pretending that the lovely old 900 North Michigan building, one of the landmarks of my parish, was not collapsing under a wrecking ball.

Ah, well, it was August and the Cubs were four and a half games ahead of the Mets. Who could expect everything?

Trust poor Suzie Wade, with her 4.0 average all through high school, to become involved with a man who really believed that he was a high priest of Lucifer, the sometime head of the angels of light.

3

BLACKIE

The Long Beach Police, I decided, pushing aside the clippings Larry Burke had left for my perusal, were a thoroughly modern, professional small-town police force.

That meant that they had some skill in harassing teenage beer consumers on the beach at night, but were of no use whatsoever in a murder case.

And the State Police were precious little better.

Wolfe Tone Quinlan had gone to his eternal reward on the night of Wednesday, July 4, in the locked study of his 1920 imitation Swiss chalet home on the shore of Lake Michigan, surrounded by his stamps, his coins, his precious stones, his daggers, his nude statues, and his suits of late medieval armor.

He was protected in the room by a specially made set of locks, the same one on each of the three doors—one from the corridor, one from a balcony overlooking the lake, and one from a bathroom that connected to the master bedroom he shared with his wife. There was but one key for all three doors, and after it had been made the plate from which copies could be constructed was smashed. If you wanted a new key (having perhaps lost the old), you bought new locks for all three doors.

The locks were double tumblers—they had to be opened and locked on either side by a key. But they were not dead-bolt locks. Thus, Wolfe Quinlan could open the door to his study, lock it from the inside while it was still open, walk into the study, close the door, and it would lock behind him. If he wanted to be undisturbed while he was working—as was usually the case—he would lock the doors and keep out the world. He could also gain access to his marital bedroom from the study, but his wife, lacking a key, could not enter that room without his consent. Nor could she, as far as that went, lock him out of the bedroom.

Not unless she had a locksmith replace the lock with a new one for which two keys had been made and then slipped one of them on her husband's key ring.

Was Suzie Wade, May-crowning heroine and fluffhead with a 4.0 average, capable of such trickery?

Not very likely. But had the Long Beach gendarmes, preoccupied as they were with their responsibility to keep beer-swilling teenage males off the beach, been intelligent enough to check the possibility?

The broadsword of one of the suits of armor, which had frequently tilted forward when winds rattled the house, had pierced his left lung. By the time his houseguests, Lawrence F. X. Burke, Burke's son Thomas, age eighteen, and Quinlan's lawyer, Kiernan O'Rourke, had broken down the door, Quinlan was dead from loss of blood. Since Mr. Quinlan had been drinking and since no one could enter his room (which locked from the inside), it was assumed that his death was either suicide or accidental. In the absence of a suicide note, the police assumed that Quinlan's death was the result of a freak accident.

The suspects? to use a word that the press avoided.

Present in the house were Burke, Suzie Quinlan, the Quinlans' two surviving children—Laurel, age sixteen, and Kevin, age twenty—Tom Burke, and Kiernan O'Rourke.

Next door were Greg Foster, Quinlan's longtime business associate (president of Quinlan Furniture, of which Wolfe Quinlan was chairman of the board) and his wife, Melanie. The Fosters had eaten dinner earlier at the Quinlan home.

Also very much in view, and loving the publicity, were Father Armande and Sister Hilaire of the Church of the

Angels of Light, to whom Quinlan was about to turn over his controlling share of his internationally famous furniture company. And to whom he had left everything in his will.

Both Father Armande and Sister Hilaire were, it was said, at an all-night service in their church.

Eleven suspects, more or less, and a locked room to which no one had access. Fascinating.

Accidental death, the police had said. Fools!

It smelled of murder and both Larry Burke and I knew it, a clever, indeed a brilliant crime. Perhaps not altogether unjustified. Time would tell about that.

I examined the newspaper pictures of those involved. They were an interesting-looking crowd: Kevin, doing his best to demonstrate to the world that he was gay; Laurel, tall, lovely, vague like her mother and not at all clear what she was supposed to do with her newfound womanly attractiveness; Foster, an overweight, balding huckster; Melanie, trying, with inconspicuous success, to radiate early middle-age sex appeal. O'Rourke, your typical smooth, red-faced, overdressed, slightly shady Irish lawyer; Tom Burke, taller than his father, a promising freshman linebacker at Notre Dame; Sister Hilaire, an outsize tart in a white gown with a massive sun on her equally massive bust, an egg fried sunny-side up.

Most interesting of all, Father Armande, whose flowing white robes were augmented by a scarlet cloak, looked more like a cardinal than Sean Cronin himself. Snow-white hair, broad shoulders, lean face, piercing eyes, hands spread in a dramatic gesture that permitted the folds of the cloak to flow elegantly around his commandingly handsome body. In an earlier age he might have worked for the inquisition. Now he was the high priest of Lucifer, the Angel of Light.

Great.

I decided that I disliked him intensely whether he was sincere or not, probably because he looked so impressing and I look so ludicrous on those rare occasions when I don my purple monsignoral robes.

Some of us, as my brother Packy remarks, certainly

not with himself in mind, appear appropriately clad only in warm-up suits that are several sizes too large.

It did not follow, however, that merely because I disliked him on sight, the so-called Armande St. Cyr was the one who killed Wolfe Quinlan.

Mrs. Carson Long?

That was, for the moment, not my problem.

Keith Moreland pounded a line drive double between short and third, giving the Cubs another one-run victory over the Mets.

The age of miracles had, perhaps, not altogether passed.

"Father Ryan," I murmured into the phone, trying to sound the way incense smells. It had buzzed at the same time Moreland pounded the ball.

"Monsignor Blackie," the teenage receptionist responded, "Mr. Burke is calling."

I listened to Larry Burke's breathless and worried message.

"Quite the contrary, Lawrence," I said, feeling a chill that could not be attributed to my nonfunctioning air conditioner. "I think Laurel Quinlan's disappearance is a matter of immediate concern. I would not be surprised if she is in grave danger. It would be a serious mistake not to call the police. What? Yes, of course she may be in Chicago with a friend. Nonetheless there is a murderer in the picture and we are not sure whether he will strike again."

Burke blustered on the other end of the line.

"Yes, I said murderer," I cut him off. "You've known that all along, haven't you?"

Gently, as if pouring water on the head of an infant, I returned the phone to its cradle. Why did I warn him about a danger to the dreamy-eyed Laurel?

I am the least psychic of humans. I wouldn't know an ESP experience if it assaulted me on the street. Occasionally, however, I have hunches, the origins of which are obscure at the time.

That Laurel was in danger was one such presently unanalyzable hunch. There was another one in tandem with it. I called Burke back.

"You're not leaving Mrs. Quinlan up there alone, are you?" I demanded.

Like sending the spider to guard the fly. All Larry needed was an excuse. Regardless of what coupling might occur, better the woman coupled and alive rather than uncoupled and dead.

"I see your point, of course. Tommy and I will drive up this afternoon."

Lots of luck, Tommy.

4

LAWRENCE F. X. BURKE

I always envied Wolfe Quinlan.

Not for his wealth, because I have more money than he had. Not for his life-style, because I could live the way he did if I wished. Not for his wife, because, as strong as my desire for her is, I would not want her as a wife.

I envied him, rather, for the ease with which he glided through life. All that I had to work for he inherited— education, business, social grace, a head start in the race of life. I've told myself often that if I'd begun with his advantages I would have made much more of them.

It is an absurd assumption. Indeed, any comparison with others is absurd. One must evaluate oneself only in terms of one's own opportunities and responsibilities. I do not have an outstanding record in my own circumstances, why should I think that I would have performed more impressively in his?

So I dismissed my envious feelings advised him well

on his investments, accepted his friendship gratefully because he was often an attractive and charismatic man, made excuses for his obvious weaknesses, and stood by him in his trials and tragedies. I was closer to him than to any of my other clients, yet I never quite liked him. Now that he's gone I wonder if the sting of envy was more powerful than I realized. I wonder if I did not secretly rejoice in his problems. I wonder, indeed, whether if I had been more generously a friend to him, I might have saved him from the ultimate tragedy.

It is hard for me to be generous. The greatest failures of my life result from my lack of generosity—often when I find myself in situations in which I do not belong, sometimes situations into which I have plunged myself in an inept and misguided effort to be generous. Under that rubric I might possibly list my present relationship as helper and friend to Suzie Quinlan, save that I suspect that my motive is sexual hunger rather than generosity. Intense and acute sexual hunger.

I am not ungenerous with my money both to organized charities and my children. It is easy to give money away when you have enough of it. I am ungenerous with myself. If I were less tight-fisted with my own person, I would not have lost my wife; and I might have managed to save Wolfe Quinlan. In that sense I am responsible for his death. If I had not cursed him that July Fourth evening... but I anticipate my story.

I am six years older than he was at the time of his death; my consciousness, unlike his, stretches back to the years before the War, back into the dim horror of the Great Depression. Nothing I experienced in my childhood would predispose me to generosity or charm. At least I do not deceive myself: I am a badly flawed human being. Some of the parts were left out when my soul was put together.

My father was a bank teller, a dour and somber man whose promising career, to hear my mother tell it, was destroyed by the Depression. He would have certainly been a vice-president of the bank, she would say sadly, if it had not been for the "Crash." Had not Mr. Roberts himself taken an interest in his career? Unfortunately, Mr. Roberts jumped out of the window of his apartment at the Edgewater Beach on a lovely spring day in 1937 during an investigation by government auditors.

When my father died in 1957, not many years older than I am now, he was an assistant cashier, a man hailed by his colleagues as an exemplar of integrity and honesty.

"He wouldn't even take home a pencil that belonged to the bank," the senior vice-president told me at his wake.

Looking back on my childhood, I am no longer satisfied with the family myth that the "Crash" destroyed his career. He was in his early forties when the Depression turned into the War and the American economy exploded. If he never quite became an officer of the bank, the reason was not that he had bad luck but that grim, honest rigidity was not quite enough to succeed in the post-war world, as we called it then.

My mother, a tall, gaunt woman with thin lips and lovely hands, which she delighted in ruining in dishwater, worshiped at the altar of his integrity, lecturing us children frequently that we were fortunate indeed to have as a father one of the few honest men in the city.

God knows there were lots of crooks in St. Ursula's in those days, "some of them daily communicants," my mother would rage, but if there were other virtues besides integrity, we did not learn about them at home.

I suppose they loved each other. Yet I cannot remember a single instance when they kissed or embraced.

There was no smoking or drinking in our bungalow, no listening to the *Lone Ranger* or *Little Orphan Annie* or *Jack Armstrong*, no movies on Saturday afternoon. As the oldest, I was responsible for cutting the lawn, shopping at the Jewel store on Division Street (every penny accounted for so that I would not sneak into the Greek ice-cream parlor and waste precious money on milk shakes), replacing the storm windows with screens in the spring and vice versa in the fall, trimming the hedges, painting the window frames, emptying the gar-

bage cans, washing the kitchen and bathroom floors. I
began to deliver newspapers—pushing a yellow cart
through the streets of the neighborhood—when I was
nine and did so until I graduated from St. Mel's. When I
protested that it was unfair that my two brothers and
two sisters did not do their share of the work, my father
told me that the responsibility came with being the oldest.

That was that.

None of us was beaten. We feared his icy anger so
much that physical violence was unnecessary. I suppose we all hated him. I have tried to deal with my own
children more tolerantly, but I doubt that I have suc-
ceeded.

Tommy, my youngest, who may want to be a priest,
laughs at my anxieties. "You don't notice any of us leaving town, do you?"

My brothers and sisters, all of whom graduated from
college, paid for by money I brought into the home, left
the city, never to return, the year after graduation. I
hear from one sister, the one to whom I was the least
close, at Christmas.

There was no time for athletics in my school years.
Too much work to do in the house. Besides, sports were
for the rich, not for us poor but respectable people. I
was strong enough to play football, and the coach at St.
Mel's high school was dismayed at my refusal and in-
credulous at my explanation that I could not give up my
paper routes.

As you can imagine, I was not popular with my con-
temporaries. Indeed, I was a figure of fun with them,
doggedly shoving my cart through the snow or bravely
peddling my Catholic papers in back of Church on hot
summer Sundays.

It was made clear as soon as I went to high school
that college was out of the question for me. My parents
believed with profound conviction that "education" was
the key to success in life: law and medicine for the sons,
nursing and teaching for the daughters. Unlike other
Irish families of that era, however, they did not anoint

their firstborn son as crown prince. On the contrary, it was explained to me that, as the oldest, I had to share in my father's responsibility to educate the others. Such a responsibility, it was explained, was more important to my education than going to school. Perhaps eventually, when the others had graduated, I could go to night school.

I've often wondered whether my father hated me. He was a bald little man, whose red nose and round face might have seemed impish if he had smiled. As he rarely did, however, he looked like an angry hobgoblin. I was, even as an infant, strong and handsome, the object of endless admiration from women, who delighted in holding me in their arms.

Did he envy me as I came later to envy Wolfe Quinlan? Perhaps. More likely, however, whatever resentment he felt merely reinforced his principles: to be eldest meant the privilege of greater responsibility.

So the day after I graduated from St. Mel's in 1948, I went to work as a clerk in the office of John S. Sweeney, a friend of my father from Commodore Barry Knights of Columbus Council. Young people were singing "Buttons and Bows" and "I'll Dance at Your Wedding," according to the young woman who worked in our office, and if they were interested in serious films, as she was, seeing *Hamlet* and *Oliver Twist*. I had time for neither songs nor films. I was still responsible for my work at home— my father even hinted that if I were not so lazy, I would have continued my morning paper route. The only free time was on my ride downtown on the Lake Street Elevated and I used that to devour books on accounting and economics. I began the morning L ride in 1948 and ended it only last year, when Tommy and I moved into our bland apartment at Water Tower Place—more than thirty-five years.

Later I would turn to other reading to make up for not going to college. Gerry, our second child, who is doing graduate work in English, says I know more about novels than any of her teachers, but I think, like the others, she is more concerned about her father's morale than about the truth.

John S. Sweeney, in my father and mother's world view, was ranked only by the members of the Blessed Trinity. Even then it seemed strange to me that parents who so abhorred gambling could admire one of the great speculators of the age. A crusty, cynical little bachelor, pink-faced, egg bald, with thick glasses and a high-pitched whine for a voice, Sweeney came home from the War convinced that there would be an enormous economic boom. While most of his generation of Irish Catholics in the "investment" business expected a return to the Great Depression, Sweeney bet on a long-term bull market and won big.

"With all that money out there," he whined, his baby-blue eyes blinking, "they're going to buy and buy and buy. The market will go through the roof."

A simple statement of what would become an economic truism—pent-up demand and the money to fund it creates prosperity and inflation. Most economists didn't realize any better than did our neighbors in St. Ursula's how much money and how much demand were about to bubble up in the United States. John S. did and made a fortune. And I rode on his coattails to a modest beginning of my own fortune.

John S. was a much more complicated man than my father; he was harsh, demanding, arrogant, secretive, frequently nasty. On the other hand, he was also generous, sentimental, witty, and, on occasion, compassionate. He didn't need a clerk, I'm sure. His investment philosophy was that all you required was a small office, a secretary, the market returns, and a pencil and notebook. I was an apprentice more than a clerk and maybe a substitute son. Quite unnecessarily, he made me a partner the day Dorrie and I were married.

I think he was fond of me, even loved me, and wanted me to love him in return. I didn't know how. When he died eighteen years ago, I inherited his accounts and his philosophy (adding a computer to the pad and pencil). I still feel guilty because I let the poor man down.

I let Dorrie down even more.

I met her at night school in 1958, a young man in his late twenties who had never dated, and was instantly captivated by her laughter and wit. The daughter of a steamfitter's widow, Dorrie operated an elevator at Marshall Field's during the day and went to DePaul at Jackson and Wabash at night. After my father's death and over my mother's objections—there was now even more "work" to be done around the house—I enrolled in my first college course.

"You looked scared stiff," the slender brown-haired girl with the snapping eyes in the seat next to me said brightly. "It's only school."

Her plaid skirt and white sweater suggested enormous womanly energy. I was both terrified and enchanted.

"I haven't been in a classroom in ten years," I mumbled, trying not to gawk.

"Must have flunked out of grammar school," she said, laughing. "Don't worry, I'll whisper the answers in your ear."

I realized with an impact not unlike a collision with an L train that I needed and wanted a woman, indeed had needed and wanted one for a long time. I was a creep. How could I possibly attract this vivacious girl (all of nineteen, I learned over coffee after class)?

She was friendly toward me partly because it was fun and partly because she was intrigued, for reasons even now I don't quite comprehend. Our song, she informed me that night, was "Catch a Falling Star." I had indeed caught a falling star all right, but I didn't realize then that she was falling.

Looking back, I can see there were signs that might have given me warning if I had known anything about life and about women. Dorrie's moods oscillated rapidly and without any obvious reason. When she was not laughing she was crying. She was using tranquilizers at a time when they were not yet as popular as aspirin. When I would kiss her good night at the end of a date, she would often cling to me and weep, for no reason that she could give.

But I was young and in love and hungry for her body.

We married three months after my mother's death,
moved into a small home on Lathrop in St. Luke's parish
in River Forest, and campaigned for Kennedy and Johnson while she was expecting Mark, our oldest.

She had a severe postpartum depressive interlude after his birth. Confused and ignorant, I took seriously the
doctor's advice that we should wait for more children,
but not so seriously as to fight against Dorrie's determination that we should have a large family as soon as
possible and our priest's advice that we should trust in
God.

We produced Mark, Gerry, Eileen, and Tommy before
Johnson rolled over Goldwater in a referendum against
war. God didn't respond to our trust. Dorrie spent six
months in the best private mental hospital I could find
after Tommy's birth. The manic depressive cycle was in
full swing. As the doctor said when she was released, "I
wish I could tell you that it won't get worse, but. . ."

I had no idea what to do. Dorrie and I were happy and
content when she was well. Our sex life was perhaps
low-key; neither of us was a particularly good lover—I
would learn those skills in a later love affair after the
psychiatrists told me that Dorrie would spend the rest
of her life in an institution. But we didn't know any
better and enjoyed our common life and our children
enormously. I worked too hard, she spread herself out
too thin; we didn't take enough time off; we both pretended that a sentence of doom was not hanging over
our heads.

Then the depression would begin again.

Mark, who is in his third year at Loyola Medical and
wants to be a psychiatrist, tells me apodictically that
there was nothing we could have done, "in the present
state of our knowledge, at any rate."

I am tempted to reach for that escape hatch. Then I
realize how I permitted our precious years together to
slip through my fingers. We should have enjoyed more
vacations together. We should have had more dates in
the evenings. We should have spent more time talking.

I visit her once a month. She looks like a woman in

HAPPY ARE THE MEEK

27

her late sixties and does not recognize me or our children. The sparkling young woman with the fresh and
elegant little breasts and lively eyes, who promised to
whisper the answers in my ear in that English Lit course
at DePaul, has become a vegetable waiting to die.

Last May was our silver wedding anniversary.

I cannot absolve myself. Perhaps I could not have
forestalled the end. Perhaps. But I should have tried
harder. If God let me down, so too did I let Dorrie down.

Eileen, who is an avid theology student, suggests that
I should seek an annulment.

"And deny the love which was there for so long?" I
ask in horror. "And make all of you illegitimate?"

"It doesn't make us illegitimate," says the gamin-
faced young woman who looks terrifyingly like her
mother at the same age. "And it doesn't deny love either. All an annulment would do is help you to continue
with the challenge of your life. You don't want one because then you'd have to finally forgive yourself and
start living again."

Smart girl. The children, astonishingly enough, don't
blame me. But I blame myself.

I have no right to forgive myself. Nor do I want to
marry again. An occasional jarring sexual affair with
someone who no more expects a sustained relationship
than I do is fine. Not the responsibility of married love,
never again.

Gerry says that I should be thankful for the love that
was. "Mom and you were terribly happy," she tells me.
"You crowded more love into a few years than most
people would in twice as much time. Don't you believe
that God wants you to be happy ever again?"

All the kids are deeply religious, more so than I ever
was.

"I don't want to hear about God," I reply lamely.

This is a lot of background, Monsignor. But if you are
to understand why I might have wanted to kill Wolfe
Tone Quinlan and why I am so deeply involved in his
family, you must realize what a convoluted mess of fear
and guilt and responsibility and tight-fisted caution I

am.

Despite the caution, I am afraid that I have blundered into a worse mistake and with even less excuse for my irresponsibility.

—————————— 5 ——————————

LAWRENCE F. X. BURKE

The first time I met Wolfe Quinlan's wife, at a weekend house party in their curiously grim house at Long Beach, I was stung, almost instantly, by a sharp pang of—there is no other word for it—lust. It was as surprising and as painful as stepping on a sharp stone while walking on the beach; the knife-like agony rushed through my whole body.

It is, I suppose, part of the ordinary experience of life that one meets another man's spouse, is immediately possessed by the transient fantasy of screwing her (I use the word because the reaction is almost entirely physical), recovers one's balance rather precariously, and then takes great care in future relations with the woman.

In our religious and ethnic group, at any rate, you do not even think about actually taking her to bed. Or, to be more precise, dragging her off to bed. It is a spontaneous reflex, an operation of hormones and nerve endings and residual adolescent fantasies (to use a phrase my son Mark likes).

There was no rational explanation for my reaction. I have sat across the table from women in sundresses who are more attractive. Dorrie was home with us and apparently in full health. We were enjoying our usual

moderate but satisfying sex life. Quinlan's wife was babbling inconsequentially and even stupidly about their
vacation in Brazil, hardly the sort of mature conversation one would expect from a woman who had already
lost two children in tragic deaths.

A shallow and vacuous woman, I told myself. You
would tire of her after one night in bed.

Nonetheless, my incipient obsession replied, it would
be a delectable night, especially if you gagged her.

"An empty woman," I said to Dorrie as we undressed
in the guest room.

"A sad woman," she replied. "Poor thing."

That was eight years ago, 1976, the bicentennial. We
watched the tall ships on Wolfe's big screen TV the next
day. My obsession continued unabated through the
whole weekend. I woke up every morning with agoniz-
ingly obscene fantasies about what I might do to her if
given a chance.

Fully awake and in the shower, I would tell myself that
my desires were completely unreal and that I ought to
be ashamed of myself.

The unreality and the shamefulness of my lusts, however, did not prevent me from mentally stripping her on
every possible occasion that weekend, an imaginative
exercise that at the time was a rare reaction in my life.
She sensed my feelings, as women do, and was, I think,
confused and embarrassed by them. She avoided speaking to me during the weekend and would not look at me.

She was in her middle thirties then, not nearly so
exquisitely delicious a morsel as she has become now.
Suzie is the kind of woman who was "cute" when she
married Wolfe, has now become "pretty," and in a few
years, if she is able to restrain a propensity to plump-
ness at the waist, will surely be accounted beautiful.

She was a vest-pocket Venus, short, with generously
curving hips, breasts large but firm and delicately
shaped, solid thighs, trim legs, pale blond hair so artfully preserved as to seem completely natural, neatly
carved oval face, and gray eyes that bounced enthusiastically but with little relationship to what she was say-

ing or doing, perhaps because when she did not wear her glasses, she could barely see across the room.

Thus stripped and examined, she was and is indeed a delicious morsel. I objectify her, of course; but my point is that even in its beginnings my obsession with Suzie Wade Quinlan was an exercise in objectification. With the passage of time it became worse, not better—and that despite the fact that, even naked in my imagination, she is hardly the most beautiful woman I have ever known.

Oh, yes, her voice. For some reason that's an important part of my feelings about her. If you call their house on the phone and she answers, you think you are talking to a receptionist at an elite law firm—low, smooth, faintly musical, and very intelligent. It's only when you listen to the words instead of the sound that you realize she's not very bright. Something like a woman who looks wholesome even though she's a hooker. I want to listen to her voice without having to hear the words.

I suppose that's objectification too. Where did I learn the word? Not from Suzie surely. From my kids. Where else?

In its beginnings, my obsession was not only harsh and even cruel, it made no sense at all. Nor does it make sense that when I finally acted on it, a few hours before her husband's death, my lust for her was so strong that I could actually contemplate murdering him.

The demon let loose in me wanted to even the score with Wolfe Quinlan, to discharge my envy, by taking his wife from him, even if it meant murder.

The demon did not win, but he terrified me.

No one noticed the currents that jumped between the two of us on that bicentennial day, not even Dorrie, who loved to needle me when she saw me appraising another woman. "Thinking of doing some impulse buying, buster?" she'd whisper in my ear. "Like the goods in this supermarket, do you?"

That was normally enough to exorcise the demon of

lust. This particular demon, I suppose, was too powerful to be obvious.

I had been Wolfe's principal investment adviser for a year and a half. The invitation to Long Beach, which delighted Dorrie, was the first step in transforming a business relationship to friendship. "God knows they need friends, after all they've been through," my good-hearted wife said.

The business relationship began in the locker room when Wolfe, stark naked (he was one of those men who love to preen themselves in locker rooms; unlike many, he had the build to carry it off), strolled up. "Hey, Larry, can I buy you lunch? Maybe talk a little business, huh?"

His grin was infectious, contagious. It caused me to reply with an untypical joke. "I don't need any furniture, Wolfe; but I'll never turn down a free meal."

He laughed enthusiastically, a big, happy-go-lucky roar of thunder, clapped me enthusiastically on the back, and bellowed, "You got a deal!"

He was a big man, over six-three—a good foot taller than his wife, I would later estimate—but slender, graceful, well-coordinated, with only a trace of bulge at his stomach. A natural athlete who was able to stay in condition with only minimal effort despite prodigious feats of eating and drinking. His hair was iron gray and curly, cut short on his head but spilling over his body, and his face full and red with thick, good-humored lips. Only his hazel eyes hinted at a trace of self-doubt or uncertainty.

We had talked before in the locker room but only casually. I knew that his plant was in Harvey, an industrial suburb at the south end of the city, and wondered how he could spend most of every morning lolling around the sauna and the steam room and the pool of the CAA.

I came away from our lunch with four impressions: 1) he was an extremely genial host and storyteller; 2) he had made a lot of money in the last ten years without giving any thought to investing it wisely against inflation; 3) he was shrewd and insightful but barely literate

despite his three years at St. Ambrose College; and 4) he
drank too many martinis by a factor of at least three.

Dorrie added more information. "A lot of tragedy in
the family; they've lost three children—a crib death, a
little girl drowned at the lake last summer. And they just
lost a boy to leukemia. I guess we should count our
blessings. Poor woman."

Wolfe Quinlan did not seem to be a man upset by
tragedy. Was he repressing the pain, I wondered, or was
he really immune to it?

"How many more children did they have?"

"Three, I think. Two girls and a boy. They used to live
in Beverly, but they moved to Elmhurst to get away from
the blacks"—she frowned in disapproval of racism—
"and they have a big old spooky house over in the
Dunes."

Elmhurst, Harvey, and Long Beach—a lot of territory
for a man who spent so much time displaying his pre-
sumptive virility at the CAA.

I learned much more about him in the next eighteen
months. Despite his money, he still had the world view
of the Garfield Boulevard lace-curtain Irish. Lace-curtain Irish with lots of money, that is—for cars, clothes,
cruises, vacations in the Orient, jewelry, homes in the
Dunes and Hawaii, but not for a house in Lake Forest,
where he could have easily lived, or membership on the
board of the Art Institute or the Lyric Opera or the
Symphony or even Catholic Charities. His musical tastes
did not rise above Lawrence Welk and his art collection
was composed of *Saturday Evening Post* originals and
nineteenth-century Italian nudes whose mocking style
he did not for a moment comprehend.

It was not that he and Suzie had considered the life-
style of the North Shore affluent and rejected it. Rather,
they hardly realized that such a world existed.

Yet his raw tastes were not totally bad. His instincts
in the manufacture of expensive furniture enabled him
to turn his father's modestly successful cabinetmaking
business into an internationally respected firm. When
he needed craftsmen, he told his employees to find the

best in the world. When he wanted his home in the Dunes remodeled, he demanded the best architect available. When he wanted an adviser in the collection of barbed wire, he sought the world expert on the subject. (Yes, he collected barbed wire.) I suppose I should have been flattered that he chose me to direct his investments.

Hiring the presumed best, however, is not always the most effective strategy. The architect's attempt to redo a Frank Lloyd Wright pseudo-Swiss chalet was an unmitigated disaster. The result was a morose, gloomy mountain castle on the shores of a lake that radiates sunlight. Yet because the architect was the best, Wolfe told himself and everyone who would listen that the house was a masterpiece.

No one disagreed. Wolfe was fundamentally ineducable because his convictions were expressed with such confidence, determination, and choler that he was rarely challenged. Politically, religiously, and socially he was an arch-conservative, one of that 25 percent of the country that was convinced Richard Nixon had done nothing wrong at Watergate. To challenge him on any of these convictions was to risk what in a child would be called a temper tantrum.

Moreover, he was deeply suspicious of the conspiracies that he believed were going on in the world. His response was not to fight them but to try to find a conspiracy of his own to join. He craved the "inside story," the "real dope," the "facts," and readily subscribed to the most outrageous conspiracy theories. He was persuaded, for example, that Dwight David Eisenhower had been a Communist agent and that Senator Joseph McCarthy had been killed by the CIA, "just like the Kennedys."

If you knew something that he did not know but which he defined as valuable—investment tax credits or the history of medieval armor, for example—he listened to you very carefully. But if your knowledge was uninteresting or worthless, he would dismiss you with a cliché and heaven help you if you tried to fight back.

Wolfe was, then, much like a little boy, with a child's exuberances and simple prejudices. He might be outrageous, but it was hard to dislike him. Even Dorrie admitted that he was a "fun person" and quickly added, "He'd be hell to live with."

I suppose what most fascinated me about him was his boyish enthusiasm for collecting. Most kids save stamps at one stage of their boyhood (I didn't, but my boyhood was hardly normal). Wolfe sustained his exuberance for collecting into adulthood and supported it with considerable sums of money (always arguing that the collections were an investment). The front of the Long Beach house had been converted into a small museum to house his collections (with a master bedroom tacked on at the end).

"Isn't it great, Larry?" he bellowed as he dragged me about the room on the third floor of the "villa," as he called it, the weekend of our first visit.

I was still trying to banish his wife's full, neatly curved breasts from my imagination and was not totally attentive to the coins, barbed wire, African masks, precious stones, and suits of armor. Nor did I think a heavily oak-paneled room with thick maroon draperies, always drawn, and matching carpet was the best way to appreciate the beauty of Lake Michigan on a summer afternoon.

The "study," as he called it, was for himself and the occasional guest who he thought would share his noisy enthusiasm. There were three doors to it, as we have seen one from the balcony that runs along the front of the house, one from the hallway, or "gallery," that leads to the master bedroom and some of the guest rooms, and one from the bathroom that connects the master bedroom with the study. One key opened all three doors and a flick of the key locked them from the inside.

"No one can get in here," he said proudly displaying the magic key, "unless I want them to. There's a bathroom for the wife at the other end of the master bedroom. She thinks this stuff is all junk anyway. You know how women are!"

He dismissed his wife and all womankind with a brisk flick of the wrist, as he would dismiss the Chicago Bears' chances of winning a championship—an inevitable but trivial part of the reality in which we lived.

The frivolity of women was, incidentally, one of his favorite themes. Women were silly, flighty, a trial to a man's patience, like an expressway traffic jam, a necessary responsibility that had to be endured cheerfully.

"If they didn't have cunts," he told me once in high good humor, "there'd be a bounty on them."

He was reported to collect beautiful and expensive women too, but about these prizes he said nothing to me, guessing quite correctly that I had a different view on the subject of marital fidelity. I could imagine him treasuring them just as he did his precious stones. "Feel this one," eyes glittering as he pressed a bloodred stone into my hand. "A ruby, worth ten thousand when I bought it. Maybe ten times that much now."

You could probably find yourself a pretty fancy woman for much less money than that.

Then he showed me his assorted collection of knives, daggers, stilettos, dirks, and other sleek instruments of mutilation.

"Feel this little beauty." He offered me a thin little flesh-colored package. "You just touch it and the blade slips out. Only six inches long extended." A wickedly sharp point emerged. "Some fifteenth-century woman wore this under her dress, probably behind her thigh, above her knee. A guy would have to feel her up pretty thoroughly"—the point slid back in—"to know that she was even wearing it. If she doesn't like his performance, she slips it out and presto"—the point emerged again—"he gets it between the ribs! Nice, huh? He's inside of her and she goes inside of him!"

"Wonderful," I said unenthusiastically, thinking of the homosexual implications of his emotion. Did he have male lovers? He certainly could not face such longings within himself.

"Sometimes I think I ought to make Suzie wear it when she drives through nigger neighborhoods, but she's so dumb she'd probably fuck up if she tried to use it. Stick it in herself instead of the crook!" He laughed raucously as he pointed the blade at me. "Here, feel the point!"

His eyes gleamed dangerously, twin blast furnaces of twisted and unrecognized desires. I breathed a sigh of relief when the knives were returned to the neat, softly lined cabinet drawers that had been designed for them and the stone collection was locked in a big safe, ingeniously disguised as a credenza.

Why, I asked myself, was I fascinated with this crude man? I could not tell myself that he did not mean the outrageous things he was saying. He meant them all right, even if he was not as deeply serious about anything as I was about everything. He had the substance of an opera bouffe tenor. Maybe it was precisely that frivolity of character that appealed to me.

While I was pondering these philosophical issues, Wolfe plunged on with his manic tour of the museum. He turned to a plush foldaway bed in a sofa at one end of the room. "Designed it myself." He stretched out luxuriously on the bed. "If I work late at night, I can fall into this without disturbing the wife. You know how women are. And"—he opened a large closet with a second key on his Florentine leather key ring—"here's a closet with all the clothes I need if I have to drive into the factory early in the morning. Look, an ice box and a little stove, so I can make breakfast before I leave."

I thought it would be rude to ask how often he had used the closet to prepare an early morning breakfast.

There were no pictures of their children anywhere in the "study." Ellen, Joseph, and Wolfe, the three who had died, were never mentioned in the family, and the three living, Margaret, Kevin, and Laurel, were quiet and sullen nonentities, gliding furtively about the gloomy house—proof enough if I needed it that Wolfe's stern and old-fashioned child rearing practices produced the desired effect of quiet children.

My father had never beaten me. Wolfe bragged that he beat his kids into line "all the time." He said it as though he were describing a combat citation of which he was patriotically proud.

"Fantastic place, isn't it?" He slammed the closet door—Wolfe never closed anything gently. Slamming was part of his battle with life.

"Yes... what the hell!"

The sound behind me was like the sanitation department emptying garbage cans at six in the morning. I turned around to see a broadsword pointed in the general direction of my neck. It was in the hands of an unfriendly being on a pedestal behind Wolfe's work table.

"That's Tancredi"—he laughed merrily—"an authentic fourteenth-century armor. His sword slips occasionally." Wolfe pushed the sword back into position in the mailed fist. "Gotta watch him. A guy could stumble in here in the dark and find himself run through by this lad. He's worth at least fifty thousand dollars, by the way. Probably a hell of a lot more."

I was not amused, but Wolfe did not notice. He rarely noticed when someone he liked—and unaccountably he liked me—was not amused.

"Be careful of him." I eased away from the swordsman, who, standing on a pedestal, was pointing his sword at Wolfe's chest.

"He'd never hurt me." Wolfe patted Tancredi's metal arm. "He knows I'm boss around here. Just like Suzie and the kids."

The irony of that statement will remain with me as long as I live.

Have I explained my fascination, which slipped into an odd friendship, with Wolfe Quinlan?

Perhaps not. Mark would probably say, without much inaccuracy, that I was obsessed with Wolfe, partly because I have obsessive tendencies anyway and partly because I saw him as the other half of myself. If I had been deprived of boyish exuberance as a child, so Wolfe had brought all of his exuberance into adulthood, at the price of lacking what I had in superabundance—responsible, cautious maturity. Put us together and you might have one reasonably adequate male.

Maybe that's why I wanted his wife. Maybe I wanted to deprive him of one of his prizes to show him that I was superior to him. He wouldn't have been convinced anyway, though he would have been furious at both of us, probably angry enough to kill us.

I think he would have mourned Tancredi more than Suzie. She was hardly worth fifty thousand dollars. Wives come cheap. You know how women are...

My desire to excel him with his wife was, as I have said, quite mad. But that did not stop me from coming perilously close to putting Tancredi's sword into his body a half hour before someone else actually did it.

––––––––––––––– 6 –––––––––––––––

LAWRENCE F. X. BURKE

Dorrie had a bad bout the next year, 1977; she wept in my arms, like a homeless waif on Christmas eve, as I drove her to the hospital, deep in depression and convinced, as I was, that this would be the last time. She insisted, over and over, that I must marry again.

"Get one of those annulment things," she said tearfully. "You need someone to love, you really do, Larry. I'll give you hell when we meet in heaven if you don't."

Even in the depths of her incipient psychosis she could still giggle at her own irreverence.

She survived somehow, thin and wan and bittersweet, a nostalgic memory of what she used to be. The psychiatrist shook his head dubiously as I talked to him in his white sterile, antiseptic-drenched office. "I wish I could tell you what to do or not to do, Mr. Burke. We have tried all the drugs which have been developed in recent years. Mrs. Burke is one of those rare patients who do not respond to lithium therapy or any similar techniques. The problem is depression, but the result often seems like schizophrenia.

"If the next episode is postponed long enough, we might discover some miracle drug. Otherwise, pray, if you believe in prayer."

"Dorrie and the kids do. I guess I do too. Anyway, we've been doing that all along."

The doctor nodded, seemed ready to say something about prayer, and then thought better of it.

"The next time will be the last?" I stood up.

"Beyond any doubt. She's a wonderful woman, Mr. Burke. We don't understand these things. Some biological process gone astray perhaps."

"You're telling me that the wonderful woman will... what's a good way to put it... go under permanently in the next episode?"

"Go under is an excellent way to put it."

Great, I had a way with metaphor. It wasn't necessary to say that my wife was fated to be a vegetable.

Wolfe insisted that we vacation in one of their condos in Maui. I didn't want to spend time with him, both because I feared my obsession for his wife and because he was hitting the bottle much more than when I first knew him.

"Don't worry," he said grinning, "I'll behave. No booze, no broads. You guys don't have to put up with us at all."

Dorrie insisted that it would be rude to decline the invitation. Besides, she'd never been to Maui.

He did behave and we did spend most of our time with them. Wolfe was genial, charming, the organizer of good, clean, nonalcoholic fun in the surf and sand, the camp director and senior counselor combined. Dorrie said that it was the best vacation we ever had. "I'll always remember it," she snickered the last night, "at least if I have anything left inside of me to remember with."

I held her in my arms and wept before we made love, nostalgic love, as everything in our lives was nostalgic in those days.

Suzie was her usual flighty, frivolous self. She worried in the morning about where we would eat dinner, raved about their vacation in Bahia, spent much of her time on shopping expeditions, read maybe twenty pages of *Trinity* on the beach, talked about children, clothes, soap operas, food, jewels, and her parents, and paraded up and down the beach in a different enticing swimsuit every day.

The woman was, I decided, constitutionally incapable of concentrating on any subject or any task for more than five minutes.

"Lovely little ass on her, huh?" Wolfe said to me as he watched her walking to the edge of the water in a two-piece floral-patterned swimsuit.

I had heard the same words about a woman's anatomy in his crowded little museum at Long Beach. His collection included three nineteenth century Italian nudes, meek, modest, partially draped women, one of them, he claimed, a Canova. He had caressed the cold marble flank of one of them while displaying it proudly to me. "A beauty, isn't she?" The hard glow in his eyes was the same as when he held a ruby or one of his daggers in his hand. There was little sexual pleasure in his gaze. The statue was an object to be enjoyed in his possession of it. He watched Suzie progress across the beach with the same harsh stare. Like a gem or a dirk or a nude statue, she was part of his collection, to be treasured and cherished indeed, but also to be kept appropriately dusted and polished.

"Absolutely sensational ass, isn't it?" He prodded me for a response.

I finally agreed, honestly enough.

"She'd let herself go to pot if I didn't keep after her, send her to spas, and buy her presents when she keeps her weight where it should be. She's as lazy as sin. You know how women are."

I remained silent, wondering what it was like to be

part of someone's collection. Perhaps there were worse fates.

"Margie's never gonna be much to look at," he continued with a sigh. "But you watch Laurel. She's gonna be tall and willowy, the kind of broad I really like."

"Margie does well in school, doesn't she?"

"So what? What good are brains in a woman anyway?" he said in disgust. "Margie thinks she knows everything. Wants to go to Yale to college. Can you imagine that? Well, excuse me, I gotta work off last night's pickled pigs or whatever the hell it was under all that sauce. It *is* a great ass, isn't it?" he persisted.

I mumbled my agreement.

He belched loudly. "I didn't realize how strong that goddamn Polynesian food was. Hey? Didn't we have a great time? Dorrie looks wonderful, doesn't she? She and Suzie get along great, don't they?"

He dashed off to the surf, a vivacious, generous, heedless child.

He was right, I reflected, as I rubbed sunscreen on my hairless chest, about our wives. Suzie was discreetly gentle with Dorrie and Dorrie patient with and even interested in her.

"Poor woman," Dorrie had said as we dressed for supper the night before. "She's not as dumb as she has to act and talk to keep that overgrown oaf happy."

"It's incurable by now," I replied, kissing her gently.

"I'm no one to talk about incurability." She giggled.

If I had only half of her courage.

"Poor woman," Dorrie repeated. "You know, I think you like her boobs more than he does."

"Dorrie!" I exclaimed.

"Doesn't bother me. They really are pretty... button me up, will you?... It's sort of weird. I think he gets his kicks from watching other men ogle her instead of ogling her himself."

I argued that she was exaggerating. We dropped the matter, while I silently resolved that I would not stare so much or at least so obviously at dinner that night.

"May I sit down for a moment?" Suzie broke into my

reverie. The halter on her swimsuit left no doubt about the deftly sculpted shape of her breasts. Wolfe had purchased the suit, of course. Great tits, Wolfe. I stared unabashedly.

"Sure, Sue, be my guest."

She curled her feet under her, the ladylike product of Catholic school and modeling class, half-bare breasts or not. Her nervous gray eyes searched my face carefully; she frowned as though she were looking for a solution to a crossword puzzle.

"You don't think much of me, do you?" She lowered her eyes. She rarely looked directly at me when the four of us were together. Perhaps, I reflected, because my hungry gaze was too obvious. "You think I'm an empty-headed ninny?"

"If you were, you wouldn't ask a question like that."

"I love him, Larry." Her magical voice was appealingly intimate even though she was speaking nonsense. "Can you understand that? I really do love him. Losing the children was so hard on him. . . ."

"Wolfe is a very lovable guy," I replied cautiously.

"Just so you understand"—she groped for the right words, stumbling as the clichés came tumbling out—"that I'm willing to sacrifice anything to protect him."

"Even from himself?"

"Especially from himself."

She stood up, dusted the sand off her calves, and walked back up to the condo.

It was indeed a wonderful little ass, I decided again. And a touching if simplistic statement of faith. I wondered how deep it went. Probably not very. That didn't mean, however, that it was insincere.

At supper that night I noticed for the first time that she looked at him for approval when she ordered her food. If his frown said too many calories, she nervously changed the order.

Poor little bitch.

Wolfe was on his good behavior in Maui, limiting himself to diet cola and soda water. But he went off the deep end as soon as were home. In late March he piled up his BMW on the Eisenhower at two o'clock in the morning. The DuPage county police told us that it was a near miracle that he had not been killed or suffered serious injury. "If you're that drunk," said the cop, "maybe you have special angels taking care of you."

"Or demons, Officer."

It was only with considerable difficulty that he managed to kill the drunken driving ticket, which would have cost him his driver's license. Tearfully Suzie told my wife on the phone that she had tried everything: he would not attend an AA meeting or see a therapist or even make a marriage encounter weekend. He didn't believe in such things. Anyway, there was nothing wrong with him. He was no slobbering alcoholic.

"Marriage encounter?" I sputtered.

"She'd try anything, poor woman."

"Do you think he pushes her around when he's drunk?"

Dorrie's eyes widened in surprise at my question. "Drunk or sober. Worse probably when he's drunk. What else is a woman for?"

I told her and she agreed enthusiastically. Dear God, why did You take her from me?

Suzie finally found something that worked—improbably enough a floating Catholic Charismatic group in the western suburbs.

"I think I finally found Jesus Christ," he said enthusiastically to me at lunch the following autumn. "All my life I haven't realized that He's my Lord and Savior. Would you believe I cried my eyes out during our prayer meeting last night?"

No, I wouldn't have believed it. Nor would I believe that he would throw himself into the Charismatic Movement with the same heedless energy with which he collected gems. His prayer group had become a substitute for collecting. And for women and booze and beating his children. He quoted scripture at me, urged me to find the Lord, prayed for me before and after our lunches, offered to find a healer to pray over Dorrie.

Wolfe's love of the secret, the mysterious, the gnostic,

the "inside story," was satisfied by the trappings of the
Charismatic Movement, even if he may perhaps have
missed the basic religious truths the sound people in
the Movement were trying to make.

He was baptized in the Spirit (spoke with tongues)
and then slain in the Spirit (passed out at a meeting). He
even told me confidentially that he thought he had
some healing power. "Not much, Larry; and it's a gift
from God to be used for others, but I really believe in
my heart that I can heal."

He prayed over Dorrie, and, God bless her, she didn't
collapse with laughter until he had gone home. His
prayers didn't work, of course. My faith was not strong
enough, he told me sadly.

I rejoiced over his transformation, I suppose. But in
truth, Wolfe as a religious enthusiast was a little hard to
take. Indeed a lot hard to take.

We were busy buying out his partner, Greg Foster,
who stood to make a big capital gain and who was
promised his job at the factory after the deal. The promise was sincere enough. Without Foster, the place
wouldn't run for more than a week. Wolfe had the ideas,
Greg administered the company.

"That's why he can spend so much time at the CAA," I
said to Foster in his office in the clean modern plant in
Harvey.

"I don't know about this Pentecostal business," Foster said lightly. "He's spending more time here. One day
a week of Wolfe is essential. Two days can be a trial.
Three days would put us out of business."

"He's likely to live a lot longer," I replied.

"Don't misunderstand me." Foster's careful brown
eyes betrayed no emotion. "Wolfe's the show. We
couldn't make it without him. I'm happy for him and
Suzie and the kids. It's just. . . ."

"You don't want him praying over new models. . . ."

We both laughed, breaking the tension.

Foster doesn't like him, I thought to myself. Friends
from grammar school days, partners in a highly successful business, neighbors in their summer homes. . . .

and he doesn't like him. Resents the flair and enthusiasm and the class, as he sees it.

Does he lust after Wolfe's wife too?

Both Wolfe's faith and mine were put to the test shortly after the election of Ronald Reagan. (I didn't vote for him, but the Democrats, having forgotten about us urban ethnics, as the media call us, deserved to lose.)

After a family dinner—it was like a wake with the corpse alive and joking—Mark and Gerry and I drove Dorrie to the hospital, hoping without any foundation that if we broke the cycle early, there might be some hope.

"Make him marry again if I don't come home," she told the kids.

And one of the last things she said to me was, "Take good care of the Quinlans; they need you so much."

I was unaware that they needed me at all.

Whatever the demons are that finally overcame my wife, they have not left her unhappy. The old woman we visit at the hospital seems content and peaceful. She watches TV most of the day and knits—something which my wife resolutely refused to do. She smiles at us, the same way she smiles at everyone else. Perhaps such a simple life is less agony than living with the knowledge that one would finally lose the battle with fear and depression.

Dorrie, I tell myself, is dead. Only, she isn't dead.

Why did God do it to me?

Margaret Quinlan, the oldest of Wolfe's surviving children, is quite dead, however, a drug overdose victim in her apartment In New Haven, the week after she failed two exams at Yale. I didn't believe that Wolfe's newfound faith would survive the crisis.

It did, even if he left the Catholic Church in the process.

They wanted a "charismatic" funeral, or at least Wolfe did. What Suzie wanted didn't much matter. The pastor of their parish, an insensitive idiot, told them that there would be none of that goddamn caterwauling in his church. Besides, the young woman was probably a suicide and didn't deserve Christian burial.

They could have found another Catholic church, I'm sure, but instead they found a Congregation of God church in the neighborhood, one to which some of their prayer group members had already drifted because they were dissatisfied with the Catholic Church's refusal to preach the literal truth of scripture.

It was the strangest ceremony I've ever attended—weeping, of course, but also singing, dancing, crying out in tongues, collapsing on the floor. The congregation whipped itself into such a frenzy that they seemed to believe the final resurrection was about to occur, that Margie would break open the cover of her casket.

"Come forth, honey," Wolfe begged, hugging the coffin. "You're alive, come forth. Come back to us."

I wondered what old Robert Emmett Quinlan, head usher at Little Flower parish, according to Greg Foster, and pillar of South Side Catholicism and militant Protestant-despising Irish nationalist would have thought.

Margie didn't rise again, but that did not seem to spoil the party, a word I use advisedly.

Suzie joined in the party, ladylike, of course, but with no hint of embarrassment or restraint. Laurel, twelve years old at the time and already well developed, seemed confused and uncertain; and Kevin, slim, blond, ethereal, was sullenly withdrawn.

Laurel had been uncertain and Kevin sullen as long as I'd known them.

At our now infrequent lunches, during which we talked about Wolfe's major investment in oil exploration (extremely successful, I might add), he spoke of Margie as though she were still alive and ate supper with them every night.

"She's the reason things are so good between Suzie and me." He dug into his salad with typical enthusiasm (the whole family was vegetarian now). "Never been better, Larry. Never been better."

I was happy for them, but something less than completely convinced. Despite Dorrie's injunction, I drifted away from them. I could not abide either Wolfe's noisy religious faith or Suzie's bland silence.

They made their journey from Elmhurst to Hyde Park, from the Congregation of God to the Church of the Angels of Light, after Kevin "came out of the closet," quit Marquette, and found a job as a part-time waiter in a Near North restaurant. I'm not sure how gay Kevin is, but there could be no better way of punishing his father than telling the world that he was. Wolfe's new religion was much more likely to denounce the gay as "an abomination unto God" than was post–Vatican Council Catholicism.

An elderly couple from the Congregation of God had joined Father Armande's church and begged Wolfe to come for just one meeting. "I've finally found peace, Larry," he told me. "Lucifer was not a wicked angel. Some Jewish and Christian leaders made that all up. He represents the life force in nature. He's the light of the world. He's preparing the way for the return of Christ, the real Christ, not the weak character we read about in the Bible. Our new faith is dignified and intelligent."

Mark, who had completed his psychiatric clerkship, offered a simple explanation. "It's a form of escalating behavior modification. Someone with a fundamentally diffuse and disorganized personality imposes on it a rigid external control, first with enthusiastic religion, then with an esoteric cult headed by a leader who assumes all responsibility for your life. Sort of like an externalization of the superego. For many people it works. For a while."

"Until they lace the Kool-Aid with poison."

"It doesn't have to end that way. Most such cults don't. Eventually the personality is threatened with total disintegration, of course. Maybe in Mr. Quinlan's case that is what will happen. There's too much diffusion for even a God figure to control."

"Satan figure."

I was invited to attend one of the "services of light" at Father Armande's Hyde Park "church." I decided not to go but made the mistake of telling my kids. They insisted that I "owed it to science," as Tommy said with a big smile, to find out what Lucifer worship was like.

It wasn't like much—white robes, candles, processions, chants in a language I was told was Babylonian (why Lucifer would understand that better than English was not clear to me), a flowery sermon by Father Armande about "life forces" and "sacred energies" that seemed devoid of religious content, bowing and kneeling before an image of the sun—in front of which Father Armande stood in white gown and red cloak as though he were the Angel of Light's grand vizier.

Nothing even remotely resembling a black mass. "How would they find a virgin in that neighborhood anyway?" Eileen sniffed.

"No hint of sex?" Mark asked.

Nothing explicit. In a common room men and women together took off their outer garments and put loose white robes on over their underwear, a titillating hint of dissolute behavior with no particular danger. I noted that many of the devout seemed uncomfortable and underwent the transformation hastily, while some of the younger ones took their sweet time—a legitimate and cautious striptease. Father Armande knew his business all right. You depersonalize your congregation and simultaneously cause both shame and minor sexual excitement.

Wolfe was in no rush to remove his shirt and trousers, a pale reflection of his locker room exhibitionism but with the same old gregarious chatter.

Suzie pulled off her blue knit dress briskly and managed to be both unhurried and modest—Catholic school instincts triumphed again. Since I was an "outsider," I could attend the service (but not chant or carry a candle) in my street clothes.

"We strip away our old selves and put on the new white self so that we may be in communion with light," Suzie said impersonally, her eyes averted from me as they always were. "It represents our inner transformation." For a moment she was unbearably lovely in a white bra and slip. My fingers twitched like break dancers' feet, yearning for her firm, pale flesh. I wanted to pick her slight form up in my arms and carry her away from that madhouse.

If I had known how mad it was, I think I would have indeed carried her away by brute force.

The robes were hardly diaphanous, and there was nothing explicitly sexual in their liturgy, which, like the white robe representing the new person, was a crude distortion of traditional Catholic symbolism.

However, Father Armande's magnetism was unmistakably sexual. Tall, virile, handsome, with incredibly blue eyes and a rich deep voice, he could have been a movie star or perhaps more likely a male model. When the women in the crowd—maybe two thirds of the fifty or so people in the group were women—knelt before him, there was no doubt about their adoration.

Sister Hilaire, despite Madonna-blue robes, was obviously a tart and exercised, as far as I could see, no magnetism over anyone.

"You are new?" Father Armande shook my hand and smiled at me warmly. Up close the mark of age was more clearly upon him. A very clever makeup job.

"An outsider." I had not bowed before anyone, goddamn it.

"No one is an outsider. Do return. Please."

I had no intention of returning to the Quinlans' latest squirrel cage. Yet in that moment, the timbre of his voice, the firmness of his hand, and the light in his eyes made me think that perhaps I should.

Sexual magnetism and hypnosis, I told myself later as I drove back to the relative sanity of River Forest and my family.

I wondered if those were Jimmy Jones's secrets.

Wolfe was his usual exuberant self after the ceremony. "Isn't this great, Larry? Isn't Father Armande sensational? Believe me, he really understands what goes on in the world. He's in communion with life and light and love like no one I've ever known. This is the happiest time in my life!"

His eyes glittered as they did when he fingered a ruby

or ogled Suzie's posterior.

She was silent and unemotional, as she had been since Margie's death.

"He hasn't touched a drop of liquor in three years," she murmured as she slipped the blue dress over her shoulders after the service. Again I wanted to carry her away, tenderness mixing temporarily with my obsession. Then I realized that I would have no idea what to do with a woman who permitted her husband to involve her in such foolishness. A touch of tenderness was merely a trick of my lust.

"Wonderful."

"Dorrie?"

I shook my head.

"Sorry." Two tears appeared on her cheek. "Very sorry." She turned away quickly, struggling with the zipper at the back of the dress. I did not offer to help.

Wolfe was on the wagon. Presumably he had given up his expensive love affairs. The money that used to go to collecting prizes was probably now going to Father Armande and Sister Hilaire. Suzie and Laurel, even Kevin, did not need to fear his savage anger.

What price did she have to pay for this family bliss?

More than anyone should pay, but that had become a habit for her.

Despite the creepiness of that night with Father Armande, I was still surprised when Wolfe told me that he could no longer invest in oil exploration.

"Father Armande says that fossil fuels are not harmonious. I can invest in wind or solar energy..."

"Fine," I said shortly, half-tempted to tell him that perhaps he could hire Father Armande as his investment adviser. It turned out that he already had.

"Of course, I'll have to get his permission for each investment."

From that moment on we were locked into a process that could only end with the broadsword puncturing his lung.

7

LAWRENCE F. X. BURKE

1983 slipped away. I had a torrid love affair in which I learned more about sex than the brothers had taught us at St. Mel's High School in the late 1940s. It ended unsatisfactorily, as such interludes must. I felt guilt and regret but, thank God (whom I normally don't feel much like thanking), no failure of responsibility.

I heard nothing from the Quinlans. Apparently Father Armande had dethroned me as investment adviser. I was just as happy to be free of Wolfe's contagious exuberance and Suzie's intense but finally inexplicable sex appeal.

Then, the last week in June of 1984, Greg Foster phoned me. At first I didn't remember him. Then I recalled that he was Wolfe Quinlan's partner and that I had heard that he'd dropped all his capital gains in commodity speculation.

"I wonder if you could be free on July Fourth for a ride up to Long Beach?" he began, his voice flat and cautious as usual. "Suzie asked me to invite you. Bring one of your children if you wish. She says you can plan to stay overnight and miss the traffic crush going home. I 90 and I 94 are both a mess from construction."

My stomach twisted violently as all my confused emotions toward the Quinlans surged up again, intense and eager.

"Why?"

"It's the craziest thing. Wolfe wants to turn all his holdings over to that crazy fool church he goes to. Make Father Armande the head of the firm."

"Suzie wants to stop it?" I asked skeptically.

"You know what she's like. He could tell her to throw herself in a blast furnace and she'd do it. But she's not enthused about it. Neither is Kevin, though he doesn't much matter. Kiernan O'Rourke and I are dead against it as you might imagine. She wants us to sit down and talk to Wolfe about the problem, work out some kind of compromise."

He sounded skeptical about the possibility of compromise.

"He agrees?"

"Sure. He's sweet reasonableness these days, but he says he won't change his mind."

"Why me?"

"Suzie says that he has always valued your judgment."

"I don't stand much of a chance against Father Armande. Will he be there?"

"Hell, no."

"I don't see that I can be any help. Still. . ."

"For the love of God, Larry, we need you."

So I agreed to go, with the dubious results you already know. Tommy was the only child free for the midweek Fourth of July.

"Any chicks there?" he asked with a yawn as he turned down the latest rock and roll noise.

"Do you remember Laurel?"

"I try not to," he sneered, but his heart was not in the dismissal. "Oh, well, I'm in the mood for a battle with the angels of darkness. Sure, I'll come and help."

"Angels of light," I corrected him.

"Baloney. Say, how old is Laurel, anyway?"

Old enough, as he decided on arrival.

And her mother was young enough, to put the matter mildly.

Despite her white-framed sunglasses, probably prescription at this age in life, Suzie had not changed at all, appealing as ever in a pink blouse and shorts from Yves Saint Laurent, unless I missed my guess (I had learned a lot about a lot of things in my ill-fated love affair). Even if Wolfe was no longer buying her clothes as part of the care and maintenance of one of his prizes, she was still a clothes horse.

"Wolfe is in his study working on his gems," she said. "He'll join us later. Kiernan, Greg, and Melanie will come over then. Kiernan is, I believe, playing pinochle with the Fosters. Tommy, darling, would you want to take Laurel waterskiing?"

"Uh, oh, yeah, why not?" He smiled broadly.

Why not indeed. Laurel was a tall and slim blond, lovely if a little ungainly. She had become beautiful overnight and wasn't sure what that meant or how to act with it. But in a white string bikini that seemed to have been designed for her, she didn't have to do much to stir the interest of an eighteen-year-old boy.

"Do you want to ski, Laurel?" her mother asked patiently.

"I don't care," Laurel said listlessly. "I guess so."

Poor Laurel. The family history had left its mark. If there was a boy on the shore of Lake Michigan who could cheer her up, it was Tommy.

Suzie showed me to the main guest bedroom in the southeast corner of the house, the same bedroom in which Dorrie and I had stayed eight summers and a couple of lifetimes before to the day. Neither of us took the risk of mentioning that visit.

I was struck again by the gloominess of the house—a Swiss villa perhaps, but designed by an architect from Transylvania with a cloak who never appeared in the daylight. As before, the sunlight and the cheerful lake were shut out by heavy draperies and the rooms were furnished with heavy—and expensive—antiques: Sheraton, Queen Anne, Early American, Second Empire, Louis XVI. I didn't know enough about the subject to distinguish between the real thing and Quinlan Furniture's respectful "reconstructions."

I pulled back the curtains, slid the glass door open, and walked out on the balcony. A swimming pool had been built next to the house, above the garage, with a high brick wall around it. Kevin, in the briefest of black briefs, was reclining on a plastic chair, reading a magazine and trying his best to look like an angry gay activist—thin, blond like his mother and sister, soft-muscled, and stoop-shouldered. The kind of son who would have driven the old Wolfe Quinlan up the wall.

"Say hello to Mr. Burke, dear."

"Hello, Mr. Burke," he sneered, imitating his mother's tone and not bothering to look up at me.

"We are in difficult times, Lawrence," she said calmly, "as you might imagine. I'm sorry to have brought you up here on what is probably a waste of time. Anyway"—she removed her glasses—"if you'd like to have a drink and a swim, I'll join you."

"Wonderful."

What had changed about her? I asked myself in the guest room as I took off my sport shirt and slacks and put on my swimming trunks. No more babble, an unnatural, almost dangerously self-possessed calm (of which there had been a hint at the Church of the Angels of Light), a bleakness in her gray eyes.

The name of the game was despair. I knew the temptation. Was there anything left in Suzie's personality to resist it?

Probably not.

I had done about a half-mile in the pool, ignoring the ignorable Kevin, before Suzie returned, wearing a long green skirt and a matching halter (Yves Saint Laurent was apparently providing all her summer clothes) and carrying a tray on which were two ham and cheese sandwiches, a glass of brown liquid straight up, and a small martini pitcher. That she would remember my penchant for Jameson's was flattering. Two martinis for herself was certainly new. Wolfe used to cut her off with one drink.

"*Slainte,*" I toasted her.

"I'm glad I was able to find a bottle of Jameson's in the Trail Creek liquor store," she said with a faint smile.

We ate our sandwiches. Kevin slammed back into the house, angry at the world. Suzie seemed not to notice.

"He's drinking again," she said so softly I barely heard

her.

"Wolfe? I thought he'd stopped."

"For four years. Since we joined the charismatics. That's why I... never mind. He came up last night and raided the wine cellar and locked himself up in his study. I don't know why."

"Because of the fight over the money?"

She shrugged her smooth shoulders. "I have no idea. The arguments have been terrible. I try to keep out of it as much as I can. But I have to think of the children, Laurel especially. I don't care what happens to me."

"You should." I sipped my Jameson's.

She still did not look at me. "I don't know anymore. ...Maybe I had better try to get some exercise. Laurel is after me all the time."

Laurel, not Wolfe.

She removed her Italian sunglasses, adjusted the straps on her halter, tossed aside the wraparound skirt, paused gracefully at the edge of the pool, and then dived in.

She swam only a few lengths—that was more than I had seen her attempt in the past—and then climbed out of the pool and sat next to me, water dripping from her skin, blond hair pasted appealingly against her head, to finish her martini.

I had learned a number of new things to fantasize about doing to her body since the last time I had seen her in a swimming suit. Realistically, I told myself, you want her even less as a victim of despair than you did as a superficial babbler. Despite such realistic admonitions, the sight of her breasts melted me as much as ever.

"I appreciate you coming, Lawrence," she said wearily. "I don't know how much longer this can continue."

"I'm here to help."

She looked up, considering my face for the first time, it seemed, in many years. "I appreciate that very much. ... I... I wish I knew what to ask for... Anyway"—she rose with an effort at decisiveness—"I'll have to ask your patience again. I ... didn't get much sleep last night. Would you mind terribly if I took a nap?"

No, I wouldn't mind at all. I'd swim the rest of my mile and then try for a nap too.

It was difficult at first to sleep. She was in the room across the hall, in which I had glimpsed pink curtains and frills earlier. Available—and this was part of my obsession—totally submissive.

It was not the sort of fantasy to help me prepare for the crisis that would surely come sometime before the Fourth of July ended. Finally, weary of my own exhortations, I fell asleep.

Tommy woke me up. "Geez, you're getting awesomely old if you take naps on the Fourth of July."

"You don't look like you've suffered," I grumbled sleepily.

"Nah, she's a pretty cool chick; it only took me a half hour to make her laugh. But the old man must be a real asshole."

"I don't like that language, Tommy."

"Yeah, but is he?"

"Some of the time."

"The old lady seems like a pretty cool chick too. Mom liked her."

Did she?

"Some of the time she is. She seemed to smile a little bit at you this morning."

"Laughed when I told her about teaching the brat to ski. Chicks dig me, Dad; you know that. Even old chicks."

Dinner would have been somber if it hadn't been for Tommy. While Suzie did not disdain ham and cheese for lunch, she honored the principles of the Church of the Angels of Light at supper. The massive fruit salad, all home grown, she told us in a brief flash of the old bubbling, babbling Suzie, was tasty enough but not what you expected on the Fourth of July on the shores of a lake.

The dining room was turn of the century—gold fabric on the walls above a dark wood base, maroon cloth on the chairs, gaslight chandelier, silver tea service on the buffet, lighted candles and Powerscourt crystal on the table. Christmas in the city, perhaps, but not Fourth of July and not with Michigan fruit salad.

Nothing to drink, of course, hard on the dinner guests, many of whom desperately needed a drink: Kiernan O'Rourke worried despite his red leprechaun face (with a hint of the meanness that is characteristic of real as opposed to Hollywood leprechauns); Greg Foster, cold-eyed and cautious, hardly speaking a word; Melanie, his wife, who coped with middle age by excessive dieting and excessive makeup; the Quinlans, much as they had been earlier in the day, quiet, anxious, perhaps frightened.

So Tommy entertained with waterskiing stories. Only Kevin and Greg Foster did not succumb to laughter. Dear God, Dorrie, you'd be proud of him. Did you really like Suzie? What did you see that I've missed? Or were you only being your usual sympathetic self?

"What the hell is all the fucking laughter about?" Wolfe Quinlan stumbled down the stairs, his paisley shirt hanging out over light blue slacks. His eyes were red, his face unshaven. I realized with some surprise that this was the first time I'd seen him drunk. With the exception of Tommy, all the others had witnessed the act before and were terrified by it.

"Will you have some supper, dear?" Suzie cooed reassuringly. "Your favorite home-grown fruit salad. Raspberries from our own garden."

"Fuck the raspberries." He swept the salad from the table, spilling fruit and dressing on the Austrian period-piece rug. Napkin in hand, Suzie scurried to clean it up.

"Leave it there!" he bellowed, shoving her away from the mess and pushing her to the floor. "Get some real food for me and my honored guests. Vultures eat meat. And wine, good wine, the 1967. It's still here; I've been drinking it all day."

Dutifully she struggled to her feet and scurried off to the kitchen, as though she were a frightened feudal serf. Laurel slipped out after her.

Wolfe slumped into his chair and buried his head on the table in the place where the salad had been. "Fucking vultures," he murmured over and over again.

I was as paralyzed as were those for whom it was a familiar event out of the past. I had a powerful urge to hit him. So, I was sure, did all the other men in the room. Wolfe's drunken rage froze us all into impotency.

However, we had come to protect the Quinlan money from an absurd gift to a church that had kept Wolfe sober for years. Did his drunkenness suggest that he was disillusioned with the church? Why had he returned to his collections, which he had abandoned with his wenches and his booze? What was going on?

Eventually Suzie and Laurel brought the steaks and the wine and timidly served them. We picked up our knives and forks and just as timidly began to eat.

Wolfe jabbed a knife into his steak and then swept it off the table to join the salad. "Fucking cunt," he screamed. "Can't you do anything right? You know I like my steaks rare. What the fuck is the matter with you? And don't try that crying shit or I'll beat the ass off you."

"Wolfe," I began firmly.

"Shut up, cocksucker," he shouted at me. "You want my money and my wife's tits. Well, you're not going to get either. None of you are going to get anything. I've already signed my will, had it witnessed, and given it to Father Armande's lawyers. All you vultures are out of luck.... Give me the fucking wine bottle, you little creep."

Trembling, Laurel brought the wine bottle.

"What a stinking bunch of vultures." He poured half the bottle on the table cloth, a spreading splotch of blood. "Foster, a dummy who's been sucking my ass since seventh grade, finally gets some money and farts it away because his hooker wife thinks it's fun to play the commodity market. You and this shyster Bunny O'Rourke have been on the take for years. Don't think I'm not going to tell the cops. You're both headed for a good long term in prison. Maybe Melanie will write to you in Statesville or Leavenworth or wherever the fuck they send you. Yeah, if she takes the time to leave the streets to write to you. Don't bet on it, loser."

I told myself that he was too drunk to know any better, that this madman was a perversion of my friend Wolfe Quinlan. It didn't do much good.

"And you, my freaking faggot wimp of a son. Counting on Daddy's money to pay for your blow jobs. Well, think again, fairy. Crawl back into your hole with your faggot friends. Hey, who's that kid at the end of the table? What's that cocksucker doing here?"

"I'm Tom Burke, Mr. Quinlan." My son's eyes glowed dangerously.

"Yeah? Hey, your mother is a fucking vegetable, isn't she? You know what? You got the same bad blood; you're going to end up the same way, you stupid little punk."

"Asshole," Tom snapped back at him.

"What did you say, fucking vegetable?" Wolfe rose from the table, a steak knife in his hand.

"I said that you were a stupid, drunken slob, a disgusting bum, one of the great assholes of the Western World. If you're dumb enough to come after me with that knife, I'll take it away from you and cut off your balls!"

My sweet, even-tempered little Tommy.

Wolfe sank back into his chair. "Fucking vegetable."

"I don't have to put up with your bullshit." Tommy was enjoying himself enormously. "I'm getting out of here. Come on, kid." He grabbed Laurel's hand. "You're coming too. We're going to the dance at Grand Beach and listen to Diamond. Maybe when we get back asshole here will have sobered up."

"You're right, Tommy." I stood up. "I don't have to put up with it either."

"The fuck you don't!" Wolfe swung at me, a clumsy, ineffectual jab at my chest.

"Asshole." I landed one punch on his jaw and sent him spinning against the buffet, then stormed out of the house, two teenage boys having put down a third.

Big hero.

Almost as though he planned it, Wolfe Quinlan had given everyone in the room an excuse to murder him.

I'd have even more excuse before midnight.

8

LAWRENCE F. X. BURKE

I walked the beach for hours, my feet jabbing into the soft sand, furious at myself for becoming involved with the Quinlans in the first place and even more furious for wasting the Fourth of July in such a madhouse. I had better things to do with my time.

Like what?

Like my family. Why bother with an empty-headed little slave who did not have the gumption to walk out on that lunatic?

She loved him, she had said in Maui. How could anyone love such an. . .

Well, use Tommy's word, such an asshole.

I walked to Grand Beach and listened to music in the distance. Rock music, of course. Probably Diamond. An ironic name for a rock group.

Then I walked in the other direction to Michigan City, watching the fireworks explode in the sky. Spent and empty after my emotional outburst, I turned wearily back to Long Beach and the Quinlan house.

A lighted cigarette glowed at the foot of their beach staircase. It was Suzie in jeans and a white T-shirt. I had never seen her smoke before, doubtless because Wolfe didn't approve.

The night air was thick and humid, the lake thumping indifferently against the beach, the stars totally uninterested in our insignificant planet. Fireworks boomed in the distance, lights from skyrockets occasionally burst

60

beneath the bored stars, mosquitoes buzzed around us.

"How is he?" I asked curtly.

"Back in his museum, sobering up, I guess. You shouldn't have hit him, Lawrence. He'll feel so guilty when he comes out of it."

"He's crazy." I touched her arm. "Why do you put up with it?"

"I'm his wife." She didn't pull her arm away. "It's too late now to decide I don't want to put up with it. Did you stop putting up with Dorrie?"

"It's different." I wanted to be furious at her but could not. My heart was beating frantically, driving hormone-drenched blood through my arteries.

"I know. Anyway, this hasn't happened since we came home from Maui and he had that terrible accident. Once in four years isn't so bad."

"At what price?" I tightened my grip on her arm.

"It's my choice if I want to pay the price," she said dully.

I was a massive dull ache of physical desire, like a tooth that had to be extracted. My pent-up desire for her, irrational, futile, foolish, bubbled toward the boiling point. You must not do anything, I warned myself. Isn't your life enough of a mess?

"What is it this time? Why did he go off the deep end today? The will? And what difference does a will make?"

"He didn't mean a will, he meant the transfer of the company to Father Armande. I suppose there is a will too. It doesn't matter."

"Is that why he's drunk?"

"I don't know, Lawrence. I simply don't know. And just now I don't care anymore."

Then I took her into my arms and kissed her, passionately, wildly, madly. She was even more delicious to hold than I had expected. She did not resist or respond. She simply submitted, as I'm sure she did to Wolfe. All her life she had submitted to men. I was one more. To be tolerated, humored, manipulated, sacrificed for.

Her mouth tasted of cigarette smoke, her lips accepted my kisses with patient resignation. Her body was limp in my arms, waiting to serve my pleasure.

I was furious. I was not interested in possessing a slave girl. What honor is there in that? I was not a savage like Wolfe Quinlan, was I?

My anger made me even more hungry for her. As long as she was going to be a slave girl, she might as well be mine instead of his. I treated slaves decently at any rate. My hot, furious hands roamed over the upper part of her body and then began to frantically explore beneath her T-shirt.

Again she submitted, patiently, inertly, defenselessly.

What the hell was I doing? Was I nothing more than a brutal rapist? I stopped, just as fingers had begun to probe the warm, moist flesh under her bra. And just as she seemed to tense in response to me.

"Sorry," I said as I forced my hands away from her.

"It's all right." She lit another cigarette with a hand I was glad to see was unsteady. "I understand."

That damn voice of hers, warm, intelligent, understanding—and totally deceptive—infuriated me.

"Do you have to understand goddamn everything?" I demanded, wanting now to replace kisses with blows.

"Yes"—she blew out smoke—"I do."

I gave up, turned away from her, and climbed up to the first floor balcony. Instead of going into the house, I continued to climb to the third floor, working out my rage, frustration, and confusion on the steps. In the darkness I stumbled over one of the elegant lounge chairs that were placed at the entrance of each bedroom. I cursed the chair and then realized that it was outside of Wolfe's room. The lights were on. I heard no sounds inside. As I told the police the next morning, I glanced at my watch and noted that it was a quarter to twelve. Fourth of July was almost over.

I gazed at the lake, more than a hundred feet beneath me, almost a sheer drop. Her cigarette was still glowing. Poor, dear woman. Trapped in her own romantic immaturity. A lost soul.

I walked around the corner, entered my room, and collapsed on my bed. Soon I was sound asleep.

Or so I told the police. There was one other incident that I saw no reason to mention to them. In fact, I couldn't sleep. I heard voices in Wolfe's room, his voice and a higher-pitched voice—a woman or perhaps Kiernan O'Rourke, whose guest room was down the hallway, next to Tommy. I got out of bed, listened for a few moments, and then, in shorts and T-shirt, slipped down to the second floor, found the Jameson's bottle, poured myself half a tumbler, and returned on noiseless bare feet to the third floor.

For a moment I hesitated in front of the door to Wolfe's study, my heart pounding, temples throbbing. I knocked on the door.

Inside there was a rumbling, shuffling noise. A key turned in the lock. The door swung open. Wolfe, in a bright red dressing gown, a Japanese kimono actually with a dragon on its back, stared at me glumly.

"Whatta ya want? Oh, it's you, Larry; what the hell you doing up here?" He rubbed his unshaved face. " 'Fraid I'm a bit under the weather." He grinned, all sheepish adolescent charm. "You wanna drink? Hey, you got one already."

"You may have forgotten about the dinner table," I began.

"Shush," he murmured, "mustn't wake the wife. You know how women are."

"I haven't forgotten it. You're out of your mind, Wolfe Quinlan, you belong in a mental institution more than my poor wife...."

"Hell of a thing to say about Dorrie this time of night. Hell of a woman, Dorrie. I wish I had married someone like her."

"If you persist in turning your money over to that phony, I will be happy to testify in court to your legal incompetency. You can count on that."

"Yeah?" He seemed confused. "You know, that's pretty funny, good buddy, real funny."

"Funny or not, it's what will happen. And if I did what I want to, I'd shove Tancredi's sword into your bloated stomach."

"Real funny." He pushed the door shut. I heard the key lock inside.

I emptied the tumbler of Jameson's in a few gulps and fell into bed. Just before I lost consciousness I thought I heard more voices from across the hall.

I suppose you can imagine why I did not report these incidents to the police. The Indiana State Prison, just the other side of Michigan City—close enough so that the inmates could see the same fireworks I watched—is a notoriously unpleasant place.

There's little more to tell. Later I was wakened from a heavy sleep by the sound of a woman's screaming. I staggered into the corridor to find Suzie in her night-gown, hands on the side of her head, screaming hysterically.

"Something terrible happened in there," she wailed. "I heard bumping noises and things crashing and then him groaning. I'm afraid he's hurt himself. Please, please do something! For the love of God, do something!"

I rousted Tom and Kiernan out of bed and we banged against the door for several minutes before we crashed into the room. You've seen the pictures. Wolfe Quinlan was spread-eagled on his work table—a company prod-uct, as the papers reported—with Tancredi's broad-sword sticking out of his chest. Everything was covered with blood, the floor, the wall, the desk, even the suit of armor that lay on top of him like an extraterrestial lov-er. He was naked under his fancy Japanese kimono, which was stained a much deeper scarlet now. He had bled to death, very rapidly. The three nude statues on the opposite side of the room from the suits of armor seemed to be watching, their meek modesty now trans-muted into horror.

"Get the Fosters," I said automatically, "and call the police. No. Wait. Let's see if anyone is in here." I checked the locks on the balcony door, the bathroom, and the closet. All were locked, as I told the police a few hours later, as was the door from the bathroom to the master bedroom. They found the Florentine leather key fob with the door key and the closet key in the pocket of his scarlet dressing gown. They all stood in the doorway and watched me. "No one here. Go ahead, make the calls."

"I'll call the priest from Notre Dame," Suzie said quietly, all hysteria gone. She meant the local parish. Tommy went down the stairs and out into the night for the Fosters. Kiernan called the police from his own room. Suzie rushed down to the kitchen on the second floor for the phone book with the parish number and called from there. I went back to the hallway to wait for the priest and the police. No one could have slipped by me at the doorway.

Suzie came back up the stairs and woke Kevin and Laurel, both deep sleepers, who had not heard the noise. Laurel became hysterical, of course, as soon as she'd looked inside the room. We couldn't keep her away from the door. Amazingly, Kevin comforted her quite tenderly.

That's the whole story. Wolfe Burke Quinlan died the way I said he ought to die, hardly an hour after I threatened him with death.

——————— **9** ———————

BLACKIE

It was an admirable presentation, objective, candid, restrained, complete with a carefully drafted chart. Lawrence Burke would have made a fine lawyer.

Or a very adroit killer.

"Is it not interesting"—I walked to the window of my office and watched the evening rush hour traffic back up on Wabash—"that you abandoned your embrace with

Ms. Quinlan just at the moment she became sexually responsive?"

I waited vainly for an explosion.

"Do you approve of adultery?" he asked quietly.

"Don't you think you were exploiting her?"

"Sure." He stirred uneasily behind me. "I told you it was an obsession."

I turned on him. "I am weary of that excuse, Lawrence, especially when it justifies using her and not letting her use you."

"I was afraid." He rested his head on his hands. He looked like a convicted prisoner waiting for a judge to hand down a harsh but deserved sentence. His father, angry hobgoblin risen from the dead, was pointing an accusing finger at him.

"Of what?" I said gently.

"Of her."

"Ah."

I let that insight sink in and then continued.

"Why is it," I asked, peering carefully at the chart, "that Laurel has such a small room and one which shares a bath with her mother? One would think that might lead to conflict."

"Actually it was the nursery when the children were young. Laurel was the last and I guess she never moved out of it."

"She and her mother are close?"

He shrugged. "Ambivalent, like most mothers and teenage daughters. More ambivalent than most, because of all that has happened in their family."

"Ah."

I wondered if he realized how much he had disclosed about himself in his description of his relationship with his children. Probably not. He was a smart man and had admirably educated himself, but there were sophisticated nuances of self-revelation that would forever escape him.

Just as well, save that he could find some consolation for his sense of guilt and loss about his wife in the thought that he was as admirable a father as his own father had been despicable.

There were also nuances, not immediately identifiable but intriguing, in his reactions to Suzie that would merit further exploration. Moreover, she sounded a little more interesting than I had expected her to be.

It was all, as Nero Wolfe might have said, rubbing his hands together, quite satisfactory.

I examined the drawing again. "You're sure the key fob was in Wolfe Quinlan's pocket."

"I didn't search for it, of course. That would be touching the body, which in the mystery stories, at any rate, you are not supposed to do."

"Hmm. . . indeed. You're quite sure than no one could have left the room?"

"How? The other doors were locked, the bathroom was empty, I even looked in the shower. And the first thing the police did was to open the door of the closet to make sure there was no one hiding in there."

"I assume the police checked to make sure that only one key had been made for the lock before the plate was destroyed?"

"Of course." His fingers locked in restrained impatience.

"And that the lock had not been changed earlier in the summer?"

"I assume so."

Assume, huh? I made a mental note to have Mike Casey check it out.

"Ah. . . you could of course see the body from your vantage point in the corridor?"

"Not all of it. Look at the perspective from the doorway." He laid a pencil across his chart. "I could see the head and chest with the sword sticking through it and the suit of armor pressing down on him, but I couldn't see the rest of the corpse because he was draped over the side of the desk."

"Indeed. Do you remember how the other members of the household were dressed?"

"Oh, were any of them hiding blood stains? No, not at all. Let me see. . . ." He folded his hands thoughtfully under his square, stubborn Irish chin. "Tommy and I were in shorts and T-shirts, Kevin in some kind of transparent black gown, poor little Laurel was wearing a dark blue college T-shirt and white panties. I remember her shivering. Her belly seemed as blue as the shirt, though it was a hot night. Suzie was dressed in a short white gown, the kind that is made for sleeping and not much else. Kiernan was decked out in old-fashioned red-and-white striped pajamas. The Fosters were in robes when they came over. The women, of course, had robes on before the police came."

It wasn't blood stains of which I was thinking. The Long Beach cops, however puerile, would have checked for that.

"Ms. Quinlan looked disheveled as I have been led to believe women do when they rise unexpectedly from bed?"

He hesitated. "No, she's a very fastidious woman. Every hair on her head was in place."

"And her makeup was undamaged?"

"You have to understand"—his square chin jutted at me defensively—"how important personal appearance is to her."

"And her gown unrumpled?"

"She is never in dishabille," he insisted. "Never. It's the kind of woman she is."

"Indeed."

He knew it was a weak argument.

"And then?"

"The rest is history. The police hassled us for several weeks. Everyone in the house and the house next door had a motive for killing Wolfe Quinlan. And the means were at hand. They never could prove opportunity against anyone. I took a lie detector test to establish that I was telling the truth about the locked room. So did Sue. They finally gave up. There was no suicide note, so they assumed that in a drunken stupor, he pulled the armor suit down on him. The angle of entry of the blade fit that theory. As you know the LaPorte County prosecutor's office closed the case last week."

"Ah... you're quite correct." I considered the chart carefully. "If the door to the house was open, as the papers say it was, the Fosters could have easily entered the house. So, in fact, could anyone else."

"But how could they have got into and escaped from the locked room?"

"Precisely. And the inestimable Father Armande, né Louis Connery, had an unshakable alibi, despite the attempt of such worthy journals as the *National Enquirer* to attribute the murder to a 'devil cult.'"

"Even if he were in northern Indiana and even if he did come into the house through the open door, he still has to enter and escape from the locked room."

"The aforementioned *National Enquirer* suggests that devils can pass through walls. An interesting hypothesis, testable in the case of Father Louie, but only with great inconvenience.... Mrs. Quinlan is contesting the will, as the papers tell us?"

"Sue didn't want to, as you can imagine. But she's virtually penniless; and she has the two kids to think about. Besides, Armande is a fraud and a thief. And probably crazy too."

"Minimally." So she had become Sue already. Ah, resiliency. Moreover, you are responsible, John Blackwood Ryan, for sending him up there to protect her. You may be excused from blame, however, on the plea that it is not yet evident that she and her daughter do not need protection. "One last point. Since you didn't tell the police about your nocturnal visit to Wolfe Quinlan, they didn't know that he had stopped drinking and was recovering from his intoxication."

"I suspected you would think of that." He watched me steadily, his eyes unblinking. "The amount of alcohol in his bloodstream, what was left of it, was compatible, according to the police, with such an accident."

"Would you say the man you talked to was likely to have such an accident?"

He hesitated and wet his lip with his tongue. "I don't think so, Blackie." He sighed wearily. "I don't think so.

"Wolfe had an enormous capacity, even after a couple

of years on the wagon. It could have happened, of course; and he might have opened another bottle of wine after we talked."

"Would he normally do that once sobriety had begun to rear its painful head?"

"I don't believe so. Of course, he hadn't had a drink in four years."

"You are not certain then of the informal verdict of death through misadventure."

There was a long pause while Lawrence F. X. Burke rubbed his face in his huge paws. "Not necessarily."

"You are sufficiently troubled to want the truth, whatever the cost?"

He nodded solemnly, like a bishop presiding from his cathedra. "There won't be peace for anyone till we know what really happened."

"Ah." I leaned forward, hoping I didn't look as passionately curious as I felt. "Now tell me about the subsequent spirit manifestations."

———— 10 ————

LAWRENCE F. X. BURKE

First of all, I must tell you that Laurel is not lost. She has moved in with the family of a friend in Elmhurst. I believe that she will come to see you with Tommy. Understandably the house at Long Beach had become too much for her. I drive up every night after work, for reasons I will explain shortly. Tommy is there all day—I won him a few weeks off from the trader for whom he is working at the Board of Trade. So Sue is safe too.

Now about the supernatural phenomena. Ten days

ago, after the LaPorte County prosecutor called off the hounds, Sue phoned me. She sounded vague and frightened. Would I please come up on Saturday morning. There was something strange happening to the house. I suggested that she ought to leave Long Beach and return home to Elmhurst. There were too many bad memories at Long Beach.

"I'm not ready for the Elmhurst memories yet. And Laurel is having fun with those nice young people over in Grand Beach to whom Tommy introduced her."

I gather that the young people are relatives of yours, Monsignor. Laurel, who has been shy the last couple of years, is particularly close to one of them who is just her age. A child, with the rather curious nickname of The Cat. She's a lifeguard, I believe.

"Tommy and I can probably get away Friday night," I said tentatively.

"Thank God." She sighed with relief. "I'm a little worried. I don't believe in ghosts, but. . . ."

Neither do I, of course. Wolfe Tone Quinlan was enough of a problem alive. I didn't want to have to contend with him dead. Nonetheless, the man's energy and exuberance still fascinated me. What, I wondered, half fun and full earnest as Dorrie would have said, would his ghost be like?

Perhaps I am as obsessed with him as I am with his wife. I wonder if I may have loved him, with all his glaring and obvious faults, more than I love her.

Or rather desire her, I told myself then. For there is little, I argued mentally as we rode through northern Indiana, listening to Tommy's favorite rock group on the car radio, in the woman to love. She did not handle the police investigation or the wake and funeral or the subsequent legal action at all well. Her typical reaction was to weep quietly and withdraw, leaving the responsibility to others. Kevin was worse than useless. Laurel was too young. Kiernan O'Rourke, who is sleaze if I've ever seen it, Greg Foster, and I were, perforce, in charge. The pastor in Elmhurst, as you know, refused Christian burial. I'm told now that if we had called the Chancery Office in

Joliet, he might have been reversed. The associate pastor, to whom Laurel was close, said prayers at the funeral parlor and prayed over the grave in the unconsecrated section of Mount Carmel cemetery.

"I loved him, I always loved him," was all that Suzie was capable of saying through her endless weeping. Surely she said it a hundred times. As though she were trying to convince herself. She doth protest too much, I thought. Nor did she pay much attention to her physical appearance. Her mourning dresses were dowdy and she wore no makeup. Wolfe's body was hardly cold and already she was permitting herself to deteriorate.

I was, you've doubtless observed, busily detaching myself from my obsession with her and with some success. I can recommend murder investigations and funerals as a cure for sexual obsession. A temporary cure at any rate.

She and Laurel returned to Long Beach after the burial and I told myself that I had bid them a permanent good-bye.

Yet when she called, I drove up on Friday night, battling the interstate construction as well as a spectacular thunderstorm.

You know how depressing a resort area can be after a couple of days of rain, soggy, dismal, faintly contaminated—its tawdry summer wrap stripped away as if by premature autumn. The Quinlan villa looked even more like Transylvanian Gothic.

"If I were a ghost, I'd haunt that place," Tommy said cheerfully as I parked our Chevrolet next to the deceased's BMW.

Sue had changed. Her hair was short and crisp, no longer fluffy. Nor did she look like a frilly matron turning plump in her midsection. Quite the contrary, she had become a trim, efficient businesswoman in summer dress. Her makeup was carefully done and she seemed in full possession of herself.

Tommy whistled and she blushed as she kissed him.

"I'll take you over to Grand Beach tomorrow to listen to Diamond instead of the brat," he said.

"You'll do no such thing, young man." She took both of my hands in hers and kissed my cheek. "It's wonderful of you to come, Lawrence."

The whole scene was designed for me, you say. Surely. Yet it was significant, I thought, that she had designed it for me and that she knew what kind of image would most intrigue me.

My obsession revived instantly.

Tommy found Laurel and they departed, promising, in response to Sue's anxious instructions, to be "home early," a phrase without meaning to young people, as she should have known.

In the huge salon on the first floor there was a bottle of Jameson's and two tumblers on the "reconstructed" Early American coffee table—the kind of coffee tables the Early Americans would have made if they had thought about making coffee tables. The drapes were open and all the lights were on, Sue's attempt to make the place bright and cheerful. It still looked like it was a nineteenth-century funeral home.

I wondered if they kept caskets for vampires in the basement.

Sue poured us both quite small drinks and we chatted. Small talk with lots of awkward silence. She was forcing herself to be relaxed and doing only a fair job. I asked her about her financial situation. While there was little doubt that there would be a settlement with Father Armande, leaving her plenty of money and control of the firm, her present situation was precarious. Wolfe had left virtually everything, including the Long Beach home, to Father Armande. She had enough money in her personal account to cover August and September. Then she would be broke. Armande's lawyers would know that and extract a high price for settlement.

"Perhaps you ought to find another lawyer. I'm not sure that Kiernan is all that straight."

"He was Wolfe's attorney and Wolfe's father's attorney. Anyway, it might be good to have to work. I don't know what I could do. I can't even type. Be a waitress maybe. I've never worked a day in my life. Wolfe didn't want his wife working."

"I'm sure you won't have to be a waitress if you don't want to." I poured us both a second drink, as modest as the first.

"I might want to. I'd be dealing with people again. Perhaps I could make them a little bit happier with a smile they didn't expect."

She tried the smile on me. It made me happier, God knows.

"If you want to. . . ."

"Or maybe I could go back to college too." She plowed on as though she had not heard me. I understood then that I was being asked for my approval, replacing Wolfe as the feudal master. "I have three years to make up. Do you think I might be able to get into law school eventually? I had good grades." She considered her drink thoughtfully. "That was twenty-five years ago, of course."

Naive and frivolous dreams, but important for her emotional well-being. I would not disturb them.

You may think it was a romantic interlude, Jameson's after a thunderstorm on the edge of the lake. It was not, I assure you. She was compellingly attractive to me again; but now I was so afraid of her superficiality that I would not have joined her in the master bedroom if she had invited me.

Of course she did not. Widows trained in Catholic schools don't think of such things. Or if they do, they don't act on their thoughts.

Gingerly I asked about the spirit manifestations, suspecting that they may have been merely an excuse to find a sympathetic man with whom to talk.

She put down her drink, folded her hands tightly, and told me about them, like a student reciting from memory in a junior high school classroom.

It had started with night noises in Wolfe's study. Then blue lights not inside the house but not exactly outside it either. The suits of armor would topple over with tremendous crashes (only Tancredi had been ejected from the house). In the morning they would find jewels,

stamps, and coins torn from their cabinets and tossed
aimlessly around the room, chairs overturned, books
pulled from the shelves, the closed draperies ripped
open.

The last couple of nights the disturbances had spread
to other rooms in the house, the guest rooms first and
then Kevin's bedroom. Even during daylight hours pictures fell off the walls and chairs would turn over, apparently of their own accord.

She and Laurel had told no one but the Fosters, who
were skeptical about ghosts and blamed the lake winds,
which indeed had been strong the last couple of days.

"I thought that if a sober and responsible business-
man like you, Lawrence"—there was a hint of mischievous twinkle in her gray eyes—"saw what was going on,
I would know that I should take them seriously and try
to do something."

"What could you possibly do?"

She glanced up, surprised. "Try to find a way that
Wolfe can have Christian burial. I'm sure that's what he
wants. He never really left the Catholic Church, Lawrence."

It seemed to me that it was one of the most stupid
things she had ever said. A few hours later I was not so
sure. About anything.

I poured myself one more Jameson's "for the road," a
good large dose to ward off evil spirits, and went up to
the main guest bedroom. Sue said she would wait up for
the kids.

Laurel, I realized, was all she had left. A thin reed.
Moreover, the girl had seemed hostile to her mother
when she and Tommy left for their date with Diamond.

I tried the door to Wolfe's study. It was firmly locked. I
wondered where the key was.

I opened the door to the balcony outside my room.
The rain had passed through, but the night air was thick
and humid, smelling of earth and storm, the kind of
summer smell I love. I felt a pang of regret that there
had been no weeks in the Dunes for me when I was a
child and that I had not tried to overcome Dorrie's fear

of spending "too much money" on a summer home.

I told myself that it was an absurd reaction, drank my Jameson's, and went to sleep.

I woke up later shivering. Had winter returned? It felt like an arctic storm had swept in from the lake. I stumbled over to the balcony door. There was no wind. The air in the doorway was warm and soft, a gentle summer night. I stepped out on the balcony. The cold—and I was now aware that it had been a clammy cold—disappeared.

I walked back into the bedroom. It was like stepping into a deep freeze. For a moment a strange little blue light bounced across the floor and seemed to pass through the door into the corridor. I was still too sleepy to think straight. I did not believe in ghosts, of that I was still sure.

Then the cold faded, slowly and, it seemed, reluctantly.

I staggered back to my bed, not sure that any of it had really happened. A dream, a nightmare, that was it.

Then I heard objects smashing against walls and a woman's terrified screams.

I dashed across the hallway to Sue's room. The door was rattling as though it were being buffeted by a wind. Inside the master bedroom, furniture was tumbling, glass was breaking, things were crashing against the walls, and Sue was screaming in pure terror.

I tried to shove the door open. It was unlocked and yielded a few inches to my pressure and then slammed shut, as if angry at my intrusion.

Then Laurel and eventually Tommy, sleepy-eyed and frightened, emerged from their rooms, Tommy from the other end of the hallway, Laurel from her room between mine and her mother's. All three of us pushed against the door and jammed it open.

I want to emphasize, Monsignor Blackie, that the three of us saw not merely the results of the phenomenon in the master bedroom after it had ended. We saw the phenomenon itself for a few moments before it ended.

Sue was pinned against the pink chintz-covered wall, seemingly tied there by one of the filmy curtains from the king-size bed, as though she were bound with chains. She was wearing a long lavender-and-white-striped gown, perfectly modest you may be sure. But the gown had been pulled from her shoulders and objects were smashing against the wall all around her—brushes, mirrors, clocks, pillows, combs, bottles of cream, even dresses and skirts that were flying out of the closet and blouses and underwear from the dresser. The terror on her face reminded me of the most disturbed patients at Dorrie's hospital—a trapped woman hesitating on the brink of insanity. The room was filled with the stench of raw, untreated sewage. The objects were hitting the wall with enormous force, as though fired from guns. Sue's bedroom had become a chaotic torture chamber in which a fiend was driving her toward madness.

We witnessed only a few seconds of this mayhem. It stopped as suddenly and as abruptly as if someone had turned off a television screen. A bottle of cream stopped dead in the air in front of us and tumbled to the floor. The sounds ceased abruptly, except for Sue's screams. There was only the quiet sound of the lake at night.

She collapsed to the floor, like a weary and ill-tempered child's rag doll discarded at the end of the day.

It required an hour for us to revive her and then calm her down. Tommy and I were very sympathetic, Laurel less so, at first. We finally got her back into bed with a sleeping pill and a promise of a guard at the door for the rest of the night. The three of us took turns. The next morning she begged me to find someone to help us put Wolfe's soul to rest.

I drove into Chicago and called Red Kane. He made an emergency appointment for me with the Cardinal. His Eminence was very gracious and suggested that I see you. The rest you know.

I've said repeatedly that I don't believe in ghosts. It is a foolish faith which is useless when you find yourself contending with the violent fury which had taken possession of Sue's room. I continue to tell myself I don't believe that the dead come back to haunt us.

Nonetheless, I know at some profound level of my being that Wolfe Quinlan came back from the dead that night to brutalize his wife in death as he had in life. My question is simple: Can you make him stop?

—————————— 11 ——————————

BLACKIE

"Could he not be punishing her because she killed him?" I asked softly.

He had been examining his huge hands. Outside, a summer thunderstorm was building up, making my Wabash Avenue office look like a rundown catacomb.

"Honestly, I'm not sure. I don't see how she could have killed him. If she did, God knows she had reason. There is such a thing as self-defense, isn't there?"

"Indeed."

"She was at the door when we battered it down to find his body. How could she have killed him?"

"Come now, Larry, you are perceptive enough to answer that yourself."

"We have no proof that he might not have been dead for fifteen minutes or so before she summoned us to break down the door?"

"Precisely."

"But there is still the problem of the locked door."

"Who else would be likely to have a secret duplicate key?"

"The police tell us that that type of key can't be copied; the plates from which the key is made are destroyed right after the key is made. It's a one-of-a-kind key."

"I suspect that someone determined enough to find a way of making a copy could do so."

"Sue doesn't have that kind of determination." His strong face was wrestling with troubling doubt.

"Don't be so sure."

"You don't think she killed him, do you? Not really?" He was almost begging me for reassurance.

"How else do you explain the phenomena?"

"I don't know. Dear God, I don't know."

"But the phenomena have stopped, have they not?"

"Yes, they have." He considered that fact thoughtfully. "It almost seems like the spirit is afraid of you."

"Ah. Perhaps."

"Well, they haven't stopped completely."

"What?" I sat up in sudden astonishment. That fact didn't fit my hypotheses. I didn't like it.

"Small scale. A cabinet in the study continues to rumble. And the Video camera comes out of the closet every night."

I felt a distinct and unpleasant chill. "Video camera?"

"We put it away every night. The next morning it's on the work table where... where his body was lying."

"How unusual." And how scary.

Hey, I'm Blackie Ryan, these things don't scare me because I can explain them all. Right? As my sister Mary Kate would say.

Right.

"You'll come up to Long Beach and investigate personally?"

"Perhaps." It would be hard now to keep me away. "I will have to interview some of the others who are involved first."

I glanced down at the folder from the diocese in which Louis Connery had served as a priest. I did not like that either. Might the two oddities fit together? There was nothing particularly supernatural about Father Armande St. Cyr's background. Yet he was scary too.

He'd been ordained thirty-five years ago, so he was

over sixty, even though he was alleged to look ten years younger. His mother was an immigrant from a Quebec farm; his father worked for the sanitation department, first as a teamster driving the horses that pulled the old wagons and then as a helper on one of the early automotive garbage trucks. Louis had not performed brilliantly in the seminary and there had been some trouble about his being ordained. The rector thought he might not be altogether trustworthy.

In those days they didn't have personality tests to sort out the potential psychopaths.

But he worked enthusiastically in two black parishes for fifteen years. Left those parishes after unspecified charges from some women in the neighborhood about his behavior toward them and their daughters. Marched on antiwar picket lines in the late sixties and then became diocesan director of the Charismatic Renewal at his own request.

So far nothing unusual. A problem priest—enthusiastic, hardworking, but lacking in balance and with a weakness for women, perhaps a little kinkier than most such weaknesses. One grows accustomed to reading between the lines in such confidential letters from chancellors: Why not turn the Charismatic Renewal over to him? It's new and it probably won't last and it gets him off our backs.

There's maybe a thousand reasons that you don't want to let marginal personalities near a legitimate but highly emotional religious movement, none of which, alas, were cautions that would occur to your typical chancery office bureaucrat of a decade and a half ago.

Then the story became strange—reputation for healing, large enthusiastic following, strange psychic manifestations, paraliturgical services featuring young women dressed in white robes called "virgins of light." Apparent accidental death of one of the virgins who was found to be pregnant. Funds missing from Diocesan Charismatic Center. Police investigation of death. No charges made. Father Connery sent to Weston Abbey for six-month retreat. Did not report to the abbey. Now heads small sect of his own in middle west.

A magnetic and dangerous madman, in other words, becoming more mad and more dangerous.

Might he be involved in locked-room tricks? And other fake or maybe not-so-fake psychic phenomena? It sounded like the sort of thing Louis Connery might want to do if he could.

In retrospect there were other conclusions I might have drawn from the report but didn't. It was late summer, I offer in my own weak defense, and not all cylinders inside my head were functioning properly. As it turned out, my lack of perceptiveness was tragic. At least four more people are dead because of it.

"I'm not sure Sue will talk to you. May I suggest you see the others first. Then perhaps drop over when you're visiting your relatives in Grand Beach."

"I had planned to talk to everyone else first." He looked at me as though he wanted once again to plead her innocence. "But why is she hesitant? Was it not her decision to seek help? Is she not concerned about the continuing, er, manifestations?"

I sure as hell would be.

"She's ashamed. She thinks you don't like her."

"That's not true, Larry." I adopted my most clerically reassuring tone. "Why wouldn't I like her?"

She was a Wade and the Wades were, God forgive them for it, Republicans, and the Ryans were, of course, Democrats, radical Democrats in my mother's case. Less serious divisions made for bitter feuding in the old 19th Ward. That was long ago. Old enmities were forgotten. Well, mostly. Besides, she was a fluffhead.

No one, however, was doomed to such a fate for all their lives. I'd be nice to Sue Quinlan, even if she is a Republican. After all, she had been born that way, so it wasn't her fault. I'd be especially nice, since she had graduated from Suzie to Sue.

There was, of course, the matter of the key. Just before Larry Burke's return, my phone had rung.

"Father Ryan," I had murmured, trying to sound like a real clerical bureaucrat, knowledgeable, discreet, wise.

"God, I thought it was the Pope.... Anyway, you were right about the key. Maybe you should write the revised edition of my book."

"Indeed."

"Right." Mike Casey was now the smooth police investigator. "There was indeed a new lock made for the door in late spring. At Mrs. Quinlan's request. With two keys. It was installed just before the Memorial Day weekend—when you were involved in the shoot-out at the Karwick shopping plaza."

"Ah." In fact, I was nowhere near the plaza, but I let it go. I was not, after all, uninvolved in that affair. I and my friend P.O./3d C.S. McLeod of the United States Coast Guard.

"Moreover, as you thought, the ninnies at Long Beach didn't bother to check to see if the lock registration in his desk drawer corresponded with the lock itself, which, as is now obvious, it didn't."

"There is or was another key? And Mrs. Quinlan had it?"

"Presumably."

"Not the kind of woman who would change her husband's lock without his knowing it," I said, more to myself than to Mike Casey.

"He might have told her to do it."

"And claimed the key for himself?"

"Why not? Maybe he gave it to your friend Father Armande."

"Indeed."

I thanked Mike for his persistence. I would not, I decided, even mention the second key to Lawrence F. X. Burke. I would reserve my little surprise for La Suzie herself.

I did not like it at all.

"I've learned a lot about her in the last few days, Blackie," Larry continued in the tone of a man describing a work of art from outer space. "She has excellent reason to be frightened. Do you want to hear about it?"

Is the Pope Catholic?

12

LAWRENCE F. X. BURKE

I can't tell the rest of my story with much objectivity. I am in no condition to make a judgment about what is right and wrong. To make matters worse, from your point of view at any rate, I no longer find myself caring what is right and wrong.

So far have I come from my father's integrity.

The day before yesterday I called my secretary and instructed her to tell those who phoned me that I was taking a day of vacation. The poor woman sounded like she had suffered a heart attack.

I drove up to Long Beach, arriving shortly before lunch. Neither Tommy nor Sue seemed surprised at my arrival. "The chick in your office said you were taking a day of vacation." Tommy barely glanced up from the computer magazine he was reading at the edge of the swimming pool. "We figured you'd appear here eventually. It's cool because I can turn over guard duty to you and play my match with Packy Jack Ryan this afternoon."

"I've had a large group of teenage protectors these last few days." Sue paused in her lap-swimming to peer up at me. "They promise to teach me to waterski when you say it's all right."

She sounded cheerful; Tommy's new friends had provided a little of the joy she had never received from her own children. I wondered if she had enough imagination and intelligence left to grasp the poignancy of that fact. And its transiency.

She served hamburgers at poolside for lunch with a

bottle of red wine, which Tommy rejected in favor of
Diet Coke.

"Better burgers than MacDonald's," he observed between bites as he wolfed down his second one, "and I'm
an expert on the subject."

"I blush, kind sir."

Tommy examined her skeptically. "Not so you'd notice it."

The two of them were getting along famously. Neither
was, of course, a threat to the other.

After he had cleared away the remains of the hamburgers and the empty wine bottle, Tommy left for the
Grand Beach golf course. Neither Sue nor I had much to
say to each other. She discarded the floral skirt she had
worn over her two-piece swimsuit and plunged back
into the pool. I read the newspapers and plunged into
Business Week.

Sue pulled herself wearily out of the pool and
wrapped a bath sheet around herself. "Darn kids are
making me exercise again."

"Tommy and you get along well?"

"He's a doll. You should be proud of him."

I would have said that indeed I was, but I was afraid to
recall Kevin to her mind. In retrospect that was absurd.
She did not envy me Tommy.

I continued to struggle through *Business Week*, hardly
noticing what I was reading and telling myself how absurd this "vacation day" was.

Sue lay on one of the thick yellow rubberized mats at
the side of the pool and, with her white-framed Italian
sunglasses in place, struggled with a book whose title I
could not see but which I suspected was a college catalog.

It was a blisteringly hot day, well above ninety, and
typical middle-western American humidity to match.
Sue loosened the straps on the back of her halter, for
the proverbial even tan (in which I'm not sure I've ever
believed).

I thought it was time for my laps in the pool. I swam
vigorously, indeed to the point of exhaustion. I prayed

that I could survive until Tommy came back. I told myself as I climbed out of the pool that I would plead the excuse of another nap.

I sat on one of the deck chairs for a few moments, merely to allow my skin to dry before beating a retreat to the guest room.

My eyes would not leave her, an almost irresistibly inviting attraction on the other side of the pool. The legal term *attractive nuisance* ran repeatedly through my head. She was a nuisance. I should never have permitted her in my life, never tolerated her image to frolic in my fantasy. She was nothing more, I told myself for perhaps the millionth time, than an empty, shallow middle-aged woman.

An attractive nuisance.

I rose from the chair, filled with virtuous determination. My traitor feet drew me not to the house but to her. I stood above her, captured by the bare back, so fragile and appealing, and all the promise and possibility that it suggested.

She had been trained to submit to men. She had submitted to others. Now she would submit to me. That was what she was for.

I'm ashamed to describe these emotions, especially after the things you often say about men exploiting and using women down through the centuries. I'm against it in principle. In practice I succumbed. I was powerful. She was fragile. I would have her.

She turned her head, conscious of my presence, though she had not heard my bare feet on the pool deck. She removed her glasses, one hand clutching at the front of her halter, to study me. She recognized what she saw on my face and turned away, in dismay and, I thought, resignation.

What I had wanted for eight years would now happen. It would be quick, perhaps harsh, certainly unsatisfying. Yet it had to happen.

I pulled her to her feet. She struggled briefly, without much force, her hand still clinging to the halter cupped against her breasts. I tore it away and dragged her into my arms, out of my mind now with desire. Her resistance ceased, and as I suspected, she submitted meekly.

The meek will inherit the earth? Perhaps. I don't know, however, why they would want it.

I kissed her, caressed her, squeezed her, pulled off the bottom of her swimsuit. Naked, she was even more lovely than in my fantasies. I pushed her down on the mat and threw myself on top of her. She smelled of wine and sweat and suntan lotion, a fastidious woman stripped even of the defenses of her perfumes.

Mine, all mine, submissively mine. An adolescent's sexual fantasy come true. A page out of a *Playboy* article.

Also, as I had anticipated, it was not much fun. I was rushing hastily and brutally toward the release of sexual tension and the discharge of a long obsession; but there would be little joy in a conquest of such a passive, silent, and resigned prize.

Then I saw that her eyes were wet. Tears, stupid womanly tears. I heard in my memory her late husband's idiot refrain, "You know how women are!"

Her tears caused a strange reaction in me, from which I have not recovered and may not ever recover. I paused in my wild dash for orgasm and kissed her eyes gently and delicately and then her lips, not devouring them as I had before but... but what? Reassuring them? Loving them? Giving her a moment of affection?

Anyway, quite unconsciously, I guess, I put in those kisses every bit of tenderness and sympathy and kindness I possessed.

For a few seconds something cracked open in my personality, a quick tidal wave of gentleness that I knew I could not sustain. Three kisses, five counting one on each breast, as light as that of a hesitant thirteen-year old lover. In the midst of my agonized struggle for sexual release, I saw out of the corner of my eye, as I would see a cabin cruiser at a distance in a hazy lake while I was reading on a sundeck, that she was a treasure to be treated with utmost care, a magical woman in whom lurked layer upon layer of fascination and mystery.

My vision faded in the mists. I felt the insidious temptation of tenderness ebbing. I sensed even greater harshness returning, now even brutality. Had she not liked brutality from her husband?

Before the last trace of tenderness slipped away, Sue changed too. Her passive submission dissolved into reckless abandon, an impassioned giving of self so total that I would not have believed any woman capable of it. It was as if she had thrown away all her clothes and offered to be totally naked for me for the rest of her life. She held back nothing, hid nothing, denied me nothing. The pleasure I experienced in her abandon was like a roaring tornado of joy, so destructive that I was not sure that I could stay alive in such a mind-destroying storm.

All else melted away. There were only the two of us, alone on a planet devoted to cosmic pleasure. My last rational thought was astonishment that this limitless joy could be happening with her, of all women.

That is not all. That first abandoned encounter was only a hint of what was to come.

We huddled in each other's arms under the implacable August sun, gasping for breath, bathed in sweat, proud of our incredible journey. She wept a little, though not, I think, from sorrow. I stroked her reassuringly, murmuring soundless words of affection.

Then she gave herself to me. Having yielded her body, she gave me everything else. She pulled a bath sheet over the two of us, pressed her body firmly against mine, and in her soft and lovely voice and now without a single tear told me the story of her life. It was not a story I wanted to hear, because I knew it would be horrifying and because I feared it would also be fascinating.

It was both, more horror and more fascination than I had expected. Some of it was sickeningly repellent. But Sue became all the more attractive as she told it. The revelation of self, I guess, is always appealing. The revealer flatters you with trust and bemuses you with vulnerability. Her trust and vulnerability were nearly total. In the end, fascination won out over horror—and brought with it admiration and respect.

I held her naked body in my arms by the side of the swimming pool and swore, to myself, that the worst of her suffering was over.

Her body, utterly peaceful in my possession, was so beautiful that I had to look away from it intermittently, as one avoids the sun on a day of an eclipse. Even its imperfections, the lines and tiny pouches of softness and flab that affect the most determined of us when youth is over, were poignantly appealing. Her facial bones and skeletal and muscular structure were such that if she were loved she would always be beautiful.

Could I love her that way? With her breasts pressed against my chest and her legs intertwined in mine beneath the now hazy but still fierce August sun, I had not the slightest doubt.

The doubts would come later.

Before I could come down to earth and reply with any effectiveness to the gifts she had given me, we heard a car pull noisily into the driveway and accompanying high-pitched adolescent voices. Sue giggled, rolled out of my arms, pulled on her swimsuit, and dived into the pool. I followed almost as quickly.

"Hi, guys, have a quiet afternoon at home?" Tommy shouted at us. "Still swimming, Mrs. Quinlan? You don't want to overdo it. Old people shouldn't exercise too much."

Despite ourselves, the two of us laughed uncontrollably. Tommy did not seem to notice.

He did notice our mixture of giddiness and nervousness at the supper table. He raised one eyebrow, in a quick flicker of significance at me, and said no more. Not that he had to.

Interestingly enough, he didn't seem to mind. I felt guilty. I was unfaithful to his poor mother. Then I realized that his mother, should she be capable of knowing, would not mind either.

After supper we watched *Wifemistress* on cable television, a mistake, all things considered, but none of us had seen it before.

"I really dig that Antonelli chick," Tommy announced.

"Even if she is real old, like almost as old as you, huh, Mrs. Quinlan?"

"Older," Sue said. "According to a movie magazine I read in the optometrist's office, she's in her fifties."

"Awesome."

"Well, I've had enough for one day. Too much exercise for an old woman, like you said, Tommy."

She kissed us both on the forehead and walked up the double staircase to the third floor. The ball was, I thought, definitely in my court.

We watched the Olympic summaries on Channel 7, Tommy marveling at the "really awesome" shoulders on the American girl swimmers. Then he went to bed.

I remained at the TV, sipping Diet Coke, paying little attention to the French mystery film that was spinning before my eyes, and marveling at what a happy family the three of us were.

If it could only go on that way...

Of course, it could not. Life is not a succession of hot summer days with hamburgers, steaks, good wine, incredible sex, interesting films, and a delightful eighteen-year-old boy.

With that in mind, I went to my room to make a decision about the rest of the night and in that decision quite possibly about the rest of my life too. I was too content, too self-satisfied, too—dare I use the word—happy to be capable of making such a monumental decision.

What had happened on the pool deck was a violent animal reaction, the hunger of a male of the species with an obsession of many years and a sparse sex life for the last several. The next step was a matter of deliberate choice, rational, conscious, reflective. I had to carefully evaluate my options, just as I would for a client who wished to invest his hard-earned savings.

Fool that I was, I thought that I still had some options.

I turned off the TV, made sure the doors were locked, switched off the lights (how like a paterfamilias!), and trudged uncertainly up to the third floor. At the top of the double staircase I was winded. Too much exercise, of various kinds, for an old man in one day.

I was an old man. What was I doing playing such foolish games?

I went into my bedroom, removed my shirt, trousers, and sneakers, and, clad only in my shorts, walked out on the balcony, as if there were no question about what was to be done. The temperature had fallen into the seventies, the lake was motionless, the moon peered graciously through a thin curtain of haze—premature hints of Indian summer for an Indian summer love affair.

The sliding door was open on her section of the balcony, pleasant night air replacing the daytime protection of air-conditioning. Transparent pink curtains stirred slightly in a faint breeze.

The serious debate about what I would do, had there ever been one, was over. I walked through the swaying curtains. Sue was sitting at her vanity table, reading carefully her college catalog. She was wearing a lace-drenched peach chemise with a matching makeup coat (I had learned a lot about such things in the last year).

I wondered if he had ever seen her in those wispy and delectable garments. It was, I insisted mentally, utterly irrelevant.

Sue heard me, looked up, put aside her catalog and rose from her vanity chair, hesitantly.

"Were you expecting me?" I paused at the door, the curtains brushing lightly against my flesh.

She took off her glasses, folded them, and placed them next to the bottle of Jameson's and the two empty glasses on her vanity table. "I thought I'd be ready if you came."

I walked carefully across the thick rose-colored carpet. I was now in the boudoir about which I had fantasized so often. Her facial expression was uncertain, a child not sure whether the teacher is angry at her.

"Complete with drinks for two?" She smelled of citrus blossoms.

"You might be thirsty." She smiled faintly.

"I don't smell nearly so pretty." I touched her face.

She winced as though I had hit her. "Yes, you do. . .

Does Tommy know?"

"I didn't tell him." I outlined her jaw with my fingers. "I think he suspects. He sure doesn't seem to mind."

She nodded solemn agreement. "Did you enjoy it down there?"

"More than anything else in my life." I caressed the muscles of her throat with feathery fingers.

"I didn't think—" She gasped as though I had stolen her breath. Her lips opened and her jaw sank toward her chest. "I didn't believe that I ever could—have you wanted me for a long time?"

"I sure have." I took her face in my hands and kissed her forehead.

"And you still do?" She seemed puzzled by the possibility.

"What do you think?" I slipped the makeup coat off her shoulders.

"I don't see how you can, after all I told you this afternoon." She was ready to cry.

"All the more." I touched the thin shoulder strap of her chemise, brushing it off.

"Really?" She was astonished, like someone who had just won a lottery they hadn't even entered. "I don't understand, but then I don't understand anything anymore."

"Don't worry about it." I brushed away the other strap. She held the garment at her breasts. The fingers of her other hand, as soft as a baby's, touched my chest, then my belly, then crept insidiously under the elastic of my shorts.

"If you want me"—she took a deep breath, like a diver at the top of the Olympic pylon—"you can have me whenever you like."

The gift wrapped up and offered a second time.

"If you want me"—I must have gulped—"you can have me whenever you like." One gift wins another.

"I was hoping you'd say that." She kissed me, lightly, then very hard. Forcing her tongue into my mouth, she threw both her arms around me and hugged me with all her strength.

Her chemise fell to the floor, followed in a moment by my shorts.

We were gentle and affectionate and even comic with one another for most of the night. I realized vaguely when I finally fell into exhausted sleep what was unmistakably clear the following mid-morning.

For the second time in my life I was in love, irrevocably and passionately in love. It might be a foolish and even destructive Indian summer love, but I would not and could not give it up.

I was older and wiser than the first time I fell in love. I knew that my decision was problematic. I knew I would probably live to regret it. I didn't care then and I don't care now.

If she did kill her husband, Monsignor Blackie, she had every right to do so and I'll do all in my power to protect her from you or anyone else who threatens her.

13

BLACKIE

"You did, of course, phone Laurel?" I said, ignoring his needless threat.

"After supper that night and the next morning—well, it was almost noon. She was safe with her friends in Elmhurst. Sue says that the child needs time to sort herself out."

The most trivial piece of wisdom spoken as though it were discovered carved on an ancient monument. You have it bad, my friend, Lawrence F. X. Burke. Not that that is necessarily bad.

"Laurel and her mother spoke?" I persisted.

"Briefly. There is tension between them, obviously; one can't expect anything different. It doesn't prove a thing."

"She had more time for you and Tommy, then?"

"Tommy especially. She was very cordial to me, however. By the way, she will come to see you if Tommy can come too."

Why not? I would check them both out with my niece The Cat O'Connor, also known as O'Connor The Cat, lifeguard in residence and reigning queen empress of Grand Beach.

There were a number of points, rather more in his favor than not, that Larry Burke, a true Israelite without guile, in the words of the scripture, had not perceived.

First of all, he was seduced. Perhaps Suzie, oops Sue, was not fully conscious of what she was about, but neither was she completely innocent of machinations. That fact did not, by the by, lower my estimation of Sue. Rather it caused me to raise my opinion of her, not much perhaps but somewhat. She had accomplished the seduction with admirable skill, given, of course, that one was to occur. Peach chemise indeed. I don't necessarily approve of seductions (nor necessarily disapprove of them either, for that matter), but I certainly disapprove of clumsy ones.

The intelligence she had tried to leave behind when she married had not completely atrophied. Her self-disclosure ploy had demonstrated some grace.

Secondly, he was mistaken in his assumption that love fell from the sky over Long Beach. It had been there for a long time. He had tried to mask it from himself by pretending that his only emotion was obsession. That he was obsessed with her was beyond debate. However, Larry Burke was not the kind of man who could sustain an obsession indefinitely without some other motive.

He had seen in fluffhead Suzie something that merited love. He could not identify it or name it, but in the murky realms of his preconscious he knew it was there.

Was it really there? On that simple question the rest of his life might very well depend. Perhaps his conviction that the unnamed lovability was present in his Sue might tease it into being.

I had grave reservations. On the other hand, who was I to question the perceptions of so keen an observer of womankind as Tommy Burke, who had said that Sue was a "cool chick."

Brigid, Patrick, and Colmucille preserve us, as my mother used to say when some unexpected wonder intruded into life.

On the other hand, Lawrence F. X. Burke was now so hopelessly in love with her that he would willingly kill or conceal killing to protect her, and do so with as clear a conscience as his father when he left his teller's window at the bank during the Great Depression without a single pencil belonging to the bank.

"You're not going to turn her over to the police?" He asked me the question a second time, interrupting my reflections.

"Mr. Burke, please. Am I an employee of the police department of Chicago or Elmhurst or Long Beach? Am I an agent of the LaPorte County prosecutor? Am I even a licensed private detective?"

"You're my pastor." He frowned deeply at that profound observation.

"Ah. So I am. I am supposed to determine the reason for certain apparent psychic phenomena in Mrs. Quinlan's house, phenomena that have apparently stopped."

"Not quite. Yesterday morning and again today, when we went down to breakfast, the camera was on the work table."

Was it really? I thought it most improbable that Tommy Burke was that kind of prankster. No, I didn't like the camera at all. Nor the chill it produced in my muscles and nerves and veins.

"As to your concerns, I have no evidence to suspect Mrs. Quinlan of murder, and even if I did it would not follow that I could consider myself bound to turn over such evidence to the police."

She might well have done it, just the same. She certainly had what many would have considered sufficient

reason. Yet the locked room was too cute a caper for
fluffhead Suzie.

But not necessarily for Sue the skillful seductress.

"After you talk to her, you will understand that even if
she did kill him, it wasn't murder."

"Ah."

Maybe. But Wolfe Tone Quinlan—attractive, brutal
moron that he was, an opera bouffe tenor in Larry
Burke's imagery—had a right to live. I could not easily
condone the violation of that right save in the most
direct and essential self-defense. Whoever had worked
the locked-room trick was either a brilliant and premed-
itating killer or an even more brilliant improvisationist.

Was my principal suspect of either sort? It remained
to be seen, but it was by no means impossible.

"You will talk to her, then? You will come up to the
lake and visit her?"

"If you and she wish."

Baloney, Blackie Ryan; you're absolutely dying to find
out whether this new Sue Wade who wears peach night-
gowns, tickles a man's chest before she pulls off his
shorts, and drinks Jameson's is for real.

"She's very fragile, you know."

"I am not the damn fool pastor from Elmhurst, you
know," I said with some heat.

"I'm sorry, Monsignor." He rose contritely. "I guess
it's obvious how much I'm in love."

Call me Blackie.

"One last thing. When you were in his study before
the murder, was the door of the closet open?"

He closed his eyes, trying to remember. "I don't think
so. No, it wasn't. I remember when I tried the handle
after we broke into the room, thinking that it was still
locked." He opened his eyes. "Is that important?"

"Could be."

"If you say so, Monsignor." He shook his head dubiously.

Call me Blackie.

After the poor besotted man left to stumble down
Wabash Avenue in the driving rain, I joined my col-

leagues in one of my usual simple midday collations—
minestrone, salami antipasto, fettuccini alfredo, veal pi-
catta, garlic bread, and tortoni, all washed down by a
perfectly adequate Chianti Classico Niocolo Machiavelli
Riservato. I declined the generous offer of My Lord Cronin, who joined our modest repast, to have a sip of Fra
Angelico liquor for digestive purposes.

I should mention that my metabolism is the despair of
my colleagues and siblings. I can eat monumentally or
fast monumentally (which I do on occasion to honor the
Church's traditions). I can exercise not at all (which I do
usually) or I can exercise recklessly (which I do on occasion, normally because of the taunts of my nieces and
nephews), and my vital measurements change not in the
least.

"He was born that way," Mary Kate says enviously,
"kind of a metabolic freak. Right?"

Right, dear sibling.

I thereupon retired to my lamentably disordered suite
of rooms, to read passages from the fathers, as the saying goes, a marvelous continental habit that I have
picked up despite the fact that I never studied on the
continent. I was diverted from this virtuous rehabilita-
tion of my resources by a delegation from the Cathedral
Associate Pastors' Teamster Local, which waited on me
with a petition that I get the hell out of the rectory, as
they colorfully put it.

This group, which has no civil or canonical standing
(and behind which I suspect the Lord Cardinal lurks), is
in fact prerevolutionary; it exists solely to overthrow
the power of the rector of the Cathedral, a power that
scarcely exists anyway.

"You're dragging around here like a worn-out lap-
dog," protested my senior associate. "Go over to Grand
Beach and leave us alone. Baptize those new babies.
Play with the teenagers. Read Willy James and White-
head and Hartshorne. Drink Jameson's all night long.
You're not indispensable."

I had no choice but to fall in with their suggestion,
especially since they threatened to lock me out of my

room and hide the key. One locked-room puzzle was enough. Give me, I pleaded, two more weeks for certain interviews and then I will leave you to your plot to move the Cathedral across State Street to the parking lot (on the site of the florist shop in which a Capone-era hood named Dion O'Bannion was sent to his reward—leaving, it is said, slug marks on the front walls of the Cathedral).

Three weeks, not two, my pitiless senior associate insisted. Lady Day in Harvest (August 15) and the rest of August.

Summer ends on August 15, not Labor Day, I contended, more for the record than seriously. Educational administrators have aborted August.

All the more reason why you should give good example, the young man (two years younger than me) responded. As hard as that is for you.

Nowadays, you don't argue with your staff.

I cite this ultimatum to prove that I was in deteriorated physical and mental condition. Indeed, far more deteriorated than I suspected. I possessed all the strands of the web—well, all but one—and all the hints of further destruction that was likely to occur. Yet I was quite incapable of pulling the facts together and taking appropriate action before it was too late.

I offer these facts not as an excuse—no one could have done any better—but as an explanation.

Quis custodit ipse custos? the Good Book asks wisely. Who watches the watchman himself?

Especially if he is falling asleep.

14

BLACKIE

Kiernan O'Rourke brought with him an invisible but noxious trail of slime. He was a classic example of an all-too frequent Irish legal type, a lawyer who reaches for distinction but, for reasons of corruption and The Drink, does not quite capture his goal and then spends the rest of his life sinking ever more deeply into sleaze while he struggles to maintain with declining skills the physical appearances of distinction. He was dressed in a rumpled white linen suit with an ill-pressed blue shirt and a white tie. His red, persecuted face terminated in a dangerously explosive whiskey nose. His shoes were white but soiled and his white straw hat was withered and depressed. The odious cigar he dared to bring into my monsignoral office was, he claimed, an illegal import from Havana—grounds for libel action if Fidel was of a mind for such entertainment. Somewhere there may have been a Mrs. O'Rourke and little O'Rourkes, but of them no one seemed to know or care. The Drink probably drove them away long ago.

It was easy to despise this pretentious, silly little man, with his pathetic hints of important political and ecclesiastical contacts and his flashy rings. On reflection, one—this one, at any rate—felt compassion. Once, long ago, he had been a very bright young man out of law school with glowing idealism and generous dreams.

Not too much compassion. My father, Ned Ryan, is of the same generation. "Watch the old buzzard carefully, Blackie," he warned me on the phone, with uncharacteristic heat. "He's played the harmless old man part since 1942 when he hid from the army in the bowels of City Hall. He was thick with the Outfit for a long time, did a little loan sharking on the side, wasn't above using enforcers, maybe even an occasional hit man. He's been a charity case for the Quinlans for a long time, the kind of guy who won't take his fee and leave but has to hang around pretending he knows something about law."

When my father talks that way about someone, you know that you'd better hold on to your wallet and not turn your back. But I was still enough moved by compassion for the poor old geek to tell him, yes, he could smoke his Havana cigar.

15

KIERNAN PATRICK O'ROURKE

Of course I'm happy to talk to you Monsignor; I've always been close to the Church. Monsignor McBride was a great friend of mine. 'Course, he was way before your time. We used to play golf every week up at Commodore Barry at Twin Lakes before the War and then almost every day at Olympia Fields after the War. He was a fabulous golfer, the monsignor was. And a wonderful human being. He could put away more bourbon than any man I've ever known. God be good to the poor man. We won't see his like again.

But that's not what we're here to talk about, is it? What are we going to do about this Quinlan business, Monsignor? A fine young man, struck down in the prime of life. Wonderful kids, marvelous wife, successful manufacturing firm—everything to live for. I said to him myself just a few days before, I said, Wolfe, I've known you since the day you were baptized and I've never seen a young fella with so much to live for. All right, you've had some tragedies, God help you. They'd do in an ordinary man, but you're no ordinary man. Get a hold on yourself, go out to Mayslake and make a retreat, talk to a priest, make a good general confession, straighten yourself out with the Church, get back on the golf course, I haven't seen you at Butterfield or Olympia in a couple of years. I bet your handicap is back up to ten.

Take time out, I said, take time out and enjoy life. Forget the past. Live for the future.

Sure, I'm kind of their legal counsel. I've been on retainer for them since back when the company was a little shop above a store on Ashland Avenue before the War and I was in law school still. My father handled their business for nothing—great friend of old Pat Nash was my father and Tom Nash too, no relation, of course. So when they started to make some money during the War and wanted to pay him, my father said hire the kid, he'll do your work long after I'm gone.

Well, sir, he was right. Forty years later I'm still doing their legal work for them. Not full-time, of course, I have a lot of other clients who would rather listen to old-fashioned shrewd legal advice instead of the pap they serve up in these huge law factories. I probably do more work for Quinlan Furniture than I do for any other single client, though I never did get around to billing them for everything. It didn't seem right. It was all in the family, if you know what I mean. You don't want to make money off your own, do you?

His whole problem, if you ask me, was the people he chose for friends and confidants. What did he need that silly religious group out in Hyde Park for? All University of Chicago mumbo jumbo anyway. Nothing good ever came out of that place; Moscow Tech we used to call it. I don't know what's happened to the Church since that council they had back in the sixties. Why do they let a crazy priest like that Father Armande wander around anyway? If he had been a curate at

Monsignor McBride's, they would have sent him off to
Coal City for the rest of his life or locked him up in
Dunning till he got hold of himself again.

Can you imagine turning the firm over to that man?
After all the work his father had put into it? And bringing those cheap shyster Jew lawyers and accountants to
look over the books? Like he never trusted me or poor
Greg Foster—and Greg dedicating his whole life to that
company and keeping it afloat while Wolfe lolled
around at the CAA or traveled to the tropics.

Look, Father, I mean Monsignor. Let me explain by an
example. Suppose one of your assistants here... that's
right; you call them associates now... well, suppose he
needs some money for, say, a young people's club theatrical. He'll make it all back on theatrical, of course, but
there isn't enough money in the treasury to pay the bills
he has to meet beforehand. Okay, does he have to come
to you and fill out a form asking for fifty or seventy-five
bucks? Of course not. A man like you, so close to the
Cardinal and all, can't be bothered with such trivia. So
he takes the money out of petty cash or maybe even out
of the Sunday collection. He knows you won't mind. He
knows that if someone comes running to you, you'll say,
Hey, he's one of my boys, that's what the money is there
for, to be used. It's all in the family. Then suppose you
are made a bishop somewhere and a new man comes in
with Jew lawyers and accountants and wants to blow
the whistle on this kid. All of a sudden it's not family
anymore. He's changed the rules without telling anyone.

Well, that's what poor Wolfe did. Greg and I kept good
family records. We paid all taxes and the social security
and government things like that. If we borrowed a few
dollars here and there, especially after Greg had that
setback in the Board of Trade, we did it because we
knew we were family and Greg wouldn't mind. Hell, if he
were around we'd ask him. But he didn't come in all that
often, especially since he got mixed up in that new-
fangled religious thing.

And I ask you, Father, why is that crazy fool priest
walking the streets? Can't the Cardinal do something

about him?

So Wolfe shows up with those Jew lawyers and accountants—you can tell a sheeny face a mile away, can't you?—and they claim we've been on the take. I tell them that, sure we have, it's no secret; Wolfe knows that we borrow money occasionally, and he doesn't mind. They say it's more than a half-million bucks. Wolfe confers with that damned priest in his white robes and red cape and says that we have to pay it back or he'll send us both to Statesville for the rest of our lives.

I ask you, Father, is that any way to treat family? In the old days when a young punk acted like that we had ways of straightening him out—a phone call here, a phone call there, a little action, and, bingo, the guy understood. You didn't have to get into serious action unless the guy was stubborn.

It saved a lot of trouble. You know what I mean?

Anyway, I also blame that crooked "adviser" of his, you know who I mean, What's-his-name Burke. A man with no quality at all, Father, nothing. His mother was a housemaid, his old man a bank teller. This guy drives his own poor wife into a funny farm. Where does he get off telling Wolfe to buy out Greg and then to invest all his money in oil? You know what's happening to oil prices these days? What did I tell you?

That punk kid of his, Burke's I mean, has a disgustingly dirty mouth on him. If you want my opinion, Father, I mean Monsignor, he's the one you should look at if you want to find out who killed poor Wolfe. Like I told the police, the punk shouted obscenities at him during dinner, merely because Wolfe, who was a little under the weather, said that the punk's mother was in the funny farm.

Well, then the police found out about everything that was said at dinner and I had a hard time calming them down. They didn't realize until I explained that Wolfe was always that way when he had a few too many under the belt and that no one took him seriously when he was in one of those moods.

I never should have been in the house, to tell the truth. Suzie—beautiful woman, Monsignor, and fine wife and mother but not too bright up in the head, if you know what I mean—wanted me to come. She thought that if we all sat down around the table we could sort out the mess about Wolfe's donation to that crazy priest—let everyone have something and avoid a public fight. I didn't want to do it. Wolfe had hurt my feelings. I felt he should come to me and apologize. After all, I was family, wasn't I? Didn't he owe me an apology?

I knew it would all work out, if we gave Wolfe some time to come to his senses. I don't blame the man for going on a tout with all those people around trying to tell him what to do. I said, Suzie, I said, leave him alone for a few days and it'll all work out. Give the man some space and he'll be all right.

She's always been a nervous little twit, Monsignor, and worried about her own money too—she couldn't do a day's honest work to save her life—so she insisted and I thought I'd come up as a favor to her. If I'd known that crook What's-his-name Burke would be sitting at the dinner table with me, I would have had some second thoughts. The man has no class, Monsignor, none at all.

A man like you, Ned Ryan your father and all, you know what class means and how important it is. Blood tells, I always say. Can you imagine it, Monsignor, Burke's old man was nothing but a fucking bank teller? Excuse my language, Father, but bloodsuckers like him really upset me. In the old days we'd get rid of his kind in a hurry, you know what I mean?

It turned out to be a lucky thing for Suzie and her kids that I was there—and one of them kids is a faggot, Father. Would you believe that? What's happening to kids nowadays, I ask you, what's happening? They sure did need an experienced lawyer around to deal with the police and the smartass twerps from the LaPorte prosecutor's office. It took me some time and some powerful talking, but I finally did sort them out. Tell you the truth, I think they still have an eye on the Burke punk; they might pick him up any day now, if you want to know what I think, as soon as they figure out how the punk got out of the room after he did poor Wolfe in.

What did you say, Monsignor? Did I have a chance to talk to Wolfe that night? No, not really. He came down for supper, under the weather, like I said, and then went right back up to his room and locked the door. I figured I'd stay overnight instead of trying to fight the traffic on the toll road, you know what that's like. I'd leave right after breakfast, maybe if Wolfe's feeling a little better we can have a word or two, but I'm not pushing him. Leave him space, I said; give him a few days to sort things out and he'll remember what family is all about, you know what I mean?

Worried about myself? Come on, Monsignor. I'm an old man. Who's going to send me to Statesville? Anyway, the thing about Chicago juries is that they understand what family is. They're not going to hold a few loans against me. Na, I wasn't worried at all.

Well, now that you mention it, yeah, I did knock on his door. Oh, about ten-thirty or so; I didn't check the exact time. Maybe about ten. No point in telling the police about it. They wouldn't have understood and it might have distracted them from the punk, who's the murderer, plain as the nose on your face, if you ask me.

Yeah, Wolfe opened the door. He was feeling better, With a body like his you can always bounce back quickly from a few drinks too many, you know what I mean? Well, we talked a few minutes, nothing much about the details, but he said what I knew he'd say. Kiernan, old buddy, don't worry. Give me a few days and all of this is going to work out. I don't really trust those sheeny lawyers either. And I don't trust that fucking priest.

His exact words, Father, so help me God!

Was the door to his closet open? Well, I wasn't really inside the room, but, yeah, I think it was. He had that home movie thing, you know the camera, set up like he was talking into it or something. Wolfe was always a great one for the gimmicks, you know what I mean? If it was new, he wanted it. A great guy, Father, a really great guy. They don't make them that way anymore.

Yeah, Father, it was set up across from his work table. I remember that I said, Wolfe, I said, you'd think you were the fucking President of the United States going on TV. He got a great kick out of that, he did. The salt of the earth, Father, the salt of the earth. We're all going to miss him.

Well, you gotta excuse me for being a bit emotional. I miss him like he were my own son, you know what I mean?

Glad to help, Father. Anytime.

It's the punk kid that did it, mark my words. Hell, he's probably as much off the wall as his old lady in the funny farm, if you want my opinion.

Keys, Father? No, I don't know anything about the keys. I've never seen a second one. Didn't the police determine that there was only one key? I believe that Mrs. Quinlan found the registration for it and the police contacted the lock manufacturers. I saw the registration form myself.

Sure, Father, anytime. Hey, give my best to Ned Ryan, will you? He and I go back a long time. Don't see him much anymore.

Remember, Father, I mean Monsignor, it was the kid. The cops will pick him up any day now. He deserves the chair or the gas chamber or whatever they use over in Indiana if anyone ever did.

16

BLACKIE

All was not well in the world. The Cubs had dropped three in a row to the Houston Astros, would you believe? Mary Decker had tripped over Zola Budd and blamed the South African kid in a display of bad sportspersonship that the poor girl would have to live with for the rest of her life. John O'Connor, the retired rear admiral who had taken over the Archdiocese of New York, was broadly hinting that Governor Cuomo was a murderer. (I'll not quote My Lord Cronin's expletives about the Rear Admiral.) The Libyans were mining the Red Sea. The Bears were pounding themselves to pieces before the other NFL teams got a shot at them. The papers were after Gerry Ferraro's husband because he wouldn't make public his income tax returns, even though there was no law that said he should. The President had jokingly told a live camera that he was outlawing the Soviet Union and the bombing would start in five minutes. Mr. Mondale didn't seem to know what to do with that bonus, nor with the news that the President routinely falls asleep at cabinet meetings.

I can't be critical. I'm a third of a century younger than the President and I fall asleep at Cathedral staff meetings.

Anyway, to make the world an even less appealing place, I had to endure the stench of Kiernan P. O'Rourke. He and my father go back a long way, do they?

However, as I waited for the arrival of Kevin Quinlan, I pondered his story. The man was despicable, but fiendishly clever. He had deliberately thrown suspicion on Tommy Burke to protect his own rear end. Doubtless he gave the police an account of Wolfe Quinlan's supper outburst that was neatly tailored to make him look good. Since the police heard the story first from him, the others not being smart enough to reveal it, they would be biased in favor of his account.

Not that Tommy Burke was home free. I had only his father's description of him; he might indeed have been furious enough to kill after the assault on his mother. Still, given the Long Beach police's fixation on teenagers, they were probably delighted to jump on the kid. If there was the slightest hint of guilt, they would have thrown him into jail, as they did to teenagers on the suspicion of having carried beer cans earlier in the night.

Presumably, since Tommy was not in jail and in fact at Long Beach, the police had not found a shred of evidence other than O'Rourke's devious hints.

I began to prepare a chart of those who had visited Wolfe Quinlan on the night he died. Kiernan at around ten, Larry Burke at twelve, two women after him, twelve-twenty and twelve-forty perhaps. Kiernan reported him sobering up with the closet door open and the TV camera set up. Larry reported the closet closed and no TV camera. He seemed to have hinted that the drinking had begun again.

I phoned him.

"A quick question, Lawrence: Was there any sign of open bottles when you visited Mr. Quinlan at midnight?"

A long pause.

"I didn't see any. I wasn't looking, however."

"But you did have the impression that he was more in possession of himself than earlier in the evening. Would you say that he had stopped drinking?"

Another long pause before a carefully measured response: "This is very tentative, Monsignor, but I think he might have stopped and then begun again. I cannot be certain of that, however."

I thanked him and hung up.

If indeed Wolfe Quinlan had sobered up somewhat, enough to play with his video machine, and then began to drink again, what might have happened between ten thirty and midnight to cause him to open another and perhaps yet another bottle of wine?

I considered the chart carefully and wrote in half hour intervals along the side margin and headings across the top about drinking and the closet in which the TV equipment was stored. Perhaps when the blanks were filled in I would be able to match this chart with Larry Burke's floor plan and find a solution.

Everyone at the house had motive and means. The

puzzle was still the opportunity. I glanced again at Larry
Burke's diagram. I thought I saw how the opportunity
could have been provided.

Kiernan O'Rourke had surely given me an edited version of his conversation with Wolfe Quinlan, in all probability edited beyond recognition. So he too had talked
to Quinlan. That meant at least four conversations:
Burke, O'Rourke, and two conversations Burke heard
from the distance of his room, one and maybe both with
women. Four people in the room between ten and
twelve-forty. The murder occurred, or rather was discovered, a few minutes after two o'clock, according to
the papers.

If the last person we knew to have been in the room
before Wolfe Quinlan's death, the woman or presumed
woman that Burke had heard from a distance shortly
after twelve-thirty, in a Jameson's-induced haze, was in
fact the killer, there would have been perhaps an hour
or a little more to accomplish the locked-room caper.

Suzie, excuse me, Sue (provisionally at any rate),
heard or claimed to have heard or thought she heard
screams and the sound of falling furniture at two. But it
didn't follow that the killing actually happened then.

Could Kiernan O'Rourke have killed Wolfe Quinlan?
He was a sly enough old bigot and cheat to figure out a
locked-room puzzle and to suggest it to someone else.
But actually thrust a sword into Wolfe Quinlan? He was
a frail little souse and it didn't seem likely.

On the other hand, all the killer really had to do was
to jump up on the pedestal holding the armor and
shove. That might require more agility than O'Rourke
possessed. Perhaps not. I would have to investigate the
physical layout of the museum. If Quinlan was partly
conscious and for one reason or another immobilized
on this work table, it would have been simplicity itself
to pull Tancredi's sword down so it was aimed at his
chest and then give the suit of armor ever so slight a
push.

Gravity could substitute for physical strength. Thus
Sue or Laurel might have sought release from their

oppressor.

Kiernan O'Rourke was wrong about Cook County juries; they would convict him after a half-hour's deliberation and send him off to prison no matter how old he was. Richie Daley was not a state's attorney who would listen for one second to a defense based on the "old days."

So O'Rourke had excellent reason to dispose of good old Wolfe before the transfer of the company to Father Armande's accountants and lawyers was complete. Whatever the condition of the deed and/or the will, they could much more easily be contested and the contest much more likely settled out of court if Wolfe Quinlan were dead.

Everyone would lose something, everyone except Tommy Burke, if Quinlan lived. But Greg Foster and Kiernan O'Rourke faced the grimmest fate—a long term in prison for a considerable variety of offenses.

There was always the blind alley of the locked room, a remarkably ingenious and well-thought-out cover-up for a killing. Brilliant either as plan or improvisation.

Or maybe it wasn't a cover-up at all. . . .

Maybe it was pure accident.

I studied the chart again.

Maybe. . .

The closet door was open at 10:30 and closed at 12:00. Interesting, not that it meant much of anything so far.

The video camera—what was that all about? And why was it involved in poltergeist manifestations after those should have stopped?

Again I felt a chill. I suppose, to be honest, I should say a warning chill.

17

BLACKIE

Kevin Quinlan was only marginally more appealing than Kiernan O'Rourke. The latter exuded corruption, the former hatred. His face wore the perpetual expression of abused petulance that John McEnroe used to display when a line fault decision went against him. He was too slight a person to be described as outraged, too blond and fair-skinned to be called choleric. He was rather so physically insignificant as to represent almost a caricature of squeaky revolt. His organism seemed capable of nothing more grandiose than nasty self-pity. Although he was only twenty, his curly hair was already receding and his thin, angry face would have been more appropriate for an aged and vicious elf.

He wore a tight white T-shirt, tighter black jeans, and various bracelets, necklaces, and rings. His clothes and his manner screamed at the world, "I'm gay, all right, screw you!"

Indeed his behavior came close to being a crude caricature of a certain kind of gay life-style. In the Cathedral parish we have enough of that proportion of the human race that finds members of its own sex more attractive than members of the opposite sex to dismiss the stereotypes and the caricatures—and to be suspicious of those who deliberately cultivate the stereotype. Some of them are surely gay, but some are not, at least in any meaningful or permanent sense. And, of course, most gays are utterly unrecognizable in ordinary contexts and circumstances.

Was Kevin faking it to offend his father and mother? I

wasn't sure and still am not sure. I don't know whether he was certain of his sexual identity either. He was certain of his hatred, however; that was his emotional lifeblood, the oxygen without which his personality would wither.

Whatever hopes his future might hold would require, even before the resolution of his problems of sexual identity, a cure for his anger. I would not have wagered much on the chances of that.

I sighed inwardly and trusted I was establishing some credit by these interviews against future pleasures that otherwise might require expiation in Purgatory.

18

KEVIN QUINLAN

I don't care. I hated him. I'm glad he's dead. The world is well rid of him. I didn't kill him, but I would have if there'd been a chance and I could have gotten away with it. I can't remember ever not hating the prick.

You have no idea how vile he was, not just occasionally but all the time. My mother is a stupid, worthless little bitch who was afraid to stand up to him; she's gutless, not mean. She sent me checks every week, even after I came out of the closet; they weren't large enough, but she had to lie to him to send me anything, so I suppose I can't blame her.

He enjoyed being mean, a complete sadist brute, and, believe me, I've learned to recognize that kind. Oh, he didn't use leather or whips, but I'm sure he would have liked to. I don't know; maybe he did with some of his expensive whores. You know about that, don't you? He was never faithful to Mother, not from the beginning of their marriage. He pretended that he was the big macho straight, you know, virile and strong and the great lover? Still, he couldn't get off on ordinary straight sex.

Mother would have done anything in bed he wanted, in bed or out of bed; that wasn't good enough for him. It had to be secret and exotic and forbidden. If you investigate his lovers, you'll find some that were into bondage and SM. And I'm the freak, huh? He was a worse freak than I am, but I'm willing to face it and go public.

He never had the guts to come out of the closet and say, "I get off on cheating and pushing my wife and kids around and on beating up an occasional whore whom I pay to let me do it."

He always despised me, I suppose from the day I was born. I was the third kid, you know, after Margaret and Wolfe. I was born after Wolfe died in the crib. He didn't like Marge either, she was not a pretty baby like Ellen and Laurel. If a girl wasn't pretty, she was useless. Wolfe was the favorite; even in his baby pictures the little shit looked like him. I'm glad he's dead too. I'm happy about anything that brought that monster pain.

So I was supposed to be the substitute for Wolfe, another big, healthy brat who slept all night and made happy faces when he showed you off. It was my fault that I was pale and sickly and didn't sleep through the night until I was almost two years old. I was a weakling, a coward, a lousy, poor replacement for poor departed Wolfe, a useless heir to family fortune and heritage.

He'd be ashamed of me if I ever tried to imitate him and walk around naked all morning at the Chicago Athletic. I was clumsy and not interested in sports. He probably decided the first day he saw me at Oak Park hospital that I was not a real man and never changed his mind. I'm not ashamed of being gay, and it's not my fault either. He made me that way.

I was ten years old when the other two died. He blamed it on me. I should have been the one who came down with leukemia, not Joseph, who wasn't as good as Wolfe maybe, but still a man even if he did cry when he lost at Little League games—and did he get beaten for that; real men don't cry, you see.

He said that I should have been on the beach watching Ellen the day she drowned. The waves were five feet high. Mother sent us both to the playground and forbade us to go near the beach. I did what I was told and Ellen, who was always a spoiled little brat, disobeyed. It was my fault she disobeyed. I was her big brother—a whole year older—I should have kept her at the playground. When she went to the beach I should have followed her and kept an eye on her. I should have died trying to save her life.

He wanted me dead, you see. He was so ashamed of me that he couldn't stand the sight of me. He beat me that day so I thought he would kill me too. Mother finally made him stop. Then he pushed her around too.

He usually didn't do that in front of us—a belt in the mouth occasionally, as he called it. I'm sure he saved it up for the bedroom. Most of us were probably conceived after SM intercourse; isn't that nice? And I'm supposed to be a pervert. What a farce!

No, I don't remember seeing any black eyes on her or anything like that. I think he was too clever to let the world know that he could get off only by beating her up. Why don't you ask her? Now that he's dead she doesn't have to pretend anymore.

That's all she is—pretense: the happy wife and mother holding the family together despite all the tragedies and despite a drunken brute of a husband. Maybe she gets off only if she's pushed around. Maybe they deserved each other. If you ask me, there's something of the masochist about her. Why stay married to such a vile brute anyway, unless you like it?

She's nothing, a weak, ineffectual nothing, just like me. You watch, she'll find some new brute, like that vile Burke person, to make the rest of her life miserable. The way he looks at her! Like he wants to tie her up and go after her with whips. He's just like my father. Maybe worse, because he doesn't go on binges.

Laurel? She's kind of a sweet kid, though a little kinky.

Psychic, you know. Weird, but nice. She was always nice
to me, nice to everybody, poor little bitch, but spaced
out. Like she was on drugs, only she wasn't. Yeah, he
pushed her around too, but not so much. Maybe he was
worn out after pounding lumps on the rest of us. She
knew how to handle his moods too, something Mom
never learned. That's what I mean by weird. She kind of
sensed what to do to him to calm him down. Sometimes
I think she could, like, hypnotize him. You ever look at
her eyes? They're dusky and murky, a little bit of a
witch, you know?

She may be the only one who genuinely loved the
bastard, worse luck for her. She'll miss him and the rest
of us will celebrate, goddamn him to hell!

Sure he changed after he joined those spooky Pente-
costals or whatever they call themselves. No more
booze, no more physical brutality, at least outside of the
bedroom. All pious and Christian, Jesus loves you, you
poor little weak kid. Pray to Jesus and He'll give you the
strength of ten, that kind of shit. Avoid sins of the abomination of the flesh. I tell you, the man was a vacuum. He
was practically illiterate. You could fill his head with
any crap you wanted to if he decided he liked you, if you
were "classy." So those creeps were "classy"? We had
to kneel down and ask his blessing whenever we left the
house. I had to pray with him to Jesus for guidance
when I failed a drama course at Marquette. Then we'd
open the Bible to find a "grace." Would you believe it?
The grace was always that I should work harder and
pray more and avoid bad companions—just what the
bastard would have told me without all the flimflam.

Finally I said screw it all. I'd rather starve to death
than live that way. So I moved out of the house, quit
Marquette, and came out of the closet.

You should have seen him! It was the happiest day of
my life! A few years before he would have kicked me in
the ass and beat the shit out of me. He probably wanted
to do that anyway. But the "grace" he found in the scripture was that he and Mom should come up to my apartment and beg me to do penance. I should pray hard to

God and I would be cured of my affliction.

I told the bastard that I didn't want to be cured and that I liked my affliction. I said that I probably inherited it anyway, since he wasn't a real man. He had to beat women to get it up; why couldn't I blow men? What was the difference? We were both weirdos.

Would you believe that he fell on his knees, tears streaming down his face, and begged me to reform my sinful ways. Mom too, of course; she always did whatever he told her. Picture it: here we are in a gay apartment building with three or four of my gay friends watching and laughing, and a couple of lesbians from the floor below us too. This middle-aged couple from the suburbs with their BMW parked outside, she in a mink coat, would you believe, are kneeling on our hardwood floor, praying and weeping.

I loved it, loved it, loved it.

Finally I told him to fuck off, I had a heavy-duty date with a forty-year-old bank vice-president.

"I beseech you in the name of Jesus our Savior"—he turns his shit stupid face up at me, glowing like he's a crucifix or something and says—"believe that Jesus is your savior!"

So I finally got some of mine back. "Fuck Jesus," I said, "and fuck you and fuck off."

Then, and this is simply delicious, I kicked his shit face, not real hard, but enough to send him sprawling on his big fat macho ass. Mother comes after me, but my friends pull her away. "You fuck off too," I go. "Keep this asshole out of my hair or we'll see if likes a blow-job rape."

You're a priest, so you can't think it was delicious, but he had it coming. Anyway, I didn't see him on his knees in my apartment again.

So I guess they kind of were excommunicated from their little nest of Christians because they didn't have the faith they needed to pray their son away from his abominable ways, and then they joined this sick little group out in Hyde Park. Talk about perverts! I bet they are heavy into SM. The old man may even need to be on the other end of it now. I think he kind of enjoyed being kicked in the face.

I don't care. I thought it was like *fun!*

So Mother calls me and goes, like he's going to give everything away to these Lucifer creeps or whatever they are; and I go I don't give a fuck and she goes I won't be able to sneak you your little check every week and I go okay, I can always sell it on the street.

Anyway, I'm pretty sure that Foster and O'Rourke will go into court and have the nut declared a nut. But Laurel gets on the phone and goes please come up for my sake. So I go what the fuck, for you I'll do it.

I had to give up a heavy-duty weekend in Dorr County with this really hot tennis pro. I should have gone to Dorr County. When the fuzz find out I'm, like, gay, they're convinced that I've stuck the sword in the bastard's gut. I go you got the symbolism wrong. If I was doing it I would have shoved it up his *ass!*

So I go to the pigs, you think because I'm gay I can walk through locked doors? Come on, man, get off my back.

Who stuck it to him? I don't care. I'm glad they did it. Probably O'Rourke and Foster; they don't want to be sent up to Statesville, where the black gays will do them four or five times every night. Maybe Mom because she wants to put on the chains for that Burke jagoff. Or maybe Burke because his whips haven't been used lately. I don't know. I'm not the detective.

Hey, how did you know I hit him up for money? Did that little creep Laurel squeal on me? Oh, about eleven-thirty or so. I was running a little short, not making the few extras I thought I could collect in Dorr County. When he was coming out of one of his binges, he was a sucker for a touch. Sure enough he gave me a fifty-dollar bill. Called me Wolfe, can you beat it? The last thing he does to me in his life, he confuses me with that little shit who died in his own puke in the crib.

The closet open? What difference does that make? I don't remember. Probably not.

The video camera, I didn't see it. I'm not sure I would have noticed.

His last words?

Well, he goes like, "I've been taken for a ride, Wolfe, for the last few years, but I'm finished with that now. A lot of things around here are going to change. You just watch."

No, not angry, kind of confused, like he was still half-drunk. There was an open wine bottle, maybe half-empty, on his desk, so I think he was going back under.

Keys? What keys? I don't know anything about another key. Why would I have it if there were one? I'd be the last one he'd trust with all his sick little treasures.

They did the bastard a favor by killing him. He would have drunk himself to death anyway in a year or two. A sword in the heart is quicker.

I only wish they'd shoved it up his fat ass.

19

BLACKIE

I withdrew from my office and complimented the young person at the switchboard on her new hairdo— my staff is astonished that I unfailingly notice such changes and comment favorably on them. Most men, they observe, not to say most clergy, are totally oblivious.

I notice because of my socialization by my mother and my sister Mary Kate. Hell would occur instantly if one failed to notice. That I comment favorably is merely courtesy and good sense.

If you comment unfavorably, you are quite likely to be the subject of a murder investigation, conducted, alas, by someone else.

These truths I learned at my mother's knee.

Kiernan O'Rourke and Kevin Quinlan had been quite enough office work for one day. I would receive the young couple who remained on the agenda in my parlor, where I have artfully created an atmosphere of musty confusion—piles of papers, books, and dust on every available surface—as to persuade a visitor that I am not a character from G. K. Chesterton so much as from Charles Dickens.

A sort of priestly Bob Cratchit, perhaps, working for Ebenezer Cardinal Scrooge—a metaphor that does not amuse my lord Cronin.

My point is that no room in the Cathedral rectory—a building reared in the style of late-nineteenth-century Ecclesiastical Ugly—can possibly be made attractive, so one might just as well settle for character. My conflict with the cleaning persons to maintain my carefully cultivated atmosphere can best be described as a running draw.

I engaged in an admirable exercise of the virtue of prudence and eschewed Mr. Jameson's nectar for soda water. (I serve Perrier for guests, to show that I am indeed a member of the academic elite, but use ordinary soda water privately.) Filled with my considerable virtue, I told myself that if ever I had merited a wee jar, it was after a morning in the office enduring O'Rourke and Quinlan. Such splendidly Irish names. For this end had the wild geese flown—a crooked lawyer and an angry would-be homosexual. Something had perhaps gone wrong somewhere in the immigrant experience.

On the other hand, it rained too much in the Old Country, too much altogether, as they would say—a discovery I had made once again only last month.

I phoned our inestimable cook and ordered three sandwiches and four Diet Pepsis. I would receive the teenagers in my parlor, disarming them, and insist that they eat lunch before we talked (like most of the species, they had probably overlooked breakfast and would arrive at the Cathedral rectory on the near edge of starvation). I ordered ham and cheese for them, with a side order of french fries (the cook is used to adolescent visitors), and for myself, a New York pastrami, heavy on the cole slaw, on pumpernickel with side orders of pastrami, cole slaw, and pumpernickel. Also a large double chocolate sundae with chocolate ice cream and nuts and whipped cream.

I was reasonably certain my young visitors would be in no condition for such a delight.

I proposed to eat my repast with them, observe how they acted toward each other, reassure them that I was more part of their culture and age group than their parents, and then interview them individually.

I had done some research on them. Packy Jack Ryan (not to be confused with his cousin Packy Mike O'Connor, the sibling of the fabled O'Connor The Cat) had assured me that Tom Burke was a "good guy," an excellent golfer, a presentable slalom skier, and not in the least flaky or spaced out or weird or nerdy or geeky or airy or any of those terms of opprobrium that adolescents use to describe those they find unusual.

The Cat was more reserved in her evaluation of Laurel. "*Well,* Uncle Punk, she is like totally *gor*geous, but kind of shy and, well, a little strange. Definitely not geeky, though. Not spaced-out either but, like sometimes far away, right? Once she knows you like her, she sort of relaxes and is lots of fun. But you've gotta be pretty explicit and say, hey, chick we think you're cool so stop trying to be a flake, because it doesn't fit, right? And her *eyes,* Uncle Punk! I've never seen such eyes! Like, you know, a smoldering furnace!"

Interesting if not reassuring—and at their worst not as exhausting as my morning visitors.

Kevin Quinlan had studied drama in high school and taken drama courses at Marquette. How much of his display of hatred, I asked myself, was a consummate cover-up for the fact that he was also a skilled leech? That he was taking money from his father as well as his mother came out quite by chance when I asked him about his visit to his father's study on the evening of July 4, a visit that was based merely on my assump-

tion—yet to be disproved—that *everyone* at the dinner
had wended their way to the museum door before the
night came to its abrupt and bloody end.

He was not prepared for that question and thus blurt-
ed out the truth, a truth that was at odds with his prepared statement/act. His father may have been all the
things Kevin suggested, but he also had a strain of in-
dulgence that Kevin had deliberately left out of his ti-
rade, although he had exploited it, probably often. And
probably of necessity, as far as that went.

A thoroughly unlikable young man, but wanting to be
unlikable, just as Kiernan O'Rourke wanted desperately
to be likable, as he had fancied himself to be with Monsignor McBride in the old days.

Thus most of his testimony could be dismissed as
part of his current persona, nothing more than an ingenious editing of the facts to meet his self-image. Perhaps he felt less anger than he presented.

Yet the anger was not all a form of self-presentation.
He hated his father and his mother too (perhaps her
more, though she was the target of less explicit rage).
He was sufficiently certain that no charge of murder
could be made to stick to him that he underwent no risk
by expressing his rage and even overexpressing it. He
might also, however, be hiding behind his mask of anger. Would not one suspect that a guilty person would
moderate his hatred of his father?

Kevin Quinlan was an ingenious young man, until
someone tricked him, as I did. It was necessary to be
suspicious of him. If all the family funds did go to Father
Armande, his sponging might be less rewarding. Even if
eventually Armande was bought off with an out-of-court
settlement, times might be hard for Kevin. He might, for
example, have to find a serious job instead of listing his
occupation as an unemployed waiter.

Hatred and greed, in an appropriate mixture, might
make him a dangerous clever criminal, a cheetah rather
than a lion.

He had also been very defensive about the question of
the missing key. Might he and his mother have

conspired. . .?

I considered once again the chart of the third floor of Wolfe Quinlan's "Transylvanian villa." Slowly a scenario was forming in my mind that would explain how the crime was committed and how the locked-room caper was perpetrated. It required only four quick and ingenious insights on the part of a killer whose mind was running in high gear, preconscious, almost poetic insights, like a quarterback's when he calls audibles at the line of scrimmage.

No, actually only three such flashes of the imagination—and a fair amount of luck. Well, only two lucky breaks, one of which could be reasonably assumed—and its absence not necessarily fatal.

I felt a certain admiration for my putative killer's alacrity. And a good deal of compassion.

I can feel compassion for geeks like Kiernan O'Rourke and Kevin Quinlan too, so don't count on my compassion.

The most important part of the morning's efforts, however, was that Kevin had touched, like a dentist probing an infected tooth, on a raw nerve of the Quinlan case that had bothered me from the beginning.

Why had Wolfe gone on his first binge in four years? No one seemed to have an explanation, other than that he had often fallen off the wagon before. Yet after four years of sobriety and two years as an initiate of Father Armande, who rejected alcohol, according to my information, as "unnatural" with as much vigor as he rejected fossil fuels. There were surely drugs in use at his church, probably pretty powerful ones; but, since they are not fermented, they could be categorized as natural and thus approved.

Why would a man so dedicated to Louis Connery that he would turn over all his earthly goods to him suddenly defy one of that magnetic leader's cardinal, you should excuse the expression, rules?

Had Wolfe Quinlan, I asked myself from the very beginning of my pokings around, become disenchanted with the Church of the Angels of Light? If so, why? And with whose help?

Now there were hints in his conversation with Kevin (whom he may or may not have called by the name of the crib death victim) that he had discovered something unexpected and disturbing in the last few years of his life. Possibly nothing more than the thievery perpetrated by Foster and O'Rourke, but also possibly something in the chicanery of that master of sleight-of-hand Father Armande de St. Cyr (a.k.a. Louis Connery).

Might the aforementioned master of sleight-of-hand have an ally or a pawn or a victim in the family who, perhaps under the influence of drugs, had done his bidding *in distans,* as we used to say in the mother tongue? The police were already closing in on him; might not he have much to fear from a suddenly clear-eyed Wolfe Quinlan?

It seemed not unreasonable and not incompatible with my still sketchy working hypothesis.

The receptionist (whose hair had been redone at the beginning of the summer and had demanded of me every day whether I still liked it) called to say that there was a young couple to see me.

Thomas McDermott Burke and Laurel Flavia (sic) Quinlan, with the ability to disconcert that marks their species, said that they would find totally awesome a double chocolate sundae with chocolate ice cream, whipped cream, and nuts.

They can't be all bad, I assured myself.

I quickly added that many folks who are not all bad nonetheless do bad things in the name of the young love that was already patent in their eyes, one pair sunny and clear blue, the other, as O'Connor The Cat had well said, like a smoldering furnace of liquid green metal.

Tommy Burke was an instantly personable young man, poised, respectful, self-possessed; enough youthful enthusiasm to be attractive, enough solid maturity to be deemed reliable. From his father he had inherited, it seemed, only his strong chin and lips and occasionally the grim determination of his eyes. The rest of him must reflect the laughing sprite that was his mother when she was not ill—lithe, tousle-haired, vibrant with a quick smile and laughter. He had dressed formally in brown for his invasion of the Cathedral rectory, suit, tie, shirt, shoes carefully coordinated with one another and blending with his medium cut wavy hair. He was the kind of presentable, promising young man that a young woman would delight in bringing home to a needlessly worried mother and father. He was quite at ease in the sanctum sanctorum of the rector's suite, a holy place into which in days of yore even the most senior curate might not venture without an advance appointment and written permission.

Laurel Quinlan, I concluded on the spot, was a bit of a witch. Maybe more than just a bit of one.

20

THOMAS M. BURKE

I sure made a fool out of myself that night, Monsignor Ryan. Oh, heck, I can't call you Blackie, not yet. And Monsignor Punk seems disrespectful.

I don't even normally use that kind of language. Sure, it's the lingua franca of teenagers—that's a pretty cool phrase, isn't it? I learned it in theology class last year. It means the Frankish language and. . . but you know what it means.

Anyway, I don't use it because my mother didn't like it and I think I should kind of respect her wishes, even if she isn't around with us anymore. I was astonished at what came out of my mouth. I guess I was trying to prove that I was as much of a man as he was. Dumb. You don't prove your manhood by foul language, as Mom always said.

I really flipped out on Laurel, you see. She is one cool chick. I really dig her. It took awhile to make her laugh, but then she laughed a lot. I wasn't ready for this man to show up and embarrass her. Yeah, he didn't say anything to her directly, but he attacked everyone else and that hurt her as much as if he had gone after her. She's real sensitive, Monsignor, poor kid. I've never known anyone that sensitive.

I didn't mind what he said about Mom. We—Mark, Gerry, Eileen, and me—we had to come to terms with that a long time ago. Even if people don't say anything, you know what they're thinking. Like, won't it be a blessing when she's gone, poor thing. No, it won't be a blessing. We miss her now and we'll miss her more then. You know you can't fight it and the best thing to do is not to make a great big deal out of it. People don't understand and it's not really their fault. If we were on the outside looking in, we might not understand either.

Mom is a tremendous woman. We were lucky to have all of her as long as we did. We're lucky to have some of her still. We don't do her any credit when we blunder into a fight because of her. Someday I'm going to be in real trouble, even if it is in heaven, when she finds out how dumb I acted.

Laurel didn't need my protection either. I mean I could have helped her a lot more if I waited until he went away and then took her over to Grand Beach to meet The Cat—a really tough broad, that one—and listen to Diamond. Laurel thinks those dudes are cute, though they're too clean-cut to be real rock types if you ask me. Anyway, I finally did take her over there, after upsetting her and making a fool of myself.

Then the cops found out about it and really leaned hard on me. Mr. O'Rourke, who is not a nice man, Monsignor, he really isn't, told them all about the supper fight and I think gave me a bigger part than I deserved. It was my own fault for blowing my cool in the first place, but I didn't blow it that much. You know what the Long Beach cops are like. If you're under twenty, they have a price on your head. There's this one cop who has watched too much TV and figures he's a character from C.H.I.P.S. or something. He kept at me all night long and into the morning till my father said he'd call a lawyer.

They would have tried to pin it on me if they could figure out how I could have flown through locked doors, like a Dracula bat or something.

Who do I think did it? Well, it was no accident, Monsignor, that's for sure. Laurel saw him later in the evening, she'll tell you about it, and he had stopped drinking and was working over his stones and knives. He had a terrible headache but he knew what he was doing. No way, she says, was he going to just run into that sword.

I figure it must have been suicide. Laurel was real worried about him. She'd been in there helping and then he told her to leave and she did. This was after we came back from Grand Beach about eleven o'clock or so. She had a bad headache and went right to bed, but then her father knocked on her door and asked her to help with the stones. She always liked the stones. He had the knives out too.

Yeah, you know, the leg knives? Oh, that's right. You haven't seen the museum. It's the weirdest place, Monsignor, really a gross-out. The poor man was probably even worse off than Mom. Anyway, he has these eight or ten knives that people back in Italy around the Borgia times would wear strapped to their thigh or calf, in case they needed it in a fight, like the kind Romeo's friends got into. Even women would wear them, so they could protect their honor—if they wanted to, which I guess wasn't all that often. They're real thin blades with an extra thin shaft. You'd hardly know you were wearing it. Sharp as a razor too. It's a wonder more of the owners didn't slice themselves up with the things. Maybe they did.

Laurel was afraid of the knives, especially when her father had too much to drink. He'd strap one on his leg and threaten to use it if anyone went after him. I'll let her tell you the rest. It was really strange. He thought someone was after him.

Anyway, he gave her one of those red stones and told her to go back to bed; he had more work to do before tomorrow, when everything would come out into the open. He was, like, confused and worried and angry, but he wouldn't tell her who he was angry at.

So of course she can't sleep. Who could? And she wants to talk to someone, so she talks to me. No way I'm going to tell the cops that, since they already want to lock me up for the long one. She gets out of bed and comes out on the balcony and around to my sliding door and taps on it. I go out on the balcony and we sit on the chaise lounge out there and she cries in my arms because she's so worried about her father.

Don't get me wrong, Monsignor; there wasn't any fooling around. Neither one of us was in any mood for it and I'm not the kind of guy who takes advantage of a girl with a broken heart.

Not that I didn't think about it. But there are some things you just don't do, even if you think about them. Anyway, she's wearing one of those sleep T-shirts that the chicks wear, you know the kind that reach practically to their knees. Not exactly wildly sexy, especially when they're Dartmouth green.

So she calms down after a long time and gets very sleepy, like I'm afraid she's going to fall asleep in my arms, which would be more than I'd want to cope with. So I wake her up and kind of drag her back to her room on the balcony. We're quiet going by my dad's room, because I don't especially want him to see me with a chick in her nightdress—even a Dartmouth T-shirt down to her knees at one-thirty in the morning.

I kiss her good night at the door, no big deal, and then guide her to the bed, cover her with a sheet, and get out of there as quick as I can. She was completely out. The next thing she knows her mother is pounding on the door and screaming that her father is dead. You can imagine what that did to her.

I'm telling you all this because Dad says you need to know all the things we didn't tell the cops. Laurel has promised to tell you everything too, but she's scared of you, even if you are O'Connor The Cat's uncle.

I'm not patting myself on the back or anything like that. It would have been easy to put the make on her that night, she was so beat out and worried. Stuff like this had been happening all her life, but never this weird. And he'd been sober for a long time.

I told myself when it started to get a little hot that night, with her leaning against me and sobbing her heart out in her totally neat and orderly bedroom (you'd think she was in a boarding school it was so neat) and nothing much on under the damn Dartmouth shirt, that if I don't care about God and I don't care about Laurel, I should at least care enough about myself to know that I'll really put the quietus—that's a neat word; it means: yeah, I know, forget it. Anyway, I'd put the quietus on things with Laurel like forever, evermore. Quoth Laurel, never, nevermore. So I left her alone and don't ask me to sort out the reasons why. Honestly, even in one of those ugly shirts she's enough to drive you out of your mind.

See, I might want to be a priest. And even if I decide I don't, maybe I wouldn't marry someone like Laurel. It's a long time away. If I become a priest, it won't be because I wouldn't like to marry. On the other hand, my father's in the investment business, you know? Being good to Laurel is a good investment, no matter what way you look at it.

Yeah, I suppose it is funny. But you're not saying I'm wrong.

A hell of a good investment, come to think of it.

I know she has lots of troubles. She scares me when she gets that dreamy-eyed, spaced-out look in her eyes. But look at all the stuff that has happened to her. If she wasn't put together with steel, would she even have survived this long? It's not like Mom, who never had a chance because it's something in the biology that they haven't figured out yet. If Laurel sees someone and talks about it, she'll end up saner than most of the rest of us.

I tell her that she should talk a little bit to Brigid Murphy's mom or dad, probably her dad; you know what a good guy he is. Yeah, I suppose you're right; he's had to be to put up with the clan.

Anyway, she's not against it, especially when I tell her about how good the psychiatrists were with Mom. So I think she will be all right, Monsignor. I can't force her to work it out; and I sure can't cure her myself. But maybe if I hang around a bit and she knows that I care about her, it'll be okay. If I end up a priest, it will be good experience, won't it?

My dad and her mom? Come on, Monsignor. I'm not making any comment on that. She's a cool chick for an old broad. I like her a lot. She digs me too. I wouldn't mind having her around. I won't say any more.

So what you're really wondering is whether Laurel might kill her father. You're thinking that I'm so far gone on this *gorg*eous blond chick that I'll say no way. Well, I don't think she did. I was with her for more than an hour on the balcony, so I ought to know what shape she was in better than anyone else. 'Scuse the unintended pun! Maybe it's true in both ways. Like, wow, Monsignor; it's *some* shape!

So I doubt that she would do something like that, you know. But I'll give you this, she is one mysterious chick. You've seen those eyes, Monsignor? What's going on inside her head? It's a lot of fun trying to find out. Peeling away mysteries, my father once told me, is more fun that peeling away clothes. Yeah, I thought it was pretty neat coming from him. Now for the first time I know what he means. I haven't pulled away any clothes yet, but the mysteries sure are fun.

Excuse me for pausing so long. There's one more thing I have to tell you, though I certainly don't want to. The next day, after the police had left, I knocked on her door. No answer. So I knock again. Still no answer. I push the door open a little bit.

Laurel is inside, sitting on her bed in jeans and... well, a bra... with a knife in her hand. Staring blankly at the wall. She sees me. Her jungle eyes are somewhere else. She jumps up and comes at me with the knife. Right at my stomach.

21

BLACKIE

"She attacked you with the knife?" I confess I was as startled by his description as he was by the event.

"Not exactly." He shut his eyes as though to blot the picture out of his mind. "I mean, no way, but she scared the hell out of me. She throws her arms around me and begins to cry again, with the knife still in her hand. I take it away from her and make her put on her shirt. Then she gets terribly embarrassed and goes, 'I'm sorry, Tommy. I was thinking about this knife and whether the women who wore it—see it's a tiny little thing you wear on your leg—ever killed anyone with it.'

"And I go, 'You shouldn't play with that on a day like this, kid. Do you want to button that shirt...'

"She gets real red and turns her back on me and goes, 'I'm a mess, I guess. I was wondering whether if I wore the knife and someone attacked me, I'd have the courage to use it.'

"I go, 'Have you ever worn it, Laurel?'

"She shakes her head, like that was a terrible question. 'I'd be afraid of it.'

"Well, I don't know what it all meant except that she was under a terrible strain. So I made her hide it because the police had sealed off the museum. Then when everything was over, we put it back in the cabinet with the other knives. They're all very ugly, Monsignor. They'd scare the living daylights out of me."

"Indeed. What interpretation do you put on the incident?"

129

He shrugged. "Nothing much. She was more spaced-out than usual, I guess. I thought I ought to tell you about it. I mean, she's real modest most of the time, Father. She wouldn't be sitting there half-dressed unless she was spaced-out, would she?"

I considered asking him about the key but decided against it. He would surely tell his father and I did not want Suzie/Sue warned that I knew about it.

"You summoned the Fosters. I take it they were in bed when you pounded on their door?"

"I don't know about Mr. Foster"—he was watching me intently, wondering about what I made of the incident of Laurel and the knife—"but Mrs. Foster was watching a video movie. She answered the door right away. With a glass of something, vodka maybe, in her hands."

"Indeed. Did she seemed surprised?"

"I couldn't tell. It was dark outside and she didn't invite me in. She ran upstairs to get her husband. I didn't wait for them."

"I understood they came over in nightclothes and robes."

He nodded. "I thought that was sort of funny. Maybe she didn't want to admit that she was still awake."

Maybe.

"Anything more I should know, Thomas?"

He thought for a moment. "That's all, Father Blackie. I hope you can help Laurel and her mother. They need more than I have to give."

"Ah."

"One more thing, to be perfectly honest with you. I have no idea what Laurel might have done or might do. But I'll stand by her no matter what she did. Anytime, anyplace. I dig her so much I don't care what she did."

22

BLACKIE

Should the young man persist in his intention to enter the seminary and the authorities who preside over it ask me for a recommendation, they will receive it by return mail, in gilt if need be. Such are, if not the kingdom of heaven, at least the kind of priest the Church desperately needs these days.

Which is not to say that his charming, artless, witty story was totally persuasive.

Is he not, you—whoever you may be—ask, very like his father, a true Israelite in whom there is no guile? Ha, I respond, no way, José!

He has far more guile than his father, who is stolid, objective, and beyond certain limits quite unperceptive. Lawrence Burke comes to see me prepared as if he were to make a presentation to a client, complete with a chart that he has asked a draftsman, oops, draftsperson, to prepare. All he knows of me, all he needs to know, is that I am supposed to be skilled with puzzles of the sort that trouble him and that I have a reputation for being fair, especially to women. He wishes to learn nothing more about Monsignor John Blackwood Ryan. It does not occur to him that he should do more research on the subject.

But his son, ah, his son is another matter altogether. He has, I am sure, consulted with such experts on the subject as The Cat, Packy Jack, Packy Mike, Caitlin, Biddy, and, heaven knows, perhaps even my father and stepmother and my sister and brother-in-law—whose praises he sings in a particularly artful flip of artlessness.

He learns that you deal with the Monsignor most effectively by doing the charming teenager bit, which he does very well anyway. You wander about, you make fun of yourself, you leap from subject to subject, you're candid, open, honest, frank. In the words of the advertising industry, you tell him the truth, a lot of the truth, more of the truth than he expects you to tell, but not necessarily the whole truth.

Consider how much truth he has told me. I learn from him about Laurel's visit to her father, which I would have guessed in any event and tricked out of her with little difficulty. He reveals the tale of the thigh knives, which is interesting but irrelevant. He feeds me a few more details concerning Wolfe Quinlan's befuddlement about something he has uncovered, but I have already discovered that. He describes with unnecessarily elaborate detail his nighttime tryst with the delectable Laurel. I do not question for a moment the accuracy of his description. I'm sure that he has been precise to the last detail. The bundle of conflicting but pleasurable emotions he feels for this vulnerable, appealing, and unfathomable child has been depicted with admirable integrity.

But of what use are they to me? Would I not have guessed, perhaps not with the richness of circumstances, his feelings toward her? Moreover, what does it matter that the two of them were huddling—or cuddling, choose your own word—on the balcony for an hour? Surely it is not an effective alibi.

Why all of that? He wishes to insinuate subtly but effectively that the young woman he had delivered with such praiseworthy chastity to her virginal bed was so exhausted, so weary, so delightfully sleepy-headed, that it is unthinkable she might have risen and, through a game of mirrors and shadows, worked a locked-room caper and dispatched forever her troublesome father.

Does he believe this to be so? Probably. But he imparts his argument in her defense so indirectly that I almost do not realize what he is about. Then, in an admirable twist of ingenious candor, he tells me frankly and disarmingly that maybe the lovely Laurel is capable of murder and escapes the possible charge of betraying her by then declaring his love regardless.

None of this is objectionable. On the contrary, it leads me to the conclusion that he can work for me any day. But it does not persuade me that he is telling me all he knows or all he suspects about the death of Wolfe Tone Quinlan. I am convinced that he would make a fine priest. I am not convinced that he is in this matter a reliable witness.

Moreover, if there was anyone in the Romanian villa who had the wit and the ingenuity to design a locked-room ploy, right out of a mystery novel, it would be this excellent young man, who is almost, but not quite, a match for Blackwood the Magnificent.

I would wager that he devours mystery novels like popcorn.

I sat by my coffee table, sipping soda water, for a long time, daydreaming about irrelevancies such as the poignancy of young love, the ambiguities of celibacy (not greater, I suppose, than the ambiguities of marriage), and the uncertainties of the human condition.

I should summon Laurel. But not yet. There was one troubling half-formed image lurking somewhere deep inside, what the ancients were pleased to call the agent intellect and which moderns call the preconscious. I knew that when I could identify and form that image fully I would have a solution to the puzzle.

And I also knew I wouldn't like the solution.

23

BLACKIE

With the teenage female of the species Homo sapiens sapiens (a needlessly arrogant redundancy it has always seemed to me) I am not totally unfamiliar. Moreover, fated to an Irish ethnic background, I am also accustomed to the strong-willed and unpredictable variety of that female type. To name but four of those available in my immediate family: O'Connor The Cat, already alluded to, Caitlin Murphy, a willowy blond comedienne who can be either a photographer's model or a model photographer; Patty Anne Kane, who aspires to be an actress and will out-Hepburn Hepburn in dramatic pyrotechnics; and Brigid Murphy, who I firmly believe is a changeling left by the banshee—a charge her mother leveled at me long ago.

Fine. With Laurel Flavia Quinlan, I am, as these relatives themselves would put it, nowheresville. She is designed on the lines of Caitlin, taller perhaps, less flesh on her thus far, and little of my niece's self-confident posture, but an almost finished dazzling blond beauty. Small wonder that poor Tommy Burke has been dazzled by her. She was wearing, with no sense of style, an attractive blue pinstripe summer dress with short sleeves. I'm sure her mother bought it for her and Laurel wore it without comment or appreciation.

She is four or five inches taller than her mother and constructed on less lush dimensions. Her face is a duplicate of Suzie's, perhaps somewhat thinner and not quite as complete a sculpture yet. The Lord God apparently decided to play bricolage with the components of

her mother's beauty. Having made a slightly undersized
Venus, She would now produce a somewhat outsize Di-
ana.

Laurel slouches, I daresay, because she is self-con-
scious about her height, as she need not be. Given a few
years and some luck (on neither of which I am at the
moment prepared to wager much), she will be regal—
no, imperial—a Viking Empress, the kind of woman toward which every eye, male and female, will turn.

A man, with the proper hormone components in his
bloodstream, would have to be dead for at least fifteen
minutes before he would be unaffected by her charms,
ungainly T shirt or not. She shares with The Cat a very
determined jaw. When she does not want to talk, she
will not talk. You can be sure that she will match Patty
Anne hysteric for hysteric when the occasion warrants.
The stateliness of her height, even when she slouches,
the flame in her eyes and her pale white skin—patently
resistant to suntan—suggest that, like Biddy, she has
been left on this planet by mischievous banshees.

And I remember that in ancient Indo-European
mythology the faerie horde is called the Troop of Di-
ana—Tuatha Dé Danann, in the Irish version. Already
this faerie was attracting her own troop.

All well and good, but for some minutes I cannot en-
tice out of her a smile, laughter, or even words. She
gives the impression that her attention is light-years
away from the atmospheric study in which we sit in the
rectory of Holy Name Cathedral. Alpha Centauri perhaps, a not distant star, but certainly not in the same
room with me. Finally she begins in a lifeless and de-
spairing tone, with little promise of finishing even a first
paragraph.

24

LAUREL FLAVIA QUINLAN

I don't know whether I want to talk.

I mean, what is there to say? He's dead; talking won't bring him back, will it?

Maybe he's better off dead. I wish he were still alive, though.

I loved him, Uncle Blackie, I really did. I loved him more than anyone else. I guess I was the only one who loved him. I'm not...

It wasn't anyone's fault. He was hard to know. I was the only one who knew him, so that's why I was the only one who loved him.

Mom was never any help. I suppose she meant well. She didn't know how to handle him. When he needed someone to stand up to him, she gave in. When he wanted someone to go along with him for a little while, she made a big fight out of it. Sometimes I used to think that she wanted things to be bad.

He needed someone to tell him that he was all wrong and that you wouldn't put up with it anymore but that you loved him anyway. Mom couldn't do that.

Sometimes I really hated her for that. Mostly I just felt sorry for her.

We're different from other people. So many bad things happened to us. Daddy needed help and there wasn't anyone to give him help except me, and what good was I?

I felt trapped all the time. You know what I mean? Like I had to do something to save him but I couldn't do anything.

I blame Daddy for what he did to poor Kevin. He really is such a sweet, gentle boy. But Daddy was a sweet, gentle man who never had a chance to act that way. He promised me that he'd be nice to Kevin and then forgot the promise because he didn't know how to keep it.

I blamed him for making Mom unhappy too, though she brought most of it on herself.

I was always his little girl, Uncle Blackie—I'd feel funny calling you Uncle Punk, and Monsignor is a silly name because you're not a lord at all—I mean I was the only one interested in his collections, the stamps and the coins and the stones and the knives. Even the armor suits, like poor Tancredi. I used to dust them every day when I was a little girl.

I don't want him dead. I want him to be back in his workroom poring over the stones and letting me hold them in my hand because I was his little girl. He was so happy doing that.

We didn't do it much in the last few years, especially after we joined that funny church in Hyde Park. I didn't like those people at all. They're real creepy. I'm a Catholic, Uncle Blackie, I always will be. I liked the parish school and didn't want to leave it when we had the fight over Margie's funeral—I don't want to think about that. It was so terrible. The nuns and the teachers in school said that the pastor did a terrible thing when he wouldn't let us have the kind of Mass we wanted. Why do priests do so many terrible things? I suppose that's a silly question. They're human like the rest of us, aren't they?

York Township High School is all right, but Mom says I can go to Immaculate Conception in Elmhurst next month if they'll take me. Do you think they will? I mean could you ask the Cardinal? He's a friend of yours, isn't he? Biddy said he was. Would you ever ask him to talk to the priests and nuns at IC? I could maybe go to Benet, but my grades are terrible and they only take real bright kids.

I went to Father Armande's church because Daddy wanted me to and because Mom didn't have enough nerve to tell him that it sort of upset me. I mean, I thought they were silly and wanted to laugh at them. But I was afraid of them too. I didn't like the way Father Armande would look at me, like he was taking my clothes off with his eyes. Sometimes that's nice when it's a real cute boy who won't do anything to hurt you.

Father Armande isn't cute and I was afraid he might hurt me. I used to get sick every Saturday morning after the services, but I didn't tell Daddy, because he had enough to worry about.

It's been a jumble the last couple of years. Sometimes I can't tell the difference between when I'm dreaming and when I'm awake. I was happy that Daddy wasn't drinking or fighting anymore and sad he wouldn't play with his stones and his knives and his coins. Does that make any sense?

I don't understand what happened that terrible day. It was a jumble like everything else, only worse. First, there was Tommy. He's really a neat boy, Uncle Blackie. I mean a lot of boys at school think I'm an easy make because I act dumb and confused all the time. Maybe I am dumb and confused. I never knew a cute boy who would treat me with respect. He was so sweet and he made me laugh and taught me to slalom ski—I wish I could go back to the lake and do it some more, but I had to get away from that place. There were so many terrible dreams....

Then all those people came for supper because Daddy was going to give our money away and Daddy got drunk for the first time in four years and said those terrible things to us, well, to everyone else. He never said them to me, because I was his little girl, you know?

Tommy told Daddy off and dragged me away from the house. I was so proud of Tommy because Daddy should have been told off when he got that way a long time ago, but I didn't know how to do it. And I felt good that Tommy liked me enough to stand up to Daddy and take me over to Grand Beach to listen to Diamond—they're really excellent, Uncle Blackie, aren't they? They're all so cute.

But I began to worry about Daddy, so I asked Tommy to take me home, supposedly because I was tired. I pretended to go to bed, but I really went to the workroom and knocked on the door and asked Daddy if I could help with the stones. He had them on the work table with those knives—I've always been terrified of knives, Uncle Blackie. He was finishing something on the video camera. He told me everything would be all right now. No matter what happened, I would not have to worry.

What time? Oh, about eleven o'clock, I suppose. No, he wasn't drinking. He was mostly himself, not all better yet, but pretty much. The closet door?

I think it was closed. I can't remember for sure, but I would have noticed it if it were open. He usually keeps it closed. No, he didn't have the video camera set up.

Anyway, I pretended to know what he meant, because he was still, like, kind of confused. I told him he had been really bad to Tommy and he didn't even remember Tommy, but he said he'd apologize to him in the morning. So he put the camera back in the closet and closed the door and we kind of played with the stones for a while like we were little kids. He was still confused and he really couldn't work on the catalog, which was terribly out-of-date anyway. I did a little work and then he told me that I should run off to bed—I had a hard day and I looked tired and I needed my sleep. He gave me a big ruby, which I didn't want, but I took it so it wouldn't hurt his feelings. He kissed me good night like he used to and said that everything would be all right.

How long was I in the room? Not very long. I mean we weren't really working on anything. It was kind of like he wanted a symbol of the old times, you know what I mean? But he wasn't well enough yet to do anything but go to bed and sleep.

I suppose I was there ten or fifteen minutes. Not much longer, but I didn't look at a clock or anything.

He wasn't drinking then, Uncle Blackie. I know he wasn't. There wasn't an empty bottle anywhere. The police found two more bottles later and they said he'd been drinking all night, but I knew he hadn't. He didn't

have anything after supper at all, not till, well, not till
after I left.

Tommy said I shouldn't tell the police about going
into the study because they would only misunderstand
and they hate teenagers anyway. They were so mean to
Tommy, I could have killed them.

The keys to the room? Oh, they were on his work
table in the corner, the one up here, nearest to the hall
and the bedroom. He always put them there because he
said that otherwise he would forget where he put them.
Or in the pocket of his dressing gown when he was
ready to leave the room. So I guess he must have been
ready to leave when... it happened.

I'm sorry, Uncle Blackie; Tommy says it's good to cry
when you feel bad. Daddy didn't like me crying. He
thought it was silly woman stuff. It made him so mad
when Mom cried.

Can I say something about Tommy? He is the most
wonderful boy. I know he told you about us out on the
balcony. I hope that won't mean that he can't be a
priest. That wouldn't be fair. I was so tired and worried
and he was so sweet that he could have done anything
to me he wanted. If he came into my bed with me, I
wouldn't have fought him off, Uncle Blackie. In a way I
guess I kind of wanted him to do that. I wanted to be
loved that night more than I'd ever been loved before.

'Course, when I thought about it, I realized that it
would have been a terrible mistake. He was not only
sweet; he was smarter than I was.

If God wants him to be a priest, I wouldn't try to stop
it. Why get in a fight with God? If God doesn't want him,
well, Uncle Blackie, I'll get in line—along with your
niece Biddy, the little brat.... I'm only kidding, I like her
a lot.

I suppose God wants all of us, one way or another,
doesn't He?

You promise that he won't get in trouble because he
held me in his arms that night? Oh, good. I'm so glad.

I don't have any right to laugh that way. My daddy is
dead. I'll never see him again till I get to heaven. If I do.

Maybe if I'd loved him a little more, he wouldn't be dead. It's my fault, not just my fault, but I'm maybe the most to blame. I hope God isn't mad at me. Do you think He is, Uncle Blackie?

I have terrible dreams about what God will do to me—like being tied on a marble table and being burned in a fire.

25

BLACKIE

Laurel Flavia Quinlan was a most disconcerting child/woman. You have doubtless perceived that she was naive and shrewd, innocent and wise, vulnerable and hard as nails, transparent and mysterious, confused and insightful. Young Tommy had his hands full with that wench.

She had obtained from Monsignor John B. Ryan two promises for which she had doubtless come prepared—a plea from Sean Cardinal Cronin to Immaculate Conception High School and a guarantee that her romance with Tommy would not be counted against him should he make application to the seminary.

In the latter matter I did not tell her the modern seminary would quickly reject a young man who did not hold her in his arms under such circumstances.

Her admission to IC was now as certain as the rising of the sun over Lake Michigan in the morning, though the Lord Cardinal would doubtless insist on meeting a young woman who was so skillful at manipulating his éminence grise.

I would not grant to him, however, that her combina-

tion of tearful childishness and clever sophistication
had manipulated me throughout the entire conversation.

Might she have killed her father? How could anyone
ask that of a young woman with such sad, tender green
eyes? Doubtless she did love him more unreservedly
and with greater understanding than anyone else, just
as she claimed she did. Doubtless too she would miss
him more than anyone else, her mother included, especially since that woman had quickly found herself a new
and, if I were to believe the patently biased testimony of
Lawrence F. X. Burke, extremely satisfying lover. What
would Laurel Flavia think when she found out about
that relationship?

On the other hand, if anyone had the quick Joe-Mon-
tana-at-the-line-of-scrimmage instincts required to
seize the opportunity of the locked-room situation, Laurel was that person. Manipulate Blackie Ryan, I say im-
modestly, and you can manipulate any situation.

There were three questions, two of them essential, I
had intended to ask her, that evaded my memory totally. Yet such is the little witch's poignant charm that I
can't even be mad at her for faking me out—like when
NFL players do not seem to mind when Sweetness Pay-
ton runs two hundred yards against them.

Her raw, primal instincts are, in any case, essential to
her survival, the only hope that she has of pulling herself out of the morass in which she has lived for so
many years. Despite her native shrewdness, she hangs
on the very brink of unreality, not always capable of
sorting out the real from the unreal, a lovely young
Olympic diver, poised in swimsuit not above a California pool but above a volcano.

Sean Cronin will lift a phone and obtain her admission to IC next month with a twitch of his marvelously
skillful vocal muscles. But her seat might well be empty.
That one could just as easily drift into a mental institution in the room next to Dorrie McDermott Burke and
remain there also for the rest of her life. Shrewdness is
not quite the same thing as resiliency.

The single tether binding her to the real world is
Thomas Burke, a stalwart young prince charming if you
are in search of one. But only eighteen years old.

Well, she tricks me again. I worry about her and do
not address myself to the issue. What did I learn? Her
father had stopped drinking and was sober enough to
play with his stones, though not yet sober enough to be
of much use in reordering the catalog. Thus if he were
more intoxicated at the time of his death, he must have
opened a new bottle of wine, several of them perhaps.

Why?

At eleven-fifteen there was no bottle displayed on his
desk. Of course, he might have hidden it from Laurel.
Kevin saw one at eleven-thirty. Or claims that he did. At
midnight Larry Burke thinks, but is not certain, that
Wolfe had begun to drink again. Did something happen
between eleven-fifteen and eleven-thirty—or perhaps
between eleven-thirty and midnight—which made him
return to the wine bottles that the police found empty
later?

Or was it merely a reactivated alcoholic's drift back
into intoxication?

And what was he recording on his video camera? The
very camera that was behaving most strangely since his
death.

I felt my accustomed chill at the camera phenomenon.

There had been no mention in the press or in Larry
Burke's admirably detailed account of events of July 4/5
of a videocassette. Surely the competent lawyers whom
Burke must have brought in by now to handle the litigation against Father Armande would have instituted a
search for documents. A loose videotape would certainly have stirred their interest.

Of course, no one knew that such a cassette might
exist, no one except Laurel and Tommy. They were not
mature enough to imagine its implications.

Or, alternatively, too shrewd to call attention to a
possibly damning voice from beyond the grave.

I did not like it one bit.

Now, let us see who, in order of their appearance, visited Wolfe Quinlan before his death: Kiernan O'Rourke, seeking reassurance that he claimed to have received; Kevin Quinlan, seeking money that he too claimed to have received; Laurel Quinlan, seeking love that she also claimed to have received; Larry Burke seeking . . .what? Quinlan's wife, perhaps, which eventually he obtained. Then a later visitor before Larry sought his Jameson's, probably a woman. Someone still later as Burke was falling asleep, a woman perhaps. Who might these women be? Suzie? Melanie? Arguably Laurel again. Seeking what? Did these later visitors, whoever they might be, have their request granted too?

Then the murderer—or the killer to be more precise—seeking to kill or seeking something else and killing in passion or mistake or mischance? A new visitor? Or a former visitor returning? Perhaps even someone Wolfe Quinlan summoned?

When and why did he begin to drink again?

That I had to know. Moreover, when I paid my respects to Suzie, or if you will, Sue, I would have to poke around for a videotape. And certain other pertinent evidence that I thought I might find.

What evidence? I asked myself uneasily.

The reluctant image almost surfaced, then I lost it again.

There was one more question that had to be faced. You'll notice how the sad, charming, clever little girl has kept me from asking it to the end: Might Laurel have killed her father?

We don't kill the one we love, do we?

Ha. As Oscar Wilde, watching from *Reading Gaol* the tiny patch of blue that prisoners call the sky, knew, we all kill the one we love. The coward with a cruel word.

The brave one with a sword.

26

BLACKIE

Mindlessly I saw no reason for urgency and much reason for caution. Laurel was safe with her friends in Elmhurst, doubtless burning up the phone lines with Tommy. Suzie was safe at Long Beach with Thomas Burke in constant attendance and Lawrence Burke in frequent attendance. The Chicago police, Mike Casey the Cop (my family has a habit of adding occupations to names, as if in the present case to distinguish him from another Mike Casey who was, let us say, a major general in the Air Force. We do not in fact know another Mike Casey) informed me that the police were tightening the net around the good Father Armande. The lawyers Larry had brought in with instructions to ease out Kiernan O'Rourke were effectively fending off Father Armande's attorneys, some of whom were apparently having second and third thoughts about their client. With the Burkes as protectors (in a number of senses of that word) there was little danger that Suzie Wade would have to seek employment as a waitress (an absurd conceit, if there ever were one). It seemed, then, that I could bide my time and approach Suzie, whose testimony was of critical import, when she was ready and eager to talk, perhaps, who knew, buoyed by her continued relationship with Larry Burke.

Unlike her daughter, Suzie would not be able to con me. I therefore would wait till she was in adequate self-control as not to view me as an agent of the Congregation of the Inquisition. Or, even worse, a 19th Ward Democrat.

The image of the evidence I needed still hid in my preconscious, skillfully ducking out of sight whenever I closed in on it.

I suppose I did not want to find it.

There was one remark of Mike Casey's to which I should have paid far more attention: "Turns out that some of his 'acolytes,' as he calls them, are pugs, presentable looking ex-cons who earn a living by being hired muscle. Maybe he needs them to protect the property in Hyde Park. They'll run like hell when the cops close in."

Foolishly I saw no hint of tragedy in his observation.

I celebrated the Feast of the Assumption (Mary's day in harvest to the Irish, the pagan feast of Lugsnada decently baptized but not quite converted) with my family and celebrated the publication of Nancy's newest SF novel for children (with the most appealing monsters), and settled in for the rest of August, waiting till my instincts told me that it was time to worry about Sue Quinlan.

With a clear conscience (easily enough achieved if you are a monsignor and thus practically confirmed in grace) I therefore consumed my Jameson's, ate my usual modest meals at Redamak's (Wisconsin cheese soup, a chili cheese dog, a plain old hamburger, and side orders of french fries, mushrooms, and potato peels, topped off by a fresh raspberry sundae at an ice cream parlor in New Buffalo—not as good as the chocolate chip with Bailey's Irish Cream at Jovan's beige restaurant on North LaSalle in Chicago, but adequate under the circumstances) with a mob of nieces and nephews who never had any money with them, harassed my various siblings, acclaimed the two new babies—Redmond Peter Kane, Jr., and Liam Curran—and entertained my father and stepmother, mostly by listening to him tell his stories. He was, incidentally, delighted with the acquittal of John DeLorean. "If the government is permitted to trick people into committing crimes, Blackie, no one will be safe, not even you." A flash of light in his pale, ice-blue eyes, "Not even me."

On the Sunday afternoon after our Christianized Lugsnada, Suzie Wade Quinlan called me at my sister Mary Kate's house. In my absence (on an absurd mission to learn how to slalom ski) she left the message that she would be delighted to see me the next day. Melanie would talk to me first. Then I should come to the Quinlan house and she would see me "for a few minutes." Then Greg would stop by on his way home from the city.

All neat and respectable and middle class.

"The poor bitch sounded terrified, Punk," my sister observed.

"What do you think of her?" I asked.

"Clinically?" She pursed her lips. "Mildly obsessive/compulsive, retarded emotional maturation, chronically indecisive. Not a bad golfer when she used to play. Kind of vanished from Long Beach Country Club when they left the Catholic Church. Looked furtive and anxious the few times I've seen her in the last couple of years. Well rid of the bastard, I'd say. She seemed rather happy, actually, a few days ago when I bumped into her at the fruit stand. Guilty for being happy too, but that's Suzie."

"Prognosis?"

"Guardedly hopeful." She shrugged. "If she wants to grow up now that she's rid of the bum."

I shudder to think what would have happened if Mary Kate ever decided that her husband was a bum. Fortunately, the family myth describes Joe Murphy, Bostonian and Jungian, as a living saint to put up with us.

Then, for no reason connected particularly to the conversation, the formless image of the evidence I needed leaped into full consciousness—perfectly delineated. As Michael Polyani observes, every intellectual breakthrough requires faith, works, and grace. Faith that there is a solution, hard intellectual work to search for it, and then a moment of blinding illumination.

I did not want this particular illuminating grace. On the contrary, it drove me to the bathroom to vomit.

Badly shaken, I stole a fresh bottle of Jameson's from the cabinet and poured myself a moderate amount of it.

It tasted terrible.

When Jameson's does not settle the stomach, there remains teenagers.

I thereupon strolled to the public beach where O'Connor The Cat, in powder blue warm-up suit and matching hair ribbon, was presiding over the young ruffians of the community with the same effectiveness attributed by history to Ivan the Terrible.

Her name has nothing to do with her physical appearance (solid, appropriately constructed, curly brown-haired, freckle-faced, impish-eyed, loud-voiced, Irish-American teenage female) nor with her disposition. In The Cat's world there was no point in being "catty" when you could shout an insult, which might well be, "Hey, space cadet, what do you think you're doing?"

My late mother, Kate Collins Ryan (God be good to her and if She isn't She's going to hear about it) was a woman of considerable presence, rather like that of the battleship *Iowa* if it made a sudden appearance at the Michigan Avenue Bridge during the rush hour. Hence the next generations boast a considerable number of young (and some not so young anymore, God help us all) women whose names are derivatives—Katie, Mary Kate, Catherine, Kathy, Kathleen, Karen, Katrinka, Catheryn, etc., etc. (no Kathi, heaven be praised). The Cat was given one of these names, I can never recall which and neither can anyone else, including, I sometimes suspect, her parents, when I poured the waters of baptism over her bald head some sixteen and a half years ago. But she was The Cat even before that sacramental moment and has been, proudly, The Cat ever since.

I commiserated with her on the beach over the absurd practice of secondary and tertiary educational institutions ending the summer a month too early (in the middle of August instead of the middle of September), a practice that I have interdicted at the Cathedral under pain of excommunication, reserved personally to Il Papa.

"Yeah, well, Uncle Punk, it is geeky. But, even if summer ends, life goes on."

A proverb to be noted in some future Book of Wisdom.

I asked her about Laurel Quinlan (pronounced, it seemed, "Laurl" though now she was called "Flavs," usually because Flavia—after Saint Flavia of Saints Flavia and Domitila, of course—was such an "excellent" name).

"That dork," she replied impatiently. "I call her every couple days in Elmhurst and tell her to get her cute little ass up here before Biddy Murphy takes Tommy away from her, and she goes, Biddy is nicer than I am, and I go, Dork, that's not the point; he likes you and she goes, I don't feel good in the house yet, and I go, Summer is almost over, Dork; I want to see you here next weekend."

"Ah."

Doubtless you are aware that in the younger generation the verb "to go" has replaced the now archaic form "to say."

"Yeah, and then I call this morning to see where she is and they go she went out this morning for her Nautilus and hasn't come back yet. Isn't that dorky?"

I agreed that it was and added the observation that many teenagers didn't check in at home, even when they were guests at a friend's home, when they changed their minds.

"Yeah, dorks," was The Cat's implacable verdict.

A dork, it turned out, can be in terrible danger.

27

LAUREL

She feels better when she leaves the Nautilus studio. Now that she knows she is going to IC next month, she wants to get her body back into shape. Her old friends must not think that she'd fallen apart in the years since her parents pulled her out of the parish school and she avoided her classmates, most of whom liked her a lot, because she was so ashamed.

Besides, she wants to look nice for Tommy.

When Mom comes home from the lake, she'll make her finally be serious about regular exercise. While Mom is real old, she is not old enough to be a widow for the rest of her life.

She seems to like Mr. Burke a real lot. Laurel considers that fact thoughtfully. She supposes it is all right. He knows how to be good to Mom, which poor Daddy never did.

'Course, she didn't give him much help or much challenge.

It still doesn't seem possible that Daddy is dead, with poor Tancredi's sword sticking in his chest and blood all over the work table and the carpet and everything. Sometimes she wakes up at night and is certain that it was all a terrible nightmare and that Daddy is still alive. Even in the morning she thinks so until she realizes that she is at Janet's house and why she is there.

It is hard to know what is real and what isn't. Maybe the primitive tribes the social studies teacher talked about are right. Maybe dreams are real and the waking world is an illusion.

She ponders that possibility and rejects it. They are silly to think that. Besides, her dreams are usually worse than anything that happens in the real world.

Still, it is terribly hard sometimes to sort out what is dream and what is real.

Tommy is real, her new friends Brigid Murphy and Kathleen O'Connor are real, Uncle Blackie is real. Mr. Burke and Mom?

She shakes her head. In bed together? That seems like a dream. Not a bad dream necessarily, just a dream.

Those weird services at Father Armande's church, they were like awesomely unreal.

Even now, on a bright summer morning, riding her bike down U.S. 45, she isn't sure that she'd ever been in that hideous place.

There were drugs in the incense and drugs in the grape juice they drank. Mom and Dad were too out of it to recognize what any teenager would know in five seconds—the worshipers at Father Armande's were stoned out of their minds.

It didn't affect Laurel very much. Most drugs didn't, not that she'd ever experimented with anything more than pot and once coke.

All they did was make her sick.

A boy had said, "Laurel's so spaced-out that she doesn't need pot."

She cried and ran out of the house. Later she thought that maybe he was right.

A maroon car, something foreign, has been following her since she left Nautilus. What do they want? Not more geeky boys?

Suddenly, when there is no traffic coming in either direction, the car lunges forward, turns toward her, and forces her down a side street.

"Geeks!" she yells at them.

Two big men tumble out of the car, one with a handkerchief in his hand. They pull her off the bike. She fights fiercely, kicking and shoving and scratching. Then one man shoves her face into the handkerchief and makes her breathe the terrible smell, sweet and sickly, *that is in it.*

Laurel's world fades away. Her last thought is that she is not sure whether she is falling asleep or waking up.

28

BLACKIE

Melanie Foster is a woman in her middle thirties who has determined that one copes with aging by diet, exercise, hair dye, and makeup, excessive quantities of each, alas. She probably has never been beautiful. But until a few years ago she had surely been accounted as attractive and sexy. If her hair was its natural black, her figure on the plump side as it ought to be, her skin relatively free from goo, the dryness of too much suntan gone, and her lips, eyebrows, and eyelashes their natural shape, the verdict would be that she is a fine-looking woman and will remain one indefinitely.

Instead, she bends every effort at redoing nature's work, reducing herself to a lean bag of bones suggesting an advanced state of anorexia. Her hair looks like straw that has rotted in the field during the winter and her face is a mass of paints—red, blue, green—in bizarre combinations, and is so thin as to suggest a vulture's beak.

She surely has excellent beauty advice from the best magazines and the most skilled beauticians, but somehow she lacks the skill or the taste to follow their advice. Maybe—and I betray the presence of psychiatrists in our family—she wants at some level in her personality to look unattractive.

Despite all the attention to her appearance, one set of

skinny, jewel-covered fingers is nervously nursing a cigarette holder and the other a large martini, very large
for what is still early afternoon. She is waiting for me, in
black slacks and a satiny white shirt, on the sun deck of
their home, a much inferior neighbor of the Quinlan
villa. I noted with interest that the sun deck, with high
fences that protect it from the ground level observer, is
directly beneath what I assume to be the north end of
Wolfe Quinlan's museum.

I think of David and Bathsheba and wonder which of
that ill-starred couple made the first move.

29

MELANIE

I'm not sure I can tell you much, Father. He was a hell
of a man. He knew what life was all about. Oh, dear God,
did he know how to live! He'd be alive and healthy today
if he hadn't married that empty-headed little bitch
who's screwing someone else with him hardly in the
grave.

I'm no one to talk, I guess. I married a wimp myself
and I mean wimp in every way you want to take that
word.

But we're not talking about my marriage, are we, even
if Wolfe and I both married sick little weaklings?

The truth is that with the right woman there would
have been nothing wrong with Wolfe. People say look at
all the tragedies, four deaths and one kid that's neither
man nor woman. Don't all of the kids, except that sexy
green-eyed bitch, take after their mother, huh? I mean
there's bad blood in that family and it sure as hell didn't

come from Wolfe.

Okay, so the drowning was an accident. But the others? A crib death? Drug OD? A faggot? Blood disease? I tell you it's something in the genes, her genes. I wouldn't be surprised that the kid who drowned had something wrong in her head too.

Bad blood, Father, bad blood.

Even the sexy little blond, and she's not so little anymore, looks real spaced-out. So, okay, she's got her father's looks and physical build, but I bet she's got her mother's brains. That means no brains—and no guts and no character and no nothing, if you ask me.

You get me? The right kind of woman who would give him what he needs in bed and the kind of kids he could be proud of, and there's nothing wrong with Wolfe Quinlan.

So he's a big kid, huh? Likes to play with knives and armor and stamps and coins and gems? So what? All men are nothing but little boys at heart. Wolfe was just more open about it and so he enjoyed it more. Played around with women? Well, most men do, face it, Father. Except wimps like my husband, but that's another story. That's the way men are, they play around. If the wife isn't a frigid little bitch, then she gives enough of what he wants in his own bed so he doesn't wander around to other beds too much. It's simple. If you get it at home, you don't have to look for it somewhere else.

Wolfe was hardly more than a kid when he married her, a pretty little girl from a Catholic convent school, you know. No disrespect, Father, I'm Catholic myself, though me and Greg don't work much at it. But you know the type. Don't wear patent leather shoes, that kind of thing. Sweet, pious, demure—and frigid and bitchy, only you don't see that till the wedding night; and by then, if you're a good St. Ambrose Catholic like Wolfe, you make the best out of a bad bargain. Only, his bargain was worse than most. He should have dumped her ten years ago. Poor guy, he was done in by his damn fool Catholic loyalty.

Then she gets him into that creepy religious stuff. I

ask you, Father, do you think a strong, sexy man like
Wolfe Quinlan will join one of them crackpot prayer
groups on his own? Or talk with tongues? Or, even
worse, stumble around in a robe like he's a Roman senator, carrying a goddamn torch? No way.

She pretends that she's going along with him on that
lunatic junk, but, believe me, she's doing it to deball
him. Okay, so he stops drinking and stops playing
around. Is that all good? He was a real man when he
drank and played around. For the last four years he's
been a pious creep. I can tell you, Father; and, believe
me, I know. Wolfe was no pious creep unless someone
deballed him first.

Greg Baby is going to tell you this, so you may as well
hear it from me: Wolfe and I had a little thing going for a
couple of years. We're neighbors up here, see? And
we're both human and we're both married to wimps. I
think he's pretty special and, well, he kind of likes me
too.

It was all fun and games, no big deal. Some kissy-face,
a few romps in the hay, that's all. Greg doesn't care
because he's not all that interested and the bitch pretends not to know about it. If she'd kept her shitty little
face—excuse me, Father, but that's just what it is—out
of things it would have worked out. I'd have been a lot
better for him than that religious mumbo jumbo crap.

We were really having good times, Father; and not
hurting anybody. He's not going to walk out on her and
the kids and I'm stuck with Greg. He's my meal ticket or
was till he turned wimp in the Board of Trade stuff too.
So it would have been fine for everyone. But, no, she has
to drag him off to the prayer group goofiness and Wolfe
turns into a goddamn celibate. Sorry, Father, but you
know what I mean. A man like Wolfe can't do without it
and shouldn't have to.

She killed him, of course. I don't know how she
worked that locked-room business. I wouldn't have figured her to be that smart. I suppose this Burke jerk
she's screwing every night planned it—somber and respectable crook is what he is. He took away Greg Baby's

share of the business and left us high and dry, so that those damn religious creeps can come in and finish us. You better believe that she's in cahoots with those devil worship freaks too. She'll have it all, the house, the money, the company, and that bastard Burke. Poor Greg may hang on to the job; she will try to keep up appearances. Maybe. She's not trying to keep them up with Burke. She's had it on for him for a long time.

They're the ones, Father, mark my words. Who else benefits by his death? Me? Greg? Poor dumb O'Rourke? Baloney. She wasn't up to a good man, so she dumped him and then killed him for a bad one.

He was good, Father. He was really good. She'd drive him up the wall with her hoity-toity ice box ways and he'd tie one on and come running to me. What the hell, for a man like that you didn't mind. I was second fiddle to her in public, but the three of us knew that I had him in bed.

He was really sweet too, generous and thoughtful and loving, not just your slam bam, thank you, ma'am, type. The finest man I ever knew, in and out of bed. I hope I live to see her get hers back. In spades. I told the cops all I knew, but I think she's bought them off. Crummy small town cops buy cheap.

See him the night he died? No way.

I thought about it, sure. It had been a long time with only dumb Greg Baby. Wolfe was coming down off of a blast. I said to myself, hey, Mel, old kid, maybe he needs you. I could have walked up those stairs real easy and into the study. It was like the house was designed for us. We'd make love in the study with her right next door in the bedroom and she wouldn't know a thing. Not a thing. She might guess, sure, but she couldn't be certain and she was afraid to ask.

So I thought about tiptoeing up those steps for a quick one. To hell with Greg. He knew better than to try to stop me. But I didn't do it. I'm sorry now. We'll never do it again. And maybe if they'd found me with him, they wouldn't have killed him. Or maybe they would have killed me.

Tell you the truth, without him to think about and
dream about, I wouldn't much mind being dead.

30

BLACKIE

Were there tears behind her heavy sunshades? Surely.
Melanie was the most pitiable of Wolfe Tone Quinlan's
survivors, hiding her own emptiness behind a pretense
of hard brass tacks realism.

Had she visited him sometime that night and offered
herself to him again?

And been rejected, perhaps again?

"Did you have any trouble sleeping after the confron-
tation at the supper table?" I asked, trying to sound
harmless. "It must have been a traumatic experience."

She shrugged indifferently "With Wolfe you got used
to those occasional explosions. It didn't bother me
much, not enough to keep me awake. I was dead to the
world when the kid woke us up. Greg had to drag me out
of bed. Mind you"—she made a disgusted face—"we
weren't in the same bedroom."

"I see."

Either she was lying or Tommy was. Why would it
matter, unless she was one of the last two women visitors and was still contemplating the result of her visit?

If she had been in his room, she would never admit it
to anyone. Perhaps because she was the only visitor
who did not get what she wanted.

"So, I didn't have any premonitions or anything like
that. I'm not the type."

"And of course you never had a second key to

the museum."

She considered me very carefully. "He changed the lock on it every year, you know. I don't think the registration that the bitch showed the cops was the right one. Anyway, no, I never had a key. Wolfe wanted to give me one before all this stuff with the creeps started. I said why bother. If you want me, just whistle. You can open the door. I'm not going to come waltzing up on my own."

"He was sober when he made that offer?"

"Of course not. Sober he wouldn't have offered God Himself a key to all those little treasures of his."

"You sound angry at him."

She began to weep.

"Why did the bastard have to go get himself killed?"

31

LAUREL

They make her take off her clothes and put on one of those creepy white robes. Then they tie her to a cold hard marble altar, like a gravestone, in the basement of the Church of the Angels of Light. She is still drugged and terribly confused. She knows she is dreaming, but it is such a different kind of dream.

She hears the men talking as they tie her hands and feet to the metal rings that have been screwed into the altar.

"I don't like it, Tony. The old man is flipped out. We've had a good thing going here. Why mess it up?"

"He wants the company, all of it. You know that. He'll let the little bitch have some money, enough to get by.

But she'll have to sign the rest of it over to him, if she doesn't want this cunt picked up off the street anytime the old man says the word."

"So she comes here and gets his terms and agrees and gets the kid back. What if she won't play?"

"She'll play. We'll shoot her up with some stuff and play some little games with her like we did the last time. Remember? Fun, wasn't it? By the time we're finished, she'll be so scared, we won't have any trouble with her ever again."

"What if she goes to the cops?"

"Have any of the old man's marks gone to the cops?"

"The Long babe said she would."

"And look what happened to her."

"Yeah, I suppose. Still, those guys hanging around outside the last few days look like fuzz. And the old man seems more wild-eyed than ever."

"He's as loony as they come, but hasn't it always worked out for us? Money? Broads? Trust me."

"I still don't like it."

"You want to have a shot at this little cunt? Nice meat, huh? You can have a lot of fun with her. Okay? Trust me?"

"I guess."

Laurel doesn't understand everything they are saying. But she knows that this will be the worst nightmare yet.

32

BLACKIE

As I considered the Quinlan villa, I accepted the accuracy of Lawrence F. X. Burke's description of it as Tran-

sylvanian Swiss. Indeed I too would want to make sure
that the architect did not spend his days in a casket
avoiding silver bullets and such like. It was a heavy,
dour, dark, depressing mass hanging against the fluffy
white clouds and the clean blue sky above the lake, a
capsule from outer space with no right to nest, however
temporarily, on the shores of Long Beach.

(Long Beach can most appropriately be described as
a place where, after you turn past the country club and
down one of the curving rows of elegant homes the like
of which, believe me, you'll never find on Martha's Vine-
yard, you note a road marker that proclaims helplessly,
"Children Everywhere.")

I shivered slightly, wondered about the video camera,
and lifted the huge knocker on the street side of the
Quinlan house.

Some of the people I had interviewed had assumed
partial responsibility for the death of Wolfe Tone Quinlan: Larry Burke for not being a better friend, Laurel for
not being a better daughter. All of them had placed the
principal blame elsewhere—most of them on the woman I was about to see. Only Tommy absolved her completely. His father changed his mind after their love affair began. Whom would Suzie blame?

No one had been more direct in her charges than
Melanie Foster, an angry, pathetic vulgarian. Could I
lend any credit to her accusation that Burke and Suzie
had conspired to do away with Suzie's husband? It was a
soap opera scenario—which did not necessarily make
it inaccurate. Suzie liked to watch the soaps. Might
Burke, by admitting his obsession and subsequent love
affair and even by summoning my aid, have laid down a
brilliant smoke screen that even my father, a DE captain
in the war, would have admired? He was, after all, a
brilliant investment manager, with a reputation for flair
as well as integrity.

But why bother with me? The LaPorte prosecutor,
desperate one would imagine for a case that would keep
his name before the public eye, had not bought Melanie's cynical analysis. Still, if anyone had reason to want

to be rid of Wolfe Quinlan, it was his long-suffering wife, as she must surely picture herself. By anyone's reckoning, Suzie must still be a prime suspect.

And by the same token, Melanie would be the least likely of suspects. She lost a sometime lover and longshot permanent love when Wolfe died. She was hardly capable of the mixture of passion and stupidity that might lead a rejected mistress to kill her ex-lover. She gained, as far as I could see, nothing. I found no reason to doubt her description of her long-standing affair with Wolfe, nor even to question her description of him as a gentle and affectionate as well as a strong and virile man. Surely that would fit with his own self-image. During his interludes with Melanie such a self-image might readily be sustained. He had been, after all, a different man to all of those I had interviewed—a sadist to Kevin, a darling if troubled father to Laurel, a fascinating and exuberant mirror image to Larry Burke, a monster who brutalized Laurel to Tommy, a successful and generous member of the family to Kiernan O'Rourke. None of these personae was necessarily false and none irreconcilable with any of the others.

The blind men and the elephant, in other words, but perhaps blind men not telling the whole truth about what they had felt.

What part of the elephant would Suzie describe?

Not that I believed Melanie completely. I was certain that a) she had put enormous pressure on Quinlan to divorce his wife and marry her, and b) that she had crept up the stairs from the garage to the study and was rebuffed by her former lover, perhaps rudely.

She couldn't admit that without becoming a suspect in the eyes of the police and the prosecutor's office. No one else, except perhaps her husband, would know about the nocturnal visit.

There was no way she would have turned down a key to Wolfe's museum if it were offered to her. And was she lying about where she was when Tommy came to collect them. For what reason?

But what reason did Tommy have to lie?

That was easy enough to answer.

Melanie is the kind of woman for whom complaint about her husband is an almost biological necessity. I have had far too many such in my parish and have long since learned to discount what they say. The complaints are not necessarily untrue but they are mostly irrelevant, filling psychological needs that do not stand in the way of commitment. If anyone else but Melanie should threaten Gregory Foster, she would be an avenging harpie.

Were they capable of the kind of secrecy necessary for a successful plot that would combine her access to Wolfe and his fear of prison?

Absolutely. I could see how it might be done.

Yet. . . I could not picture Melanie Foster carrying off the elaborate trick of the locked doors, either by premeditation or brilliant on-the-spot decisions.

It would solve a lot of problems, especially for people I found myself liking, if Melanie had indeed run her lover through with Tancredi's sword.

"Sorry, Monsignor," Suzie opened the door breathlessly. "I've been trying to hunt down Laurel. You know what teenagers are like."

At first I was inundated by a wave of poignant sadness. The woman who nervously admitted me was indeed lovely, but she was not the fresh, dew-covered child who had crowned the blessed mother when I was in fifth grade. Why must we grow old, goddamn it? Well, in Paradise we would all be young again.

Call me Blackie.

"I can't do that, even if I knew you when you were crossing 93rd and Glenwood and I was the crossing guard. You were a terrible little imp in those days. Cute but terrible."

Ah.

Score one for Suzie—indeed, score a lot of initial points for her.

She was certainly as lovely as Larry Burke had described, not perhaps like totally *gor*geous, as her daughter was currently described, but a carefully packaged and well-cared-for rosy-cheeked little specimen of womanly attractiveness who would brighten any man's life; a cleverly wrapped box of candy that said "open and taste" and now said it with a confidence that came from experiencing beyond doubt how delightful she could be. Her image that day was sensible and business-like: white dirndle skirt, campshirt in khaki and white stripes, navy blue blazer with two copper buttons, beige shoes with short heels and dark stockings (pantyhose at this state of our cultural development, not that it was any of my business), minimal but skillful makeup, short blond hair (with natural and artifical colors indistin-guishable even to my trained eye) combed severely back from her face—a competent professional woman in a resort area dressing for a visit from a member of the papal household.

Her clean, sharply drawn face and neatly curving body, the kind that seems to cry out for fondling, were made even more attractive by the radiant glow that suf-fused her skin. Sex, good sex, and lots of it. Not what one expects to see in a widow of six weeks.

Good for you, Lawrence F. X. Burke.

Maybe.

I was conducted to the "salon," which indeed made me want to search for the casket and bow over it, mut-tering how natural the deceased look. Idly I wondered if Wolfe's wake had been held here.

Of course not. He was buried in Elmhurst, with the curate defying his pastor to say some prayers at the funeral home. I would have to learn his name. He sound-ed like an admirable young priest.

Suzie thanked me and asked that I thank the Cardinal for obtaining Laurel's admission to IC. "It's time we all return to the Church, Monsignor."

She appreciated my visiting her here. She wasn't quite ready for Chicago yet.

She thought that perhaps she might want to study philosophy at Loyola. Would I recommend courses? That was what I did my doctorate in, wasn't it?

How long did a doctorate take? Was there an upper

age limit?

This was a conceit less improbable (though still highly improbable) than her becoming a waitress. Larry
Burke's description of her personality had been as precisely accurate as his description of her physical and
sexual attractiveness. Suzie/Sue was two women, the
fluffhead who had married Wolfe Quinlan and endured
him for twenty-four years, and another, more intelligent
and resourceful woman who had been buried when she
graduated from high school. The latter was striving for
resurrection; her chances were not good, not good at
all, but she wasn't giving up easily.

The latter was also more likely to kill and perhaps
with better reason.

We sat at a coffee table. I declined a drink and coffee.
I wanted no distractions in this conversation. Sue, as I
shall call her henceforward, giving her the benefit of the
hope, picked up from the table—Reconstructed Early
American it had been called, I believe—a notebook
bound in red leather and her glasses. Her hands were
trembling. One of them reached, Suzie-like, for her
throat.

"I'm scared, Monsignor. I want to do this and I don't
want to do it. You were always a nice little imp. I have to
talk to a priest. Maybe when this is over we can come
back and call it a confession. I have so much to confess.
I'm not sure I'm sorry for everything, so I probably don't
deserve absolution."

"There's nothing to be afraid of, Sue. I'm not a police-
man."

How's that for reassuring dialogue from your friendly
parish priest detective? I was beginning to wish I had
accepted her offer of a drink.

"I know. It's not you. It's me. I have been so evil. I
know it's a sin against the Holy Spirit to despair. Then I
wonder how anyone as empty and as worthless as I am
can commit such a big sin as despair."

"We must instantly rule out of consideration any discussion of either worthlessness or despair. Those are
unacceptable terms with regard to you. I wouldn't be

here if I thought you were worthless."

A cute little blond a few years older than me and I begin to sound like a cardinal. "A cardinal or something," as The Cat would have noted.

"Here, give me your glasses, Monsignor; I'll clean them." She removed them firmly from my hand and produced from the purse next to her on the over-stuffed maroon leather couch a small spray container and some tissue.

Watch your step, Blackwood.

"I tell myself I should try contacts again. I could see better in bed—"

Her hands froze on my spectacles.

"I'm sorry I said that, Monsignor."

Call me Blackie.

"I wish I could say I was ashamed of what I'm doing. I ought to be ashamed. Poor Wolfe hardly cold in the ground. If someone else was doing it, I would be the first to condemn her. But I'm not sorry and I'm not ashamed and I'm not going to stop. Isn't that horrible?"

"What do you think?" I recovered my glasses.

"I can hardly wait for the sound of his car. If things were good between us, I was happy when Wolfe came home because he was my husband and I loved him and I was a little lonely without him. Now I almost go out of my mind. I want him to touch me so badly that I can hardly stand it. I want to tease him, drive him mad with desire, turn him on so he can't think of anything or anyone but me... I... I had no idea I was that kind of person...."

"Do you like yourself less now that you know?"

She shook her head vigorously in the negative. "I'm terribly curious about myself and I try to be disgusted but I can't. It's hard to explain, Monsignor—and I didn't want to get into this till much later." She put on her glasses, opened the notebook, which matched the couch, I noted, and ruffled through her notes. "If I'm a whore, Monsignor, and I think I might be, I like myself more as a whore than as a dutiful Catholic wife and mother. Is that so terrible?"

You will observe what I mean by scoring points. The woman not only cleans my glasses; she leaps into a central problem and speaks with candor. She is timid and uncertain about her love affair, but seeks to justify it, if at all, on the grounds that she enjoys it. Not sweet Suzie anymore save in her question of whether it is terrible.

"For the present, Sue, I don't want to take a stand on your relationship with Lawrence. I certainly won't at the moment condemn it. After all, it's not my purpose in this particular conversation to make any judgments on that subject. I'm here to find out about the psychic phenomena that have been happening and their possible relationship to your husband's as yet unexplained death. I will say this, however; if you do nothing worse in your life than make love to Lawrence Burke, you don't have much to worry about."

She nodded solemnly and flipped back to the beginning of her notebook. "That's the problem, Monsignor"—wide-eyed and solemn. "I've committed far more terrible sins, so terrible that I can't quite believe them myself."

— 33 —

FATHER ARMANDE

He was trembling when he put down the telephone, shaking from head to foot like dune grass in a windstorm on the bay when he was growing up.

So long ago.

He removed an elaborate gold container from his desk, dipped a gold snifter in it, and inhaled. Ah, that

*was more like it. Now he could see clearly again, think
properly for a half hour or so. Proper thought, in harmony with the music of the spheres, was essential.*

*He looked at himself in the mirror and quickly turned
away. He was not an old man. No, not at all. He had
many years of useful service ahead of him. Why should
it be cut short by the stupidity of two people he had
saved from the gutter, figuratively if not literally? First
Mrs. Carson Long, the foolish old woman with her private detectives, and now this unbearably stupid Quinlan, loud-voiced, vulgar, crude, a really unbearable
man. He had become so pliable, so ready to give everything to the sacred cause.*

*He smiled at the thought of Quinlan's wife. Bending
her to his will had been intensely pleasurable. A delightful reassertion of the life energies and forces of the universe. She was a far more promising neophyte than her
husband.*

*However, he must not waste precious time with pleas-
ant memories. Should he inform Hilaire? No, that would
not do at all. She would want to run, of course. He had
run too often. Now might be the time for the ultimate
sacrifice, not as crude as that man Jones whose lust for
quantity destroyed any sense of quality. Poison in Kool-
Aid, how unseemly.*

*No, if he were to go finally to the Prince of Light,
leaving behind a proper judgment on a faithless and
unresponsive world, it would be with a work of quality,
of high art, the kind of ultimate liturgical gesture of
which he had always dreamed.*

*It was either that or jail. He and Hilaire would not
escape this time. The police knew too much; they had
done their work too well. He had understood the risk
clearly enough. Either Long must be ultimately joined to
energies of the cosmos or grave charges would be leveled against him. Why had she changed? She seemed to
enjoy the advanced rituals well enough. Had he been
too interested in some of the neophytes? The Quinlan
woman perhaps? A harsh irony if that were true.*

He had given the necessary instructions, the maid ar-

ranged for an overdose, and the matter was consummated. No one contested the will. The maid was sent away, with a supply of drugs, to be suitably removed when such a measure would not create undue notice. Perhaps she would even save them the necessity of such intervention by removing herself.

There was no medical surprise; the woman had a serious heart condition. No postmortem, and no contested will. The police might have their suspicions, but he had carefully calculated their ability to respond to him when there were so many more pressing demands on their energies.

How was he to know that there might be one or two more stubborn investigators who would keep track of the idiot maid and that, arrested for shoplifting to support her childish addiction, she might succumb to pressure from the Chicago police?

The critical mistake had been to tolerate her continued existence. He had been guilty of an error in judgment.

How often in his life had a combination of his honest mistakes and the malice of others aborted his important work?

Then the Quinlan fool, suddenly filled with suspicion, asking impertinent questions, demanding answers, making charges, forgetting his place. Armande had pointedly reminded him of his position, of his own cooperation in certain activities of which the police could hardly be expected to approve.

He had responded with vulgarity and obscenity, knowing full well that such language was intolerable among the followers of the Angel of Light.

Well, that ungrateful and faithless man had been punished. Armande had prayed to Lucifer and the sword had done its work. Beautifully.

He chuckled to himself at how it had been done, not quite remembering once again how in fact Lucifer had carried out his wishes. If only the others had gone so quietly.

He clenched his fists. Damn them all, they never un-

derstood that he was born for greatness. They owed him recognition, acclaim, reward, opportunity to test his theories of sexual harmonies and integration. He had accomplished so much. He had come so far. Why must it end?

He steadied his nerve with more cocaine. What would be, would be. He of all in the universe must understand that. It was now important to be reabsorbed into the dazzling light from which he had come so that he might reemerge, more radiant than ever, when the world was ready for him.

He had once told the spiritual director in the seminary that the world was not ready for him. The foolish old man had wanted him expelled.

How might he most radiantly leave? How best to burn his image into the memory of the world?

The immolation, of course. Now was the time, now was the hour, the fullness of time, the proper hour. Ah, it is later than you think. Rise up! The enemy is at hand! It is later than you think!

He struggled to his feet. He must prepare for Armageddon.

The acolytes must be eliminated first. They did not count. They were of no importance and could not be expected to be welcome should he bring them on his pilgrimage to the center of light.

For the Sacrifice, three would be necessary. Where would they come from? The black clerk and stenographer? Worthless, of course. He would in his mercy send them away. But how, then, would there be three?

There had to be three. It was the proper number. Without three the music would be wrong, the radiance improper.

Ah, but of course, it was obvious, as it should always have been. Perhaps his time has come. He had made too many mistakes, overlooked too many dynamisms that flowed with the basic energies. Soon there would be only peace and light.

He opened his private safe, failing to work the combination properly on his first two attempts because of trembling fingers. He removed the massive .45 caliber gun. Enough power he had been told to destroy a man's head or chest with a single bullet. He slipped the gun into his desk. The acolytes were of no importance. When their work was done, they would be reduced to their basic energies.

He would wait a bit, perhaps take a nap, and then make the required phone call.

Fire and sword, that was what the sacrifice demanded—beautiful cleansing fire, ravishing and sweeping away impurity; and sharp, penetrating sword, cutting to the very source of life. Fire and sword, the instruments of grace, the media by which one made the great leap into the very core of light itself.

He donned his blazing cloak, removed his slender graceful sword from its richly tooled sheath, and turned to pray to the giant eye that occupied the wall behind him. The cloak fell in elegant folds. He lifted one of the braziers from its stand next to him. He stretched out one arm with the sword and the other with the fire in the position of heroic, sacrificial prayer.

"Lucifer, God the Father, God the Mother, Angel of Light, Angel of Darkness, Demon of Fire, Demon of the Sword, Source of Life, Source of Death, give me the strength and courage I need to cut and burn and destroy in Thy service. May my hand be steady and my heart be as ice as I do Your will. Then take me home until it please You to send me into the world again."

As he tottered off for his nap he was momentarily distracted by the thought that, ideally, two of the votives should be virgins. It had always been planned that way. Now there would be only one. It was too bad, but nothing could be done about it.

So it had always been. They conspired to force upon him the imperfect when he was entitled to perfection.

The single virgin would have to suffer enough for two.

34

SUZIE WADE QUINLAN

I killed him, Monsignor.

If you're looking for the person who put Wolfe Quinlan in his tomb, it was his wife, the wife that loved him and tried to do her best to be a good wife.

The wife who ruined their marriage for both of them. She'd try to tell you that she did her best. Maybe she'd even mean it. Her best was not good enough and it was her fault that it was not good enough.

At the end he was a terrible man, cruel, hateful, sick, maybe much crazier than poor Dorrie McDermott. It wasn't his fault, Monsignor; it really wasn't. He was caught up in evil he didn't understand and it finally destroyed him. I forced him into that evil. I could have pulled him out of it. When I finally tried, it was already too late.

I don't mean I drove that terrible sword into his chest. I was asleep in our bedroom when that happened. I suppose that someone from Father Armande actually killed him. It was still my fault.

So Wolfe is in Mount Carmel Cemetery and I'm in bed every night with one of his friends, loving it the way I've never loved anything before. What kind of a woman combines murder and adultery in a month?

I'm being hysterical, just like you thought I would be. That's no help, is it? One part of me is filled with guilt and another part of me is rejoicing in freedom and pleasure. The first me says you killed him, you little bitch, and you're glad. The second says you're damn right I'm glad and I'd have done it a lot sooner if I knew what wonderful things my lover would do to me.

Give me a few seconds to get hold of myself.

What I just said was terribly dumb, wasn't it? Poor pathetic Suzie who was once the brightest kid in her class and hasn't had an idea since 1970. Yet it's true. I'm glad he's dead. Poor man—poor, dear man. I loved him so much and I killed him anyway.

Don't look at me that way, like you think I'm a silly little fool who is taking responsibility on herself to which she has no claim.

I know I'm a silly little fool. I always have been. Give me a few more seconds. I didn't plan to begin this way. I wrote out my notes very carefully. I wanted to explain what happened calmly and rationally, so I could hear a philosopher's reaction. I haven't paid any attention to my notes. I will from now on. I promise.

Did you know that I got A's in Logic and Metaphysics the year I went to college? Wolfe made fun of that on our dates. What good is metaphysics when you're taking care of babies? I couldn't think of any answer.

Well, to begin at the beginning. I was born in 1941, which meant I graduated from Mother Macauley in 1958, did my one year in college in 1959, and married Wolfe in the spring of 1960, six months before Kennedy was elected. We didn't vote because we forgot to change our registration. We would have voted for Nixon anyway. Wolfe was always a strong Nixon supporter, even after Watergate.

The Wades were always Republicans, which you Ryans didn't like at all. I remember...

Never mind. No one seems to remember anymore what it was like to be a young woman getting married in 1960. That's where I want to start.

We were taught by our parents and by the Church that the finest accomplishment for a woman was to have a husband and a family. Nothing else mattered. If we were too intelligent or too good at something, like art or music, that might even be bad because men didn't like bright or talented women. A woman's task was to raise her children, keep the husband happy, and help him become a success in his career. If he was a success, then she was too.

Mrs. Reagan is a perfect example of the ideal in which we were raised.

The worst calamity that could happen to a woman was not to marry. No one said it, of course, because there were always unmarried aunts around who were useful as baby-sitters and you didn't want to hurt their feelings. Still, you knew you had about seven years— between eighteen and twenty-five—to find a husband. If you didn't, your life would be wasted.

Why go to college? First of all, to find a man. Once you found a man, college was less important. Also, it was a matter of pride for parents to be able to afford to send their daughters to college. It was expected to add a kind of polish that made us even more attractive in the marriage market. Furthermore, college might train you for a career that you'd need if anything happened to your husband and you had to be the brave and tragic widow who kept the family going. Finally, a few of my friends said that when their children were raised—and we all expected to have six at least—they would find themselves some kind of career and use what they'd learned in college to start with.

My mom and dad didn't expect any of their four daughters to graduate from college. They would have been horrified if we had, afraid we might be having big ideas about ourselves. "A year or two," Mom would say. "Don't rush into marriage; it lasts long enough anyway."

That was one of the mixed signals we received, although we didn't pay much attention to them. Marriage and family were our dignity and our destiny, but they were hard, serious, and unrewarding work. "Now you'll find out what the world is really like," one of my sisters said grimly to me on my wedding day.

Why, I wondered fleetingly, sacrifice everything for a vocation that didn't make you happy?

My three older sisters were married and pregnant before they were twenty, shockingly early, according to some of the families in the neighborhood, and it was expected by all of us that I'd do the same thing. Why break the family string? The race went to the fastest, didn't it? You only had a few years, so why take chances of being left behind?

Our Cana Conference teacher in high school told us that when his secretary married, he made her give up her job because if she brought money into the family that would be an embarrassment to her husband. And he was a great liberal too!

I liked college more than I wanted to admit at home. I wanted to finish and graduate. But Wolfe was in a hurry, of course. He was four years older, a big, mature, passionate twenty-three, and my parents and sisters wanted to know who I thought I was that I expected someone would wait three more years for me.

Besides, Wolfe was a better catch than I deserved. If I lost him, I might be out of luck.

You think I'm a fleabrain so maybe you won't believe that I held out for six months before I agreed to marry him. I panicked at the end of my freshman year. Ten girls in my class had diamonds. It was now, I thought, or never. I went back to school for a few weeks in September, left college, worked in Daddy's office till Christmas, and then quit so I could help my mother between January and May in the wedding preparations like the older girls. She prepared, I helped. She was experienced at weddings and I wasn't. I remember thinking that it really wasn't my wedding at all.

I didn't have any second thoughts about Wolfe. He was big and handsome and lots of fun. He drank a little too much but most boys his age did. He was sweet and generous to me. Like all boys, he wanted to cross the border lines on sex we had been taught by the nuns to defend at all costs. Like all girls, I let him cross those lines a little bit some of the time, sinful touches, passionate kisses I used to tell the bored priest in confession on Saturday night. Later on, after we were married, I wished I had some of that necking and petting back. It was a lot more fun than anything that was happening in marriage.

Wolfe was a good guy, Monsignor. No one who knew him at that age would have expected any of what has happened. He didn't finish college, but that didn't make any difference because he would inherit his father's company, which we all knew was very successful. His career and his wealth were already assured, so he didn't need an education.

I didn't know him, of course; but even if I had, it wouldn't have made any difference. I could never have expected what our life together would become.

I say that most of what went wrong was my fault, not because he was perfect, poor man, but because I believed that it was up to the wife and mother to hold the family together. I still believe that. At least I think I do. A woman is the heart of the family. She goes along with what the husband wants, accepts his decisions, fulfills his requests. Sometimes she gently redirects him for his own good, and he doesn't really mind, so long as she doesn't embarrass him. Women are wiser than men, but they must exercise their influence indirectly, by affection and gentle persuasion.

If you were cynical you would say that the husband thinks he's the boss and the wife knows she is. My mother certainly ran our family, but she never gave an order and always seemed to be doing what my father wanted. We give in so we can have our way. We stoop to conquer.

Well, I stooped but I never did conquer. I didn't know how to hold a family together under pressure. Somehow I never learned that. I couldn't control my family the way Mom controlled her family. That was one of my many failures.

A lot of women made something out of men far worse than Wolfe. No one quite warned me that you had to be a mother to your husband too, making something out of him the way you made something out of your other children. I suppose the message was there. God knows I heard it often enough from my sisters after marriage when we had trouble. I guess I never understood what it meant or learned how you did it.

Divorce was something whose existence you did not admit, not in our neighborhood at that time. It was an admission of failure. It was like a man going bankrupt or losing his business, only worse because you could always earn your money back. It was proof that you had failed as a wife and a mother and as a woman. What good were you then?

It didn't matter what provocation you had, except maybe public adultery; the fault was always yours, regardless. There were a few divorced and remarried women in the parish, but they couldn't receive the sacraments and were a bit of an embarrassment to the rest of us. Maybe there would be a divorce in your family, like my aunt Martha. Since she was family we'd make an exception for her and blamed, or pretended to blame, her husband. We knew that our neighbors would not give her the same exemption from the rules. There were whispers about an annulment, which we knew would be very hard to obtain (a lot of money and influence in Rome helped, we were told). That would somehow make things right, not only because her new marriage could be blessed in Church but because it would be like the Church's verdict that it wasn't her fault after all.

Anyway, divorce was as unreal for me in 1960 as flying to the moon. It wasn't an option and it wouldn't be necessary because my Wolfe and I were going to be deliriously happy for the rest of our lives. I'd show my sisters that marriage wasn't as bad as they said it would be.

I look at my wedding pictures and realize what an innocent kid I was, no older and probably less prepared than the teenagers down on the beach today. Yet I was on top of the world. I knew everything, I understood everything, I would be the perfect wife and mother. I would make all my dreams come true.

Such a little fool! I didn't know a thing about marriage or sex or life. Neither did Wolfe, poor man. We were young, we were in love, the world was our apple. We knew what we had to do and we were going to do it.

Now he's dead and I'm committing adultery

every night.

Not everyone was raised that way in the 1950s, not even in our neighborhood. . . . Your sisters weren't. Do you realize I had three children by the time I was as old as Mary Kate was when she was married? We all thought she'd be an old maid when she went to medical school without having found herself a husband. Wasn't that absurd! Yet we believed it like it was gospel.

Maybe a lot of the other kids didn't buy it as completely as I did. I was the sweet, naive youngest child who trusted everyone and believed everyone. It wasn't all bad, Monsignor. Many, many women of my generation have made it work. I don't think they're any less happy than the younger women with their careers and their independence. I don't know which is better. All I know is that I didn't have a choice. I did what I was supposed to do.

Then someone changed the rules.

— 35 —

SUZIE WADE QUINLAN

I was a terrible lover, Monsignor, an awful bed partner, a total bust in bed.

Oh, I'm sorry for the pun. I didn't mean it. I suppose I wouldn't even have noticed it if I wasn't. . .

Never mind that. You know what I mean. I'd made the retreats in high school in which the priest talked in whispers about sex. I'd studied the biology textbook and looked up the words in the dictionary, so I knew how the parts fit together. I'd yawned through the Christian Marriage course the year I was in college. But

I had no idea. . . .

Wolfe wasn't much better, to be perfectly honest. I had no experience at all. He had a little. No, I'm sure he had a lot of experience before we were married, but it didn't seem to help him much. The wedding night was terrible and the honeymoon not much better. I wanted to be a wonderful lover. I thought I would be one without any trouble. I was a total failure.

Maybe the change was too abrupt. You're supposed to give yourself completely to a man against whom you were drawing firm and unnegotiable lines even the day before. "Wait till we're married." Well, when you're married, you find out that there's not much there to give once the lines are crossed. I mean, you let him do what he wants to your body and that's that.

He told me once when he was drunk that he went to a prostitute during our honeymoon in Lake Louise. Have you ever been there, Monsignor? It's so beautiful. I don't know where he could find a hooker, but I'm sure he did. I think I knew it even then.

The hotel was filled with honeymoon couples. Some of them seemed very unhappy, and others were glowing with contentment. I envied the happy ones and blamed myself for being such a twit. The walls of the hotel rooms are thin, so we could even hear the couple in the room next door to us grunting and squealing and the woman exclaiming as though she'd been hurt. I knew even then that it wasn't pain that was making her cry out. I wondered if I would ever experience that sensation.

I tried, Monsignor. I read books, that was back in the days when I could sit in one place long enough to read more than a few pages. I talked to my friends, even the one sister I was close to. They all said, "Give it time. Who do you think you are that it should be special for you?" I tried to talk to Wolfe, but he refused to discuss it. What happened in bed at night was something completely isolated from the rest of our life. Looking back on it, he probably felt that he was a failure too, poor man.

I think he was a better lover with the others. Melanie makes her vulgar little hints whenever she dares. Maybe it was different for him with someone who was not his wife. Maybe I was too pure, too good, too Catholic, to turn him on the way the others did.

I was pregnant with poor Wolfe Junior when we came home from our honeymoon, bored and frustrated (you can take just so much of that glacial beauty and you want to scream for the next slide). I was sick every morning and much of the day too. So that didn't help.

There was a little pleasure in our marriage. I wasn't completely frigid. Some times were better than others. I didn't like it when he went to the others. I even told him so. Well, once. He told me that he wasn't getting it at home so he had to get it somewhere. I wept for three straight days.

What he said was true; he certainly wasn't getting it at home. I decided that I was an undersexed woman and he an oversexed man. If I wanted to keep the family together, I would have to accept that and live with it. I accepted everything, you see, Monsignor. Everything.

The best time for us, as far as sex was concerned, was when we were in the Charismatic Renewal, before we joined the Congregation of God. The husband was supposed to give his wife sexual pleasure. People even gave public thanks for their pleasure the night before (I never did that, too ladylike, I guess). Wolfe approached the problem like he did everything else. Spend money, buy big picture books, work at it long and hard, spare no effort or time. It was pretty somber and heavy-handed, but still better than anything before or since in our marriage. I faked it a lot to keep him happy—he'd become so impatient with me. But sometimes I didn't have to fake it.

Then I would scream like the girl in the room next to me at Lake Louise and really mean it. Wolfe was embarrassed because when I finally became passionate I went really wild. I guess he wanted me to have orgasms but not unseemly orgasms.

Often the orgasms didn't seem worth all the effort.

They were helping to hold the marriage together and making our family happy for Margie and Kevin and little Laurel.

I was having orgasms, pretty mild ones, I now realize, for others more than for myself. My whole life had become a sacrifice for others. I knew no other way to live, no other way to feel I was worth anything.

Our sex life slowed down when we joined the Congregation and even more after we became part of Father Armande's group. Wolfe found other interests, but I'll explain that later. In a way I didn't mind. I could understand why so many other women retired from sex after forty.

Other men? Sure, they made passes, which I promptly rejected, sometimes without any hesitation and sometimes only after being tempted by curiosity and maybe loneliness too. In the last few years, after we stopped seeing our old friends and stayed away from the country clubs (we belonged to three—Olympia, Butterfield, and Long Beach), there weren't any men around who would make routine passes as easily as ordering a Scotch and water.

I missed that kind of man. They were a lot more human than the ones in our new churches.

Lawrence.

I suppose if I were honest with myself I would admit that I've known for a long time that he wanted me. I was flattered and puzzled. Why would such an attractive and powerful man like him be interested in an empty flake? I tried not to think about it.

I was simply not that much interested in sex, I told myself. There were other things in life that meant more, just as the priests and nuns told us when we were young.

So now look what has happened. I've become a sexual glutton. I tingle when I think of him, I want to take my clothes off as soon as he comes into the room, I can't get enough of him, I wear the poor man out. Not that he complains. I cry out much more loudly than the girl in the next room at Lake Louise. It's like a honeymoon twenty-four years too late.

I'd feel guilty for Dorrie except that she explicitly told me that she wanted us together if anything happened to Wolfe.

"You two will do fine," she said with that crinkly, wicked grin of hers. "Just fine."

Why can I be that way for a man who is almost a stranger when I couldn't for my husband, whom I really did love despite everything that happened in our marriage?

Both men wanted me to yield to them. I wanted to yield to both of them. Why did I succeed with one and fail with the other? Why does Lawrence make me feel like a woman when poor Wolfe only made me feel like a thing?

It's not that Larry... well, I'm sure he told you. I mean at first it wasn't any different than with Wolfe—a man sees you and wants you and finally takes you. Any man might react that way. It's not worth the effort to say no or to fight him off.

Then something happened. Excuse me for crying again. He must have seen something in me that made him change. I could tell he was looking at a different woman. It was all in the twinkling of an eye. He saw this different woman and became very tender with her. I hated him for it. I didn't want to be seen that way. I would submit to his lust, I wouldn't let him... let him have that woman he saw. I would push him away or say something mean. I saw her slipping out of his eyes. The twinkling was almost over. One push, one word, would finish. I made up my mind.

Then—well, maybe I shouldn't be saying this to a priest—I turned on. I quit trying to pretend. I gave in completely to my feelings. I mean I let all the passion tied up inside of me explode. As Laurel would say, I freaked out.

I was good, Monsignor, though I shouldn't be saying it. I was incredibly good and I knew it. I've been that way with him ever since. I'm blushing terribly; but I'll finish what I started to say. I'm good and I'm getting better.

Maybe there's something wrong with me. Maybe I'm like Wolfe. Maybe I only get my kicks when there's sin in it. Maybe if Lawrence and I should marry it would soon be the same way.

I won't marry if that's true. I don't think God would want me to. He made me the way I am, didn't He?

Every day since—well, I'll use the words, though I've never spoken them about myself before—every day since my... my love affair—see, I can say it—began I've asked myself whether if I had been a glutton in bed with Wolfe our lives would have been different.

I'm not even sure he would have liked it. He would have been horrified at his wife acting like a cheap hooker—he said that once when I bought some very revealing lingerie. Still, maybe if I could have been then the kind of bed partner I am now, our whole life might have changed. We would have survived the deaths with less suffering, we would have never had to leave the Church—and I'm still a Catholic, Monsignor, I always will be. I heard Mary Kate say at a dance at Long Beach Country Club, "Once a Catholic, always a Catholic. Give the goddamn papists the first five years and they have your imagination for the rest of your life."

Why does a woman want to do an instant strip for one man she loves after a life of cringing at the sight of another man she also loves?

I did love him, Monsignor. I did. I'm not saying that to convince you or to reassure myself. There wasn't enough in me to love him the way he should have been loved. It wasn't merely in bed that I was an empty nothing. That was only the most obvious place.

So I'm good in bed now for Larry, so good that I can't believe it's me. What would Laurel think if she knew the things I'm doing? Should I tell her before she's married? I think I will, all the disgusting, glorious details. I would have been a much better wife if someone had told me long ago.

Not really. It doesn't work that way. You have to be someone outside of the bedroom before you're someone in the bedroom. Doesn't that sound profound, Monsignor? I'm sure I heard something like that in the Christian Marriage course at Clarke and thought it was boring like everything else in the course.

I haven't been someone outside the bedroom for a long, long time. Ever, I guess. I'm not sure how long I can be someone in the bedroom either.

I'm going to try, even if I have to break into Mary Kate Murphy's office and force her to spend a whole day listening to me. You tell her that too.

It's my last chance to be someone and I'm going to try, if it's the last thing I do.

So, Monsignor John Blackwood Ryan—I will not call you Blackie, not yet anyway—I'm sorry my husband died. I'm sorry that I was such a poor wife to him. I'm sorry that I am almost as guilty of his death as the person who killed him with that terrible sword.

Don't expect me to be a proper, weeping, broken little widow woman. I've had a taste of life in the last week, the first taste in a long time. I like it. I want more of it. I may lose, but it won't be because I haven't done my damnedest to make something out of myself.

Am I grateful that the burden of Wolfe has finally been lifted? I've never said it this way before, but you better believe I am. I thank God every day that the horror is over.

36

BLACKIE

"What did you do with the second key?" I broke into her narration, partly because it seemed the appropriate time to spring my trap and partly because her calm and candid narrative of tragedy and despair was creating odd, stinging reactions behind my eyes.

She looked up from her notebook and removed her reading glasses. "I threw it in the lake."

"And didn't tell the police?"

"No." She closed the notebook, finger in place. "I mean I threw it in the lake the day the lock was installed. I knew the police might not believe that, so I let them check up on the old lock."

"Wasn't that a risk? What if they had learned you deceived them?"

"They weren't very smart cops, Monsignor."

Sue, as opposed to Suzie, was a woman capable of desperate gambles.

"Why did you throw it in the lake?"

"Well"—she drew her arms around her chest as if in self-protection—"Wolfe often told me to change the lock. He was kind of paranoid about his little treasures. He never asked for two keys before. When he came up here that night, I gave him the one key and he demanded the other. I told him I wouldn't give it to him unless he told me who was getting it. He became very angry and said it was none of my business... he used some other words too.

" 'You're giving it to Father Armande, aren't you?' I shouted at him.

"He tried to grab me and I slipped away from him, ran out on the balcony and threw it as far out into the lake as I could."

"Then?"

She put her glasses back on and opened the notebook. "He beat me, of course. Terribly. So I knew it was for Father Armande. Then... well, I guess you can use the term now even of husbands... he... raped me. Brutally. I didn't care. I didn't want that man holding a key to my bedroom."

"Not quite the bedroom?" I said, my fists clenching.

"Same thing.... For a few moments I was afraid he would throw me after the key. I didn't care. I wanted to die. But who would take care of poor Laurel?"

"Indeed. He was strongly attached to Father Armande?"

"Totally." She closed the notebook, sensing another line of questions.

"Sexually?"

She put the notebook aside and pressed clenched fists against her forehead. "Good God, Monsignor, I don't know. I suppose so. In some of the soaps I used to watch they said that a man who plays around a lot really is trying to disprove his own homosexuality."

"Ah."

"Sometimes... well, sometimes"—she frowned as though trying to think it through—"I wondered if that was why he was fond of Larry. I mean, he admired Larry's integrity and ability, but... but there seemed to be something more, if you know what I mean."

"You think that Mr. Burke responded in kind?"

"Oh, no, Monsignor." She grinned shyly at first, then slyly. "That's not his kind of problem at all."

Who would know better than she?

I found myself thinking, not for the first time, that whoever had removed Wolfe Tone Quinlan from her life had done a very good piece of work indeed.

As I have said, I fall in love very easily.

37

SUZIE WADE QUINLAN

You've got to understand, I'm no one, Monsignor. The youngest of six kids, four girls, spoiled and petted, pampered and protected, made to feel naive and silly and innocent. I was pretty or at least cute. I crowned the Blessed Mother in eighth grade. I had the highest marks in school. I was class president my senior year in high school.

Beyond that I am or have done nothing. I brought six children into the world, which requires only a woman's biology, some sexual intercourse, and a good obstetrician. I fed them and clothed them and tried, unsuccessfully in most cases, to protect them from harm, drove them to school and to lessons, put Band-Aids on their hurts. I thought that was all you had to be.

Now I find out. . .well, I'm not sure what. Maybe I should put it this way: I find out that if all you are is a good mother, you can't be a good mother.

You must have interests and ideas and concerns and commitments beyond motherhood to be a good mother. If you're not somebody when you're not playing the mother role, then you won't be a good mother. That's obvious, isn't it? But no one told me. They told me just the opposite: be a good mother and you'll be a good woman.

After twenty-four years of marriage and six children, I discover that you have to be a good woman, a good

person, a good human being first. It makes me so goddamn mad. I'm sorry, Monsignor.

That thought—and it's not much as a thought, is
it?—is the first thought I've had since I married Wolfe.
He wanted a dumb little bunny. My family told me I
should be a dumb little bunny. My church seemed to
agree that I was most pleasing to God when I was a
dumb little bunny. So I acted like one. It wasn't hard
because that's all I was. All I am. With another man or
even with Wolfe in a different life, one without so much
tragedy, I might have made it as a dumb bunny. God
knows there's enough women like me sitting over on the
veranda of Long Beach Country Club sipping martinis
now who are as much dumb bunnies as I am, and happy
and content too. Or so they'd say.

Maybe my problem has always been that I knew deep
down that I was nothing but a baby-making and feeding
machine, a silly, giddy, unstable little twit. If that's all
you are, what do you have to give those you love when
they need something more than breasts and a womb?

Nothing. So you go along. You give in. You accept.
You sacrifice. You demean yourself. Oh, God, how you
demean yourself! What else is there to do?

I'm a hollow woman, Monsignor—goddamn it, I won't
call you Blackie till I'm ready to. If you don't want to be
called a monsignor, you shouldn't have accepted the
title. Give me your goddamn glasses. Can't all those
bright sisters of yours put a container of this spray into
your pocket?

All right, that doesn't sound like a hollow woman.
Temper tantrums are not much substitute for a mind.
I'm sorry. I guess I'm pretty much a mess. Here are your
glasses.

Anyway, the only thing that's not hollow in me is that
I have enough of a rusty brain left to know that I'm
hollow. I haven't read a serious book, any book, in
years. I glance at the women's magazines, barely look at
the newspapers, don't even think about concerts or art
galleries, worry whenever I miss my soaps. I lived
through Vietnam and Watergate, the sixties and the sev-

enties, like they were something happening in another universe. When I'm caught in a serious conversation, I don't say anything, because I don't have anything to say. The dumb bunny role fits me so well that it's become me. My brain, my tastes, my common sense are atrophied. When you look for my self, there's nothing there. And that's a line I heard somewhere twenty-five years ago.

Oakland, California? Really? I've never been there.

So you see what happened? Because I was a dumb bunny I accepted the little things like staying up late every night to watch Johnny Carson, then the bigger things like his whores and his drink, then really big things like his beating the kids and beating me too, then the biggest things of all.

I should have drawn the line early. I should have said, you can watch TV as long as you want, but I'm going to bed and don't wake me up when you finally turn that damn machine off. I should have said, sure, fuck your whores if you want, but don't expect me to be waiting for you when you come home. I should have said, join AA, buster, or I'm moving out. I should have said, you raise a finger to one of us ever again and I'm calling the police and a divorce lawyer.

You see, I know the words. I had the thoughts. They were on the tip of my tongue time and again. I never said them. I was afraid to, afraid that he would hit me even harder, afraid that I'd lose him, afraid that I would be called a failure in marriage, afraid that I didn't have the gumption to make the words stick.

I don't know what would have happened. Would he have straightened out? Maybe. Maybe not. But it was the only chance I had to make things better. Worse, it was the only chance he had. If I had drawn the line early, he might still be alive. I'm not sure. I finally did draw the line, very late in the day, God knows, and now he is dead.

I'll explain that later. If I work up enough nerve.

So the role of the accepting, long-suffering dumb bunny, the "poor woman" that others talk about at the back of church on Sunday morning, the martyr to a drunken husband and ungrateful children *became* me. I degraded myself instead of drawing the line. I knew, somehow, what I was doing was wrong at first. After a while accepting degradation became so much of a habit that I didn't give it a second thought. Hit me again, Wolfe, darling, that's what I'm here for.

There was a tiny corner somewhere in my brain where a soft little voice occasionally whispered, "Suzie, you're a damn fool to put up with this shit." The last couple of years I didn't even hear her telling me off.

How long have I been thinking this way? I didn't make it up on the spur of the moment when Lawrence took off my clothes by the swimming pool. A long time. Some things happened, I'll get to them, that stopped me in my tracks. I would sneak off to Mass at Notre Dame of Long Beach in the morning after Wolfe had left for work or for the CAA and stay in the church after Mass to think and pray. It was kind of formless at first. Then Wolfe's death forced me to crystallize it: I had been a self-degrading little dumb bunny all my life, the kind of wife Wolfe thought he wanted but exactly the kind he didn't need.

I drew the line on him because he had finally crossed the last line on me, the son of a bitch.

I can express anger at him now that he's gone, poor man. I did it once or twice to his face toward the end. Too late, much too late.

I should have shouted at him the first week at Lake Louise. Do I shout at Lawrence? Well, a little bit. He doesn't do that much that requires shouting.

Having said all this, and I've really dumped on Wolfe, I must also say that I did love him and that I never stopped loving him.

There was so much good in him, Monsignor. When he was sober, he would read the kids stories at night, play ball with the boys, work on coloring books with the girls, let them help him with his collections, take me to dinner and a movie every week, buy me anything he thought I might need or want, like this great big gloomy, useless house.

When he went away on his "golf vacations"—that meant hookers and booze and the best of both because nothing was too expensive for him—I was angry, of course, and relieved because I could do without the drunken tantrums. But I was lonely because I missed the laughter and the jokes and the good times. Despite myself I'd hug him enthusiastically when he came back. Later I found out that he'd stop at Melanie's for something I couldn't give him before he came to me. That upset me, of course, but I was so far down the road in degrading myself that it didn't much matter.

Each time he came back into the house, I hoped and prayed to God that life would change. When I saw his big smile and felt his arms around me, I'd be convinced for a few minutes or a few hours or a few days that he had changed.

You see, Monsignor, the poor man loved me too. He had no more clue what to do with me than I did with him.

A real mess, huh? And now I think maybe, just maybe, if I'd drawn that line early instead of late, the laughter and good times might have won out and we might still have them.

When he finally did give up drink and women and beating us, he gave up his charm and jokes and fun too.

Before that happened, I prayed and prayed and prayed that he could find the strength to be the man I thought I'd married and the man I really loved all the time.

Prayer is never enough. He wouldn't talk about therapy, swore he would beat me within an inch of my life if I ever suggested it again. So I tried more prayer. The Charismatic prayer group was my idea, God forgive me for it. I mean, they were nice people and it's a fine movement and only a tiny number end up with someone like Father Armande dominating their life.

With Wolfe's personality, his hunger to be ahead of others, to know mysterious secrets, to have power that others don't have, to do things others don't do... that kind of religion was the worst thing in the world for him.

It pulled him together, like I always hoped he would pull himself together. But it was from the outside, not inside him. The community held him together, then Father Armande. That's why he's dead.

If I hadn't talked him into going to the prayer group meeting, he'd still be alive.

That's one more way I killed him.

38

FATHER ARMANDE

Twice, while he was engaged in the remote preparation for the Immolation, he had to rescue the Virgin from his acolytes. Normally he did not mind if they amused themselves, in moderation, with the women who were undergoing spiritual transformation. It was, in fact, a critical element in the process of conditioning them out of their illusions and into harmony with the life forces and energies. The acolytes barely understood this, but their lust was nonetheless useful in the redevelopment of a soul even if they did not understand they were mere instruments. Some of the women were horrified by the necessities of transformation, others patently delighted. The Peace Potions were helpful in producing the latter highly desirable reaction.

However, the Virgin was another matter. She must remain a virgin until the time of the final Immolation; otherwise she would not accompany him as his bride on his long journey through the Realms of Light.

The second time he caught them fondling her, they had pulled off the top of her gown and were amusing themselves vigorously. The Virgin herself, drugged with

the Peace Potion and bound to the high altar, was powerless and scarcely aware of what was being done.

There was here no question of conditioning because
her transformation would be virtually instantaneous.
Moreover, she was his virgin, his queenly companion on
the celestial pilgrimage; no one else should be permitted
to fondle her.

He chastised them harshly and dismissed them from
the sanctuary. To mollify them for the time being, however, he promised them full use of her after the Sacrifice.
This seemed to be enough.

"Anything we want, Father?"

"Anything. It won't matter. The other one also."

He chuckled to himself at the hard lust in their eyes.
They were quite unaware, poor foolish instruments, that
they would be dead by then.

He returned to the basement of the house to continue
his preparations. The tins of kerosene he carried, at the
expense of exhausting exertion, to the sanctuary and
placed them in the corner near the sacrificial altars,
carefully covering them with one of the red garments
that were used in ordinary services.

He kissed his Virgin Queen gently on the lips and the
breasts. Soon, my darling, we will be riding on our char-
iot together, into the purifying rays of the rising sun.

Then he descended again to the basement to spread
the gasoline on the musty concrete floor and on the old
and dry wooden walls. An interesting liquid, colorless
with a strong odor, a fossil fuel but under the circumstances a necessary evil.

Whence came that phrase?

From his seminary days. Yes, there was much laughter
and good times then, even if his classmates did not understand his greatness and often made him a figure of
fun.

He thought about the seminary and his work in the
parish when he was young. Was it too late to recapture
that part of his life? Was the Immolation the only way?

He paused, gasoline drum tilted sideways. He expected no pain in the Ascension into Light. The others would

experience intense pain, especially the Virgin, as an essential prerequisite for their transformation. But as a high priest, he would feel nothing but a slight twinge as his astral body freed itself from his aging earthly body. Yet who could be sure?

Might there not be another way?

The acrid smell of gasoline, reminding him of the service station in which he had worked on vacations from the seminary, stirred him out of his foolish reverie. Of course not. It was too late now. Fortunately. The Immolation was the only way, the sacred way, the preordained way. So it had been written, so it would always be.

Humming one of the Babylonian chants he had copied from the book in the library of the Oriental Institute, he completed the spilling of the gasoline. When, as the last act of the ceremony, he cast the blazing torch from the sanctuary into the basement, the old house would become a glorious inferno of Immolation.

He washed his hands carefully in the sacristy so that the smell of gasoline would not be upon them and removed the hose they used to clean the holy place so that it would always be spotless. It would be necessary to extinguish each of the preliminary oblations so that they did not cause the final Supreme Oblation to come before its proper time.

In what order would they occur? The Virgin at the end?

No, that would be crude. She should be offered between her two handmaids. But which handmaid first?

He heard a low moan of pain from the sanctuary.

He flung open the door. Hilaire, of course. The woman was totally without discipline. All his efforts to train her had been in vain. She wanted only pleasure and money, like the acolytes.

"You are hurting my Virgin!" he shouted at her.

"How come you're so sure she's a virgin?" Hilaire sneered with a total lack of respect. "Here, shall we have a look?"

There were black-and-blue marks on the child's

thighs. He was sickened at the disgrace, the sacrilege of this low woman violating his bride and queen.

"Depart," he thundered.

"All right, all right. I'll be glad when we straighten these folks out. You haven't been yourself since Quinlan kicked the bucket."

"It was the work of Lucifer at my bidding," he roared after her. Praise to the powers of light, he was still able to intimidate her with his rage.

Might not such a crude creature contaminate the ritual? Even transformed, was she worthy of a journey to the Realms of Light? Perhaps. At first she had been quite amusing. So she would be permitted to join them, but only as the most lowly of servants. Even that was more than she deserved.

There was no longer a question of which would be immolated first.

He sighed at the woman's vulgarity and went to his office to place the crucial phone call.

39

SUZIE WADE QUINLAN

Between May of 1960, when we were married, and January of 1968, when Laurel was born, I was pregnant fifty-four out of ninety months, more than half the time. They were all hard pregnancies and hard deliveries, except for poor Laurel. Margaret and Wolfe Junior were Irish twins, born eleven months apart.

I wanted to take a breather then. It was about the time Catholic women began to use the pill. My OB man recommended I go on it. Wolfe wouldn't hear of it. It was our solemn obligation as Catholics to have children, as many as God would send us. You'd think a man who always had one or more mistresses on the line, all of whom were using some kind of contraception, would permit his wife to do the same thing, wouldn't you?

I'm being bitter. Mistresses are for pleasure, wives for having babies. Even more bitter.

Two of those children were dead before Laurel was more than a baby. When I feel like being soft on myself, I say, well, it's something for even a dumb bunny to keep her sanity under those circumstances. Babies, diapers, midnight feedings, inoculations, pediatricians, noise, smell, mess, fights between the kids—and then two little caskets.

Wolfe Junior was a crib death. We didn't know as much about them as we do now. People always suspected the parents of negligence if not murder. Now they say it's that the breathing apparatus forgets to work. I felt guilty about Wolfe for a long time. Everyone, Wolfe, my family, his family, even the police, thought it was my fault. The woman police officer even said, "Lady, if you weren't a rich bitch from Beverly, we'd drag your little ass into the station on murder one."

I was already pregnant again with Kevin, though I hadn't even seen the doctor to make sure—no time. I was nursing Margaret and trying to talk to Mom on the phone. She called up every day with long lectures on having too many children too soon. She wouldn't let me get rid of her so I could go back to my work, almost as though she were enjoying my attempts to end the conversation.

Well, she finally hung up. With Margie still on my nipple, I went into the nursery to check on Wolfe Junior, who'd been unnaturally quiet.

He was dead, Monsignor, already turning blue. I had hysterics, of course. I phoned Wolfe and he came home and beat me till I was almost unconscious. It was my fault, he said, I was no good as a wife and no good as a mother.

I don't know how I survived those next few days. I knew deep down that our marriage would never be really happy after that. There would be some good times maybe, but Wolfe would never forgive me for Wolfe Junior's death and I would never forgive him for the beating. We pretended that none of it happened. I pretended that it wasn't my fault. But it was never quite right again.

Well, we had Kevin and Joe and Ellen and then finally Laurel. While I was carrying Laurel, the doctor told me there would have to be a hysterectomy. I was delighted, God help me. I pleaded with him not to tell Wolfe because I'm sure he would have refused permission.

When Ellen was swept away by the wave, I was haunted for days with the thought that God was punishing me for deceiving my husband. I asked a priest in confession if that were possible. He said there would be worse punishments ahead. He was right.

Wolfe blamed me for all the deaths, even Joe's leukemia. He would not read the articles written more recently about crib deaths. If I were not on the phone blabbing away to my mother, Wolfe would still be alive. That was that.

Joe's death was the hardest of all. He was a real person, kind of like what Tommy Burke must have been when he was a little boy, not just an infant in a crib. He was the healthiest of all the kiddies, never sick a day until he... I think I gave up hope then. The others—Ellen, Margie—I was numb. I'd gone through it so many times that all the funerals blur together. His family and my family blamed me. They didn't quite say it, but you could tell what they thought; and the priests in our parish, especially after we moved away from Beverly, allegedly to escape the blacks but actually to escape all the wagging tongues....

Do you think there's an upper limit of suffering beyond which we can't go without losing our minds? I know Wolfe was pushed beyond his limit. Whatever hope there was for us ended completely when Joe died. The things that happened after that, what I'm so ashamed to tell you, were not the actions of the happy, cheerful young man I married. He'd been buried with Wolfe Junior and Joe. I can find fault with my husband for what happened in the first eight years we were together. After that he was doomed.

Me? As I told you, I didn't have much character to begin with. If I wasn't a strong enough woman to cope with one death, how was I going to endure four of them?

I suppose I went over the line too. Looking back, I see only a nightmare, twenty years of nightmares, from the honeymoon at Lake Louise to Margie's overdose. It all blurs together sometimes. I can't remember which pain goes with what loss. If I were told it all happened to another woman, I would say that she probably belonged in an asylum.

So I'm not in an asylum. I'm having sex every night with a man whose wife is in an asylum. I suppose that proves how empty I really am.

What comes next is the worst of all. Everything else is building up to it. I'll try to tell you that I'm merely trying to explain what happened. Actually, Monsignor, I'm looking for excuses. I'm trying to convince you and me that after all that had happened to Wolfe and me, we were both in a stage of madness during the last two years and that we really can't be blamed.

Don't let me get away with such cheap excuses.

I didn't want a Charismatic Funeral mass for Margie. Neither did Wolfe at first until the members of the group began to work on him. I certainly didn't want to go over to the Congregation of God; I'd already had enough of our prayer group, to tell you the truth. I was so locked into acceptance and so numbed with, well, pain, I guess, though I don't want to sound self-pitying, that I went along, more or less in a daze. I told myself that Wolfe would change his mind eventually, that he'd always been such a sincere Catholic he would someday want to return, and that, after all, he wasn't drinking, he wasn't having love affairs, he wasn't beating Kevin or Laurel or me. It was the first peaceful time in our marriage. I'd settle for it.

Kevin's decision that he was gay was the final straw
for Wolfe. But instead of getting drunk and finding the
most expensive hookers in Chicago—or inviting Melanie up to his museum—he became more serious and
more deeply religious. The Congregation of God practically expelled us because Kevin wouldn't go back into
the closet. So we went to Hyde Park and Father
Armande.

I could see that it was mostly crap—you should excuse the expression, Monsignor—right away. White
robes, torches, "natural" food and drinks, Father Armande's gobbledygook. It seemed harmless; and it kept
poor Wolfe sane. I didn't like Father Armande and I worried about how much power he seemed to have over
Wolfe. I did my best to keep Laurel away from there,
especially since she didn't want to go. Sometimes Wolfe
insisted.

Now the really terrible part. As short and sour as I can
make it.

In the Church of the Angels of Light there is an inner
group of "The Perfect," chosen by Father Armande for
special initiation. They are assigned to spiritual marriages with other members, I mean others who are not
their spouses. Wolfe was assigned a pretty but crazy
little girl from the university. I was assigned to Father
Armande.

The spiritual marriages weren't very spiritual, as I
soon found out. They gave me something to drink that
had a hallucinogenic drug in it, so that I hardly knew
what I was doing. Then they made me enter one of the
"Secret Sanctuaries," little white rooms off the main
sanctuary, take off my clothes, and have sex with Father
Armande.

It was oral sex, Monsignor. I was in such a daze I
barely realized what I was doing. It seemed like I was
watching another woman being degraded. He had a
great time. I didn't enjoy it at all.

I told Wolfe afterward, expecting him to hit the ceil-
ing. He told me I was very fortunate to be honored by
the High Priest of the Angel of Light. He wasn't much

interested in me. He couldn't stop talking about the
wonders of his new bride.

He had it all now, you see, Monsignor. Religion and
young bodies.

I was nearly out of my mind for days; I felt cheap,
debased, used—like a soiled paper plate or a used section of toilet tissue. I wanted to die. I thought about
killing myself with one of those knives Wolfe keeps—
kept—up in his museum. I swore I'd never return to
that Church.

I got over it more or less and Wolfe insisted. Of
course, I gave in. Hadn't I been doing that all my life? So
I went back for a Saturday morning service. Nothing
happened. The spiritual marriages were "reconsummat-
ed" at Father Armande's pleasure, whenever he felt we
deserved a reward. A word would be whispered in our
ear during the regular service that we should stay after
for a festival.

I would pray to God, our God, the real God, that it
wouldn't happen this week, that I could get through
another week without sinking into the slime again.

It always seemed to occur just when there had been
enough time so that I thought I'd never be forced into
that little room again. It wasn't so bad, not till you
thought about it afterward, because you were pretty
well drugged when it was happening. You did sex in a
trance with tilting walls and wild colors and strange
smells and soothing noises. Once they made me do it to
three other men, then the four of them—Father Armande and the other three did. . . did things to me, none
of them regular sex. Do I have to say I didn't enjoy it?

To make it worse, Father Armande's face glowed like
he was in ecstasy when I was. . . was being degraded. It
seemed as if he were anticipating something that would
bring him even more pleasure. I'm free of him now,
thank God, but it still makes me shiver to think about it.

I almost killed myself the next day. I'd started swal-
lowing the sleeping pills and then I thought of Laurel.
She saved my life, not that it's worth much.

If I heard this story about another woman, I would say

the stupid little fool should have left him after Wolfe
Junior's death. I should leave him with a sick little baby
girl and pregnant again? Where would I go? What would
I do?

There were always reasons.

How many times, if I were watching another woman
so degrade herself, I would have shouted with outrage,
"You goddamn asshole, get out."

After a while you have been degraded so often that a
little kinky sex every month or six weeks for a half-year
is hardly more than frosting on the cake.

Well, I finally drew the line. I had to. If it killed him,
that's too bad. It was like killing a dog with rabies. I
mourn the man I dated at Christmastime the year we
were all singing "Chanson d'Amour" who slipped an en-
gagement ring on my finger at Midnight Mass. I didn't
mourn the religious fanatic who, in the beginning of
May, wanted me to give Laurel to Father Armande. The
two of us together.

A bomb exploded in my brain when he asked me that.
I said no to Wolfe Tone Quinlan for the first time since I
refused to go to bed with him before we were married. I
said no and meant it. At first he couldn't believe it, then
he knew I was serious and began to beg, plead, cajole.

I said no again about the second key. Now you know
why. Then I did it again, but that comes later. . . .

I could see clearly again, not everything, but enough
to know what a terrible, hollow, foolish, degraded woman I was.

I refused to attend the church's services again. I refused to permit him to take Laurel. I said that if he
forced her to go even once, I would call the police. He
believed me.

He felt terribly guilty about spoiling Father Armande's
"beautiful design." I told him if he ever mentioned Father Armande in my presence again, I would call a divorce lawyer.

Real brave, wasn't I, so late in the game?

Telling you this makes me feel more anger than I've
felt ever in my life. The dumb, crazy bastard.

Anyway, I suppose Father Armande must have exploited the guilt to get the money and the firm instead of Laurel. I told Wolfe, now quite coolly, that I'd fight him in court. I also said—I was making it up but I bet I was right—that I had heard the two acolytes whispering about how they had conspired to murder Mrs. Carson Long.

He stormed out of here accusing me of calumniating the greatest religious leader since Jesus Christ; I was a modern Pharisee and he'd prove me wrong.

I guess I must have impressed him, however. He didn't beat me and rape me that time.

The rest you know. We tried to have a dinner conference with him up here; he was drunk all day, someone killed him that night. I don't know why he was drunk; I suspect from our conversation at one o'clock that he'd found out I was right about Father Armande.

You don't know about that detail, do you?

I walked the beach for hours, fretting, fuming, stewing. I was terribly impressed with the way Tom Burke dragged Laurel out of the room. I kept saying to myself that long ago I should have dragged Margie and Kevin and Laurel out of the house the same way.

I went to our bedroom, got ready for bed, still furious, and then put on a negligee and banged on the bathroom door that connects to the study. Finally, Wolfe opened it.

He was wobbly and unshaven, but better than he had been at supper, conscious enough to hear what I intended to say.

"Whatta ya want?" he snarled at me.

"I have endured my final dinner party humiliation, Wolfe Tone Quinlan. I'm finished. My twenty-four years of hell with you are over. As of now. By noon tomorrow you will be out of this house or I will. In your own elegant language, fuck you!"

At first he didn't believe me. Then he saw by the look on my face that I meant it. Funny, he almost seemed to admire me.

He opened a bottle of wine, which he took from the

closet, and began to drink again. He begged me to re-consider; he promised things would be better. There were a lot of mistakes he'd just discovered. He'd take care of them, if I only gave him a few more days.

I weakened. He seemed so sincere and so confused. Even at his worst, Monsignor, he was a charming, per-suasive man. Finally, I said, "I'm still leaving if you're not. If you go into therapy and stay for six months, then I might consider a reconciliation."

"There's nothing wrong with me, honey, that a little loving won't cure. I don't need no head shrinker."

Then he become amorous. I refused him for the first time in twenty-four years of marriage. He tried to force me but not like the time I threw the key into the lake. I kicked him in the shins hard and ran through the bath to our bedroom and slammed the door in his face. I waited, terrified now, for him to come through the door. I made up my mind that if he touched me, I would scream and wake up the whole house. Instead, I heard him turn the lock in the door. An hour later he was dead. Maybe I drove him over the brink, Monsignor. As I said, I'm sorry he's dead, I'm sorry I wasn't enough of a woman to draw the line twenty-four years ago. Maybe then he would have begun to admire and respect me before the last hour of his life.

If what I said and did those last few weeks and that last night did cause his death, then I'm not sorry at all. I'd do it all again.

40

BLACKIE

I weighed my words, as one may imagine, very carefully indeed.

"Permit me, Sue, a preliminary comment. As you know, the issue before me is Christian burial as a possible response to a plea from the grave. I'm authorized to make no judgment on your life."

"I understand." She was quite composed, hands folded, shoulders straight, gray eyes serene, a demure little novice.

"I don't question the general accuracy of your descriptions or interpretations." I was sliding carefully to the critical issue. "I do most strongly question your evaluation of your own responsibility. In this respect: While both you and your husband made disastrous mistakes, the blame for which we can leave to a God who is pathetically eager to forgive at the slightest hint of any emotion that can be called compunction (fortunately for us, he is not a member of the Roman Curia)"—still sliding but getting there—"there was one fundamental difference. Your deficiencies, often, as you yourself admit, considerable, were the results of the aborted maturation of attributes of character that you did in fact and do in fact in some residual way possess. His failures were the result of the total absence of certain essential character attributes that were simply not in his personality. A different man might have called forth the required traits from you—one seems to be doing so at the present moment, but, note well, woman, only because you gave him a chance to. No wife on earth could have compensated for what Wolfe Quinlan, tragically, did not and could not possess in his character. Am I too obscure?"

She smiled faintly. "Oh, no, Monsignor Blackie, too precise if anything. You absolve me too easily."

"God absolves, Sue, with scandalous ease. Confessors, with more caution perhaps, absolve in his name. I'm not talking about forgiveness at the moment. I'm talking about a realistic analysis of the dynamics of your life."

She nodded. "Somehow I know you're right. I've known it for a while, I guess. It will take some getting used to. Still, it should make the future easier."

"And more challenging."

The phone rang. She answered it in another room. It was necessary to drive to Chicago to pick up Laurel. Would I mind? Greg Foster would be over shortly.

She went up the stairs and returned a few moments later wearing, I noted rather abstractly, darker hose.

I was as happy that she had departed, since in her presence I would be in no emotional shape to consider her narrative. Moreover, I could, perhaps, after disposing of the colorless little Mr. Foster, make certain, uh, reconnaissances of the house, search for evidence that might still linger.

All right, snoop.

For evidence that I didn't want to find.

I certainly understood the impact of her self-disclosure on Lawrence Burke. Doubtless the story was even more tellingly recounted with me—if in less emotionally charged circumstances—both because it was now told for the second time and because she had acquired the self-possession that comes from experiencing herself as a partner in deeply felt physical love.

There were not exactly tears in my eyes when she snatched my glasses to clean them for the second time. No, not really.

Sue Quinlan was, astonishingly, a survivor. In the depths of that pathetic fluffhead there was to be found a sufficient amount of biblical meekness to bring her through twenty-four years of hell. Some of the hell was self-made, the rest was senselessly endured. Nonetheless, she had managed to survive because of residual intelligence (whose existence at one time in her life no one denied) and residual toughness (whose existence no one, not least her husband, had suspected).

Moreover, she had moved Blackie Ryan very close to tears—a most unusual phenomenon.

The problem in which I was involved was, as surely the reader will have perceived, God's fault. He is a notoriously unprincipled character, which presumably is not objectionable, since He made up the principles to begin with. The Lady God dances around us through most of our lives, desiring us with an obsession that makes Larry Burke's hunger for Suzie look mild and waiting for those occasional moments of meekness that permit Her to intrude and possess, to seize and to transform.

The two of them are together at the side of the pool; they begin to engage in routine human behavior. The Lord God is lurking there, prancing around them with unseemly delight; perhaps there will be a slim chance to steer them both in His direction, a flicker of an eyebrow, a touch of a hand that will open them both up to a more demanding Lover than either can imagine.

Then Suzie, perhaps in a weariness that approaches despair and under the impulse of sexual needs she hardly recognizes, abandons her life-long mask of submission and momentarily replaces it with surrender. In those same few seconds Larry perceives her not as an object to be used but as a woman to be cherished. Caught in his own despair and in the grip of a passion he does not begin to understand, he cherishes her. She perceives herself as being cherished and for the first time in her life possibly, though it seems unlikely, worth cherishing.

That is all the unprincipled Lady God needs. Their love affair is now a ménage à trois. God's delight is infinitely greater than the orgasms of the two lovers, who may understand dimly at the fringes of their consciousness that they have been trapped by the

Great Voyeur.

Larry now devotes his commendably ruthless energy to cherishing her; Sue, as she has become, luxuriates like a spoiled house pet in his challenging affection and discovers a strong self that she did not know she had, and indeed only traces of which had previously existed.

Hooray for the Lord God! Love triumphs. Right? Right!

Are there minor tangles and details to clean up, like murder and adultery and devil worship? The Lady God sniffs disdainfully. Why else do I have people like you, Blackie Ryan the Priest, save to dispose of such matters while I cavort around the cosmos, pursuing the needs of my insatiable passions?

I anthropomorphize and metaphorize, you say? Certainly! How else can we deal with the Absolute? However, the metaphor is not greater than the reality, but less.

So Blackie Ryan the Priest had better dispose of the mess before the Lord God comes back and requires an explanation. No one wants to explain to an angry lover.

Sue (née Suzie) was being given in God's providence a second chance. Would she blow it? We all do, in part. Would she make enough of it to progress in meekness?

There would be a lot of us around to offer help. What more can be said?

I tell you what more must be said. If she blows her second chance, the Lady God will require an explanation of her. If those who, without asking for the task, have been assigned to help Sue avoid returning to Suzie fail to do their part, God will be most unhappy with us. Under such circumstances, She can be exceedingly unpleasant: I needed to be cherished in My newfound worth and you did not cherish Me.

All right, all right. I suppose You've permitted the woman to turn my head more than a little just to make sure I don't slough off. Still a sweetmeat, but now one to be respected and revered—and hence even sweeter. Ah, well, as Professor Whitehead would have said, truth without interest is irrelevant.

Was my new charge's story unusual? Perhaps, in the mixture of elements and in her survival. But there are many husband/wife relationships like the one in which she lived. And many religious cults that use mysticism and sex and drugs to dominate the personalities of their members. The power of abused religion to control was demonstrated at Jonestown so forcefully that it need not be demonstrated again. Moreover, some families seem to be the victims of a concatenation of tragedies that would seem, a priori, quite impossible. Two-, three-, even four-death families do exist. A couple of them in my parish. Often the survivors deteriorate completely. I know of one case where a mother sought surcease in a bizarre Catholic religious cult.

There are probably other women in the country who might tell similar stories. Only the ending would be different.

And it was my unfortunate task to question the ending. She admitted that she was in her husband's study and indeed had set him off drinking again. She said that, in effect, he tried to rape her. Implausibly, he seemed to have changed his mind. She was careful to note the small detail of his locking the door, obviously for my edification.

But had he locked it? Might she not, then or subsequently, have pushed the statue over on her husband, escaped through the open door of the connecting bathroom, raised a commotion by pounding on the main doors to the study, and then persuaded her paramour to lock the bathroom door with the keys on the desk (where Laurel said they were always left) and drop the keys into the dead man's pocket?

It was a plausible scenario. Kevin and Laurel were still asleep. Tommy would be a willing co-conspirator. The Fosters had yet to arrive, Kiernan O'Rourke was in his room, phoning the police. Resourcefulness and courage and quick wit would be required. Lawrence Burke had all those qualities in abundance and powerful motives besides.

And to protect the story, Sue could have told me the

entire truth—even to her regret at Wolfe's death—and protected herself with only a single small lie: Her husband did not lock the door between the connecting bathroom and the master bedroom.

Locked-room puzzle solved. Brilliantly.

Damn it.

Surely no jury in the Republic would convict her, especially not with the attempted rape defense and the wild tales of fun and games with Father Armande. Indeed, not every prosecutor would bring such a case to trial, convinced that he would certainly lose it—despite the steady drumbeat of publicity.

The image in my brain of the evidence I knew I would find was now clear, steady, and demanding.

A very reasonable scenario, quite probably true. Hard to prove, however. Indeed, virtually impossible. Of course, proof of murder—or killing—was not my responsibility. Could one disprove it?

I thought for a long, long time and saw one way that it might be possible to disprove Larry Burke's complicity. A thin thread of a possibility, but worth trying. I then thought for an even longer time, searching for another scenario in which she could have carried off the locked-room deception without Larry's complicity. She and Tommy perhaps. . .

Hey, you say, what's a matter with you, Blackie Ryan the Priest? We thought you liked the woman. Had she not adroitly summoned from you suppressed memories of gazing up adoringly at her when she was a crossing guard at 93rd and Glenwood, an astonishingly pretty crossing guard? Why are you trying to make her into a murderer?

I didn't say murderer, I said killer. There's a difference.

Because I admire the survival of meekness, as the scripture defines it, in her soul—and she was never more meek than when she told that pair of loonies there was no way they were going to mess around with her Laurel Flavia—it does not follow that I am indifferent to the truth of what happened to her husband. Or even indifferent to the puzzle of the locked room.

I would search, like a good philosopher, for the truth. Then decide what, if anything, to do about it.

I trusted Rich Daley's wisdom a good deal more than that of a prosecutor in LaPorte, Indiana, with all due respect to that old and lovely town.

Was that like *really gorge*ous little blond matron, sitting across from me on the maroon sofa, fists clenched, eyes blazing, lovely body taut with remembered pain, really capable of killing her psychopathic brute of a husband?

Do bears excrete in the forest?

Before I could pursue that ingenious observation further or examine my remaining provisional scenarios, Mr. Gregory Foster—small, overweight, pasty, disappearing hairline, nervous darting fingers, wet lips, cold, hard, expressionless eyes—appeared at the door of Quinlan manse.

---------- 41 ----------

SUE

Furious from her battle with the rush-hour traffic on Stony Island and the construction on the toll road and even more furious at that creep Armande for picking up her daughter, she jams her BMW into an empty parking place, slams the door shut, and strides down the street to the big old frame house on a large lot at the corner.

The nerve of that geek. She'd had it with him. The police would be told everything tomorrow, everything, regardless of what happened. That would be the end of him.

210   Andrew M. Greeley

*She had tried to call Lawrence from Long Beach, but
he was out with a customer. Tommy was at football
practice. So she will face them down herself, take Laurel
by the hand, and walk out of that place forever.*

*My, you've become an angry little bitch, haven't you,
Suzie? After putting tears in the eyes of that poor, cute
little priest.*

*That priest listening to you patiently all afternoon
made you even more angry at all the shit you've put up
with. Well, no more from Armande.*

*She had not called the police, not because the crazy
old fool had told her not to, but because she knew that
she could handle Armande herself and because she
wanted to avoid newspaper publicity—to protect Laurel—if she possibly could.*

*Against her thigh she feels the faint pressure of the
wafer-thin leg knife she has snatched from Wolfe's collection and fixed above the inside of her knee with
transparent tape as she dashed from the house.*

*You're also getting to be pretty bloody-minded, aren't
you?*

Well, if they lay a hand on Laurel...

*The black receptionist doesn't answer the door. Prob-
ably gone home from work. Instead one of Armande's
"acolytes," looking handsome and brutal in his business
suit, opens the door. "Good afternoon, Mrs. Quinlan.
Nice to see you again. Do you want to take your clothes
off now or later?"*

*She strides by him, heels clicking furiously, and
through the receptionist's office into Armande's "library." The bigger acolyte is sitting at the big oak desk,
his feet parked comfortably on top of it.*

"I want Laurel and I want her now."

"Do you, now?" *He grins viciously.*

"You heard me," *she snaps.*

"Well, suppose we tell you that you can't have her?"

"I demand her. Now."

"You can't have her. She's with the Messenger."

"All right, I'll be back with the police. Then we'll see."

She turns on her heel and storms into the reception-

ist's office. She is halfway to the door when the man grabs her from behind.

"No fucking police, lady. The Messenger has some big plans to teach you and your hop-head little cunt the lesson you need."

She kicks and struggles and screams. The shorter man comes in from the front door and slaps her brutally across the face.

"Shut up, cunt."

As she gasps for breath the first man quickly ties a gag around her mouth. Then they wrestle and drag her into the "library."

The first man rips the buttons off her blouse.

——— 42 ———

GREGORY FOSTER

I'll help you however I can, Father. I promised Mrs. Quinlan that I would. There's not much I can tell you that you don't already know. I'd do anything for her. She's real class, always has been. While I'll miss Wolfe—God knows everyone at the company will—it will be good to have her in charge. She'll keep a steady hand on the controls.

I don't think anything will come of this business with Father Armande. It won't be hard to beat them in court. We'll have to pay off a few hundred grand, I suppose, to keep him quiet. That's lawyer stuff. It'll never come to trial. Meantime I have to do what I've been doing for more than twenty years—keep the company running.

Mind you, I'm not complaining. I like what I do and I'm well paid for it. Wolfe was always a generous man. I'm not sure you understand the way we worked. I was sort of the inside man and Wolfe the outside man. He made the contacts, developed the concepts, designed the lines in a general sort of way, found the designers and even some of our skilled craftsmen, met with the regular clients, showed up at the industry meetings and conventions, personally submitted our big bids.

No one in the world was better at it, Father. No one. He had all the moves. In his own kooky way he was a genius, a self-destructive genius, God knows, but a genius just the same.

I'm more the stay-at-home type, the inside man. I administer the firm on a day-to-day basis, everything from production schedules to paying the bills. The company doesn't run a day without my being in charge of it. But it has nothing to run on unless Wolfe is out getting the ideas and beating the bushes for clients.

People used to say, how can you run the firm with him hanging around the CAA or the locker rooms at Olympia or Butterfield every day?

I'd answer, I don't care where he is so long as he's dreaming up his ideas and meeting the clients. Only, keep him away from the premises because he's a bull in the china shop when he comes in.

The last couple of years, with all the trouble they've been having in the family, he hasn't been so good. We're running on our spare tank, so to speak. Not so many brilliant innovations in the product line or big new accounts. One of the first things the missus will have to do is find someone to take over in that area. There's a lot of young people out there who are first rate. I'll give it to you straight, Father: none of them will be as good as Wolfe.

And you know something? It doesn't have to be a furniture specialty company. It could have been TV sets, it could have been an airline. It could have been anything. People say his father did him a big favor leaving him the company. Baloney. The old man may have hindered him. Maybe he would have been bigger in something else. Anyway, it isn't the same company we took over in 1965, almost twenty years ago—yeah, after his first kid died but before the second.

Look, the old man ran a furniture shop out of a loft on Ashland Avenue all through the Depression. He gets government money for a defense plant out in Harvey during the War, manufactures seats for bombers or something like that. Then in 1945 he settles down to a nice little business, riding the prosperity of the years after the War without working very hard or thinking about it very much. He figures he knows all there is to know about the game because he's made so much money.

Even when we're in high school, like in the early fifties, Wolfe sees this is dumb. The old man really hasn't made much money at all. And he puts it in bonds and bank accounts where inflation is going to eat it up, instead of plowing it back into expansion. When I graduate from college, Wolfe is already working at the company, even though he knows it's a nothing outfit. He's got the old man wrapped around his little finger because he agrees with him on everything.

It's a lot of shit, Wolfe, I say. I know it is, he says, but look, if the geezer thinks I'm like him, he'll turn the place over to me in a few years and then we'll go to the moon. Do you want to play? If you do, I'll talk him in to hiring you to work out our accounting problems and we'll have fun for the rest of our lives.

I don't mind telling you I jumped at it. I'd been carrying Wolfe's glove since grammar school and I'm proud of it. He's a bit of nut, booze, dames, you know the stuff, and Suzie, poor girl, is just not the kind who can slow him down. But, as far as I'm concerned, so what? It's always fun to be with him.

Maybe I was always afraid something like this would happen and the private life would catch up. God knows they went through hell. I stayed out of it. Melanie—I married much later than Wolfe—she tried to help and it only leads to misunderstanding. So we stay out of it as much as we can. Yeah, we live next door to him up here. But, see, the place next door was my family's summer home. Wolfe buys this big dump so we can be together like we were in the old days, you know? Only, he doesn't spend all that much time up here and Melanie and Suzie are different types, so there's not all that much social life. Still, we're friends. Always have been, always will be.

Let me tell you about the company. When we take it over, Wolfe is the president then and I'm the vice-president and we're still in our twenties, so the sky's the limit. We're doing all right, but if we want to really go big we need more capital than we can scare up with bank loans. I have some money my parents left me, a pretty good chunk of it in those days, and it has performed nicely on the stock market. I watch the market closely and make some lucky deals, get some lucky breaks. So I says to him—mind you, Father, it's my idea—do you want to borrow my money to use for the firm? Borrow it, hell, he says, I'll sell you forty-five percent of it. That way you'll have a big capital gains in ten years.

No way, Father, I could buy forty-five percent of the firm even then with my money. That's how Wolfe was. The big gesture, the sweeping gift, and never once look back. So I own forty-five percent of the company, just when inflation starts to eat up the stock market. When I sell ten years later, my profits after taxes, in constant dollars, are over three hundred percent. Wolfe never blinks his eye.

Sure, I always planned to sell out. We both planned it that way. When Burke suggests it—and he's a heads-up guy—we both say, yeah, it's time. Wolfe insists, not me or Burke, that I get a lifetime contract with the company and a salary in inflation-free dollars. Father Armande would have a hell of a time breaking that, not that he'll ever get a chance to try. That's Wolfe's doing. I'd have never thought to ask.

I did some pretty dumb things with the money in the next five or six years. You know what it was like on the Board of Trade in those days. The government had destroyed the action in the stock market and there was no way you could stay ahead of inflation there. So the smart money boys moved over to the CBOT. I've been following the action in the papers for a couple of years and think I see a way to pile up enough bucks to become a millionaire ten times over. Kind of the Richard Dennis of the late seventies, if you know what I mean.

I won't bore you with my tale of woe, Father. I blew it all, every last cent of it. I learned that it was one thing to play the pits in your imagination and another to play them for real. So... so, I've still got my job, our life-style isn't going to change. Melanie is a little upset, but, hell, she gets over things. So what difference does it make? I still do a little investing here and there, just for the fun of it, and I'm ending up about even. The firm is my life, though. And life is going to be pretty empty over there without him, even if he hasn't been up to par for the last couple of years.

Trouble with Armande's accountants? A bunch of assholes, if you ask me. You should excuse the expression, Father. Look, poor old Kiernan has been on the take since the beginning, phony retainer fees, that sort of stuff. I picked it up the first week out of college. Wolfe says, never mind the poor bastard; let him have it. I says, you better put that in writing. I've got the memos to prove it.

They think they have something on me. Sure, Wolfe knows I make myself an occasional loan and pay it back in a month or two or a year at the most, particularly after I blow my wad. He doesn't care. I've got notes from him to show it. Armande's sleazy lawyers—and in their own high-powered, LaSalle Street way, they're as much sleaze as poor Kiernan—can't lay a glove on me.

What bothers me, Father, is Wolfe. He's a different man, not the guy I knew back in the old days in Little Flower, not the guy that smashed a hundred windows in the public school in one night, not the guy that necked dames out of their minds in the backseat of my car in Ryan's wood. I become Mr. Foster. He talks to that creep in the red robes and then tells me I will have to pay for my crimes.

He's gone off the wall, Father. I feel sorry for him, but I have to protect my own ass, so I don't say anything to him while those lawyers are around. When Suzie sets up this meeting on July 4, I say fine. Hell, maybe we can work it out like in the old days. But he's off on a tout, first one in a long time. I figure that Armande has finally got to him and in a few weeks Wolfe is going to be in a hospital for a long stay. Small wonder when you think about what they've gone through. I don't figure him dying on us, though, Father. I didn't think he was that far gone.

Yeah, he was pretty wild-eyed and Suzie tells me he's spaced-out. But to throw himself on a sword? Wow! I still can't quite believe it.

It's the only explanation that makes sense, isn't it? You know, in a way, it's all for the best. I would hate to see Wolfe—a real free spirit, Father, if there ever was one—in a loony bin for the rest of his life. And it does make it a hell of a lot easier to fight off that creep Armande Whatever-his-name-is.

It's my company, and no one is going to take it away from me, especially some off-the-wall ex-priest. Take away my company and you take away my life.

43

SUE

She continues to resist even though they beat her. If you fight back, she tells herself, you are not degraded. They have been ordered not to rape her or they would have done it already. Moreover, by twisting and turning and kicking, despite her bound hands and bruised body, she keeps on her pantyhose and protects the thin sliver of steel that is Scotch-taped to her thigh. She is angry enough to kill without a twinge of conscience.

They fondle and play with her, squeeze and pinch her, hurting her terribly. She does not give up.

Finally, Armande comes. He raves at his pugs, gibberish about spoiling the Immolation. He makes them carry her down to the first floor and into the sanctuary. Torches burn on the cold clean white walls, casting wild shadows around the room. She is tied with thick bandages, hands at her sides, to one of the marble altars, chill and deathly against her flesh. The old man—he now looks old and haggard, like he is ready to die, dismisses his pugs. He leans over her and caresses her with his filthy claws, murmuring more unintelligible gibberish. She accepts his attentions, even feigning pleasure, because she knows her hand is near enough to the knife that she will be able eventually to grab it. The old man, his breath smelling like a sewer, kisses her lasciviously. She sighs in mock contentment. He pats her approvingly, covers her with a red cloth, and leaves.

Only after he has left and she has begun to twist and turn under the cloth to get her fingers on the knife does she realize that the softly breathing object on the altar next to her is Laurel.

Don't worry, honey, she tries to think the message through her gag, I'll kill all of them for you.

It is a struggle to free the knife. Stockings run when you don't want them to and are tough and strong when you do. Her fingers barely touch the cold blade when the old man and the pugs return with another burden, a twisting, protesting gagged bundle of white robe. Sister Hilaire.

She is stripped brutally of her robe and tied to the empty altar on the other side of Laurel.

The old man whispers a word of approval to his thugs. "This one first, not the others till I tell you."

She reaches again for her knife, wondering which one she will stab first. The odds are rising against her but she is so angry she does not care.

The thugs are playing with Sister Hilaire, in no great rush to pursue their amusements rapidly. The woman protests noisily, but the gag reduces her complaints to muffled sobs.

The old man returns and once again she lowers her thigh against the now-liberated blade and pretends to be motionless. He is carrying a large object gingerly in both his hands. Quietly he steals up behind the bigger of the two men and holds the object at his head.

There is a burst of light, a wrenching explosion, and the acolyte's head disappears in the darkness. Calmly the old man points the gun at the other and blows a vast hole in his chest. The second acolyte slumps wearily to the floor.

Bile surges from her stomach to her chest. She chokes it back. She does not want him near her, not yet.

He opens a sliding door. She sees a light and a staircase going down. Slowly, as though he has all the time in the world, Armande de St. Cyr, Messenger of Light and High Priest of Lucifer, drags a dead body toward the door and sends it tumbling down the staircase.

44

BLACKIE

"Neither you nor Mrs. Foster returned to the Quinlan house after dinner?" I asked cautiously.

He shifted uneasily, but the flat hardness of his eyes did not change.

"No. We talked about it, of course. Mel—she's more emotional than I am—thought we ought to try to help. I said that anything we did would be misunderstood.

When Wolfe was on one of his binges, the only thing to do was to let him play it out. If I had any idea of what would happen, I might have thought differently. Still, I don't know what we could have done."

"And you both were asleep when Tommy Burke came to tell you about Wolfe's death?"

"I was out like a light. I'm a very heavy sleeper. Mel heard the noise and slipped out of bed without waking me up. She had to shake me so I could hear the bad news. At first I couldn't believe it."

"You've never heard of a second key to Wolfe's library?"

He seemed to relax, as if I had been steering closely to dangerous waters and now had turned away. His eyes were as blank as ever. "I wasn't much interested in that collection of his. It was all right, mind you, kids' stuff but harmless, part of Wolfe's creativity, I suppose. A business partnership is like a marriage, I guess. You get used to your partner's peculiarities. I respected Wolfe's thing about collections and he respected my lack of interest."

"I see. Do you think his death was accidental?"

His eyes twitched momentarily. "That's what the coroner said, wasn't it?"

"Indeed."

He exhaled slowly, wearily. "I'll be damned if I know, Father. There doesn't seem to be any other explanation. But it's damn strange if you ask me. We all had reason to want him dead, if it comes to that, yet we all miss him. With Wolfe gone, life will never be the same. We all have to go, don't we? Still, I wish he had more time."

He meant it and he didn't mean it. Gregory Foster's emotions about his life-long hero and rival were so confused that it was just possible he himself didn't understand them.

Or that he wanted me to think he didn't understand them.

45

BLACKIE

As I began my, ah, explorations of the Quinlan manor I pondered the contrast between Melanie Foster's image of her husband and the man's presentation of himself. She insisted that he would tell of her love affair with Quinlan and he in fact did not. She described him as a stupid wimp and in fact he appeared to be a dedicated administrator and a very clever operator who made sure that he covered every base.

His admiration for Wolfe was surely sincere. But the envy, which he hid so well save from his granitelike eyes, was certainly profound, an envy made even worse, if I understand the dynamics of that worst of human vices, by Wolfe's open-handed generosity.

Was he as secure in the firm as he pretended to be? That would bear further investigation. Perhaps. As he himself said, they were all better off with Wolfe dead. The company had been slipping since his excursion into first Pentecostalism and then diabolism. They needed new blood, men and women with new ideas. Wolfe would certainly not approve of that. Perhaps Foster, anticipating Wolfe's emotional collapse, had been making plans about new personnel and new goals. Maybe, having failed on the CBOT, he now aspired to the top position in his own company. Then the creative people would work for him, not the other way around. Turnabout was fair play, was it not?

Almost without warning Wolfe arrives at the plant with Armande and his lawyers and accountants. An audit begins. Greg is threatened, no matter how firm he sees his long-run position. Prolonged litigation could be an intolerable hardship for a man who has little money of his own—and still likes to speculate at the CBOT. The new owners could challenge his contract, hold back his salary, destroy his vision of a company that belonged, for all practical purposes, to him.

Suzie certainly could not run it without him, could she?

If Wolfe were only a shell of his childhood hero and was doomed to a lingering death in an institution, why not sneak up the stairs, creep down the corridor, slip into the museum, and send Wolfe on his way to the haven of eternal reward for twisted Charismatic geniuses?

Few of our suspects had stronger motives, and few could do it so easily.

But there was still the mystery of the locked room. Might Melanie have a duplicate key? Might she and Greg have organized their own tight little conspiracy and sworn to protect each other no matter what happened? They were hiding something, all right. Perhaps nothing more than a late-night visit to Wolfe. A man like Foster, who had always felt inferior to his partner and rival, might fear that he would be set up with blame for the murder.

Whatever might be true of the relationship of the Fosters, they would be completely loyal to each other in this crisis. If they did engage in a conspiracy, successful or not, how would I ever find out?

With that happy thought I ascended to the third floor, removed Larry Burke's chart from my large briefcase, and began my explorations.

At the head of the stairwell I bumped into Wolfe Tone Quinlan.

46

SUE

The old man cleans away the remnants of his double murder slowly and serenely. The bodies are dumped in the basement. He descends to do something with them. She hears the sounds of a liquid being swished over them.

He climbs up the stairs, humming softly, brings a hose in from the sacristy, and begins to hose down and mop up the mess at Hilaire's feet. The woman whimpers pathetically, but he ignores her. Sue works carefully on the bandage that binds her right wrist, jabbing and cutting at it with the slippery blade, which slices into her skin almost as often as it cuts the bandage. She is perhaps halfway through it.

She thinks to herself that the old man did her a big favor when he killed the two hoods. It is now one-on-one. With Laurel as the prize. She is suddenly afraid. The blade slips from her fingers and desperately she recaptures it.

She could lose—that thought has not come before. He might kill them both. She thinks of Wolfe and his wasted life. She thinks of Lawrence and how much she has come to love him in so short a time. She wants to live a little longer if only to make up for the mistakes of the past.

Please, she prays to the real God, the one she's always believed in, it's up to You. I'm grateful even for the last week. If You don't mind giving me a few more weeks, I'd be very grateful.

Reassured, she begins hacking again.

The old man leaves the hose on the floor and removes

*the buckets and mop. He pulls a crimson robe away
from the corner of the room—more containers, maybe
fire extinguishers. Her blood runs cold. He's going to
burn us.*

*He discards his scarlet cloak and white robe. His body,
wasted since the last time she was made to look at it only
a few months ago, is clad in a satin loincloth. He pulls
the crimson blanket away from Hilaire and then from
Laurel. Quickly she slides the knife under her leg as he
removes her blanket and throws it with the others in the
corner of the room.*

*"My dear friends"—he sounds like the old monsignor
at St. Praxides when she was a child—"we are about to
embark on our long-awaited pilgrimage into the region
of light, indeed into the very center of light. We shall
rejoice and reign there until the Prince of Light sees fit to
send us back for his and our second coming."*

*It probably all started as put-on, she thinks, shivering
with terror; now the madman believes it.*

*"It will be a long journey and a pleasant one. We will
frolic through the cosmos, my Virgin Queen, her two
handmaidens, and my regal self. The first part of the
journey will be briefly arduous, particularly for the Virgin. Suffering is a necessary part of transformation. If
the suffering is terribly painful, be assured that the rewards of transformation are glorious. Now I will bathe
you and anoint you for our journey."*

*He brings two basins from the sacristy, and returns for
a cloth and sponge. He begins with her, cutting away her
pantyhose with a long knife. She cringes with shame.*

*"Come now, handmaiden," he murmurs reassuringly,
"be not ashamed of your mature beauty. Give yourself
over to the sweet natural energies of the cosmos."*

*She wills herself to be compliant. The sooner he is
finished, the sooner she can begin hacking again.*

*He scrubs her body with a sponge, briskly as though it
were covered with dirt. Then he anoints her with cheap
bath oil. He gives special attention to her breasts and
lingers on them as though he cannot leave.*

She thinks of Lawrence and prays.

The bastard wouldn't even buy expensive ointment,
she thinks irrelevantly to herself, trying to exorcise the
degradation and humiliation. The smell is like the taste
of coffee with too much sugar. Will he ever finish? she
thinks. Her nipples harden not from pleasure but from
the chill of the room. He twists them playfully, again and
again, and then leaves her.

It was too dark and he was too busy feeling me up to
see the knife, she thinks, and reaches for it.

He is upon her again, scattering flower blossoms on
her body.

Oh, my God, she thinks, this is absurd. She hides the
knife quickly, lest he see it this time. She will have plenty
of opportunity to free herself while he is playing around
with the others.

Her fingernails scrape the slippery marble. The knife
is beyond their reach; she has thrust it too far under-
neath her knee to be recaptured.

She has lost.

---------------- **47** ----------------

BLACKIE

I picked up my briefcase and restored its contents.

No one had told me that there would be a full-length
portrait of the dead man at the head of the third-floor
hallway. Why had Sue left it on the wall?

Perhaps because it had become so much a part of the
scenery that one hardly noticed it anymore.

It was a good job, Wolfe had obviously searched for
the best portrait painter money could buy—and pretended to be delighted with it even though the painter

had been scrupulously honest about his subject.

I had never met the man, even though we had grown up in adjoining neighborhoods. But then, perhaps worse luck for me, I was not given to necking girls out of their minds in the backseats of cars in Ryan's woods.

Yet the artist must have been honest to permit that ever-so-slight hint of uncertainty and fear into his subject's hazel eyes, a hint that beneath the bonhomie and aggressive geniality of this handsome, successful, clever man there was an emptiness of which he himself was dimly aware.

Character defect, I muttered to myself and thus slipped into the fault, endlessly denounced by my sister Mary Kate, of confusing a label with a diagnosis.

What was it Larry Burke called him? A comic opera tenor? A man behind the door when substance was distributed? Old T.S.'s classic hollow man?

In any case, enough vulernability so that it would be hard to hate him. Was he killed in a moment of passionate hatred? If the evidence I anticipated and dreaded was indeed where I thought it would be, the killer would have ample reason for hatred.

But the crime might not have been committed in a burst of hatred, not at all. That was, if my scenario was right, the ultimate question.

So I ignored Wolfe Tone Quinlan's watchful eyes and continued my investigation. Resting my briefcase on the landing, I stood at the top of the staircase on the third floor, with Lawrence Burke's chart in my hand. I had already opened the doors to all the rooms. If I am Lawrence F. X. Burke early on the morning of July 5, in the year of Our Lord nineteen hundred and eighty-four, I can look directly across to the open door of the study or museum or whatever one chooses to call it. I can see the work table where the body lay in a weird erotic embrace with Tancredi. I can see in that room the sliding door in the glass screen that surrounds the whole third floor. I cannot see either the closet or the door that leads to the connecting bathroom.

All as Lawrence has said.

Moreover, I can see the open door to the master bedroom, which is empty because Suzie, as she still was, had fled downstairs to find the phone number of Notre Dame Church. Or was said to have done so. Surely the priest did come eventually.

I can see the closed door of Laurel's bedroom. Heavy sleeper that she is, she has heard nothing. Similarly Kevin's bedroom, across the top of the staircase, is also closed. My own bedroom door is open, but since there is no connection between my room and Kevin's, he cannot emerge through my bedroom, should he for some reason be of such a mind. Kiernan is immediately next to me at the phone inside the door of his room, making a 911 call. I can see him and he can see me. Tommy has already sped down the stairs to the garage to fetch the Fosters. No one can move about the corridor unless I see them.

No one can enter or exit from the murder room without both Kiernan and Larry seeing them. Nor can I move without Kiernan seeing me nor Kiernan move without my seeing him.

Then Suzie returns, hysterical, and the bereaved offspring are awakened.

Ah.

I step into Kiernan's room, pick up the phone, and, having gleaned his number from the phone book in the kitchen on the second floor (where, sure enough, in a list of emergency numbers, is that of the local parish), call that worthy attorney at his Chicago office. No answer. Then his home. Still no answer.

Probably in some bar, the oily bastard.

Nonetheless, I think I know what happened. I'm afraid I know.

I ran through it all in my head again. It's a solution, all right. Let's see if it can be done.

I went into the museum, a much more cheerful place than I had expected now that Sue had pulled back the drapes and let the bright Lake Michigan sunlight in. One suit of armor was still in place. Tancredi's mate. I felt the tip of the broadsword. Oh, yes, it would do the job nicely, all right.

The room was pleasantly cluttered: velvet drapes, cane-backed chairs, small littered antique tables, mahogany bookshelves and cabinets. A little overdone, but tasteful enough. The three submissive little marble Italian girls would doubtless shock my parishioners, who would, if they could, put an athletic supporter on Michelangelo's Risen Jesus and a bra on his Eve, but they were chaste enough and appealing enough to be presentable works of art.

My theology, more orthodox than that of my prudish weekly contributors, told me that the ingeniously shaped marble and even more the three lovely peasant girls, now doubtless home and even more lovely, on which they were modeled were sacraments of God's appealing beauty, hints of Her life-giving, nurturing tenderness.

Presumably Wolfe Quinlan had not seen them that way. Poor man. Such an insight made the work of art more enjoyable rather than less.

No, dirty the statues were not. They were owned by a man with a dirty mind perhaps, and the dirtiness might not have been altogether his fault.

Meek they were not either, not by my definition. To reflect the passionate modesty of the Lady God there would have to be some hint that under the proper circumstances they too would slip their fingers down a man's chest and under the elastic of his shorts (or the nineteenth-century Italian functional equivalent thereof). For all their appeal, they were too passive for such a sentiment.

Maybe the hint wasn't in the models or maybe the artist was afraid to see it. If the hint had been reflected in the statues, Wolfe Quinlan would not have bought them. He would not have liked the challenge.

I sighed my west of Ireland sigh even though there was no one to hear it. Except the Lord God, who was by now immune to it.

The world was not well ordered.

More to my immediate concern, could someone hide

behind one of the statues? Not very likely, but there were lots of other places to hide, though hardly from the intent eyes of Larry Burke. The closet door was open, plenty of room for storage as well as for the icebox and stove. I borrowed a bottle of soda water from the ice box.

Then I entered the connecting bathroom to the rose and pink filmy master bedroom. Feminine, to say the least. Well, Sue was entitled. The bed was made too. A fastidious woman, obsessively so perhaps. Every jar and comb in its exact place. Morning makeup would be a solemn high pontifical ritual.

Then into Laurel Flavia's room, as impeccable as described by the estimable Thomas Burke—only the Michael Jackson and Ryne Sandberg pictures and the Notre Dame pennant above the bed would hint that it belonged to a sixteen-year-old woman. Beige rather than pink like her mother's room, with an Apple Macintosh computer and printer beneath a shelf of Penguin classics, the abode of Laurel Flavia suggested that she was a young intellectual rather than a tribal witch.

Of course, one could be both.

I walked around to each of the exits to make sure the locks were as described. Then I reenacted the murder, even to the extent of pushing Baldwin (as I tentatively named the surviving knight) off his stand and against the work table. He fell easily and with a resounding thud and cut a sharp gash across its mirror-polished desk.

Sorry about that.

The killer had performed with astonishing brilliance. No wonder the police had been tricked.

All that remained was to hunt for the evidence that I thought I might find. Its absence would prove nothing. Its presence would prove everything.

I found it, exactly where I thought I would find it. Looking exactly as I thought it would look.

This time I did not vomit.

I came close, however.

Poor fool, I said mentally to the killer.

Poor damn fool.

48

SUE

She gives up, panics, quits, while he anoints the angry Hilaire and the barely conscious Laurel. Her daughter stirs painfully under his kisses.

Fury restores her energy; she stretches herself as far as she can against her bindings, forces her hand under her thigh, and into the hollow of her knee.

Her fingernails touch the knife, scratch it, lose it. She tries again. It slips farther away.

He walks out of the room, whistling softly.

In sheer desperation she lunges again; pain rips into her arms and legs.

But the knife is hers.

He returns and lays a long rapierlike sword on the floor. Oh, my God! What's he going to do with that?

Her exclamation becomes a prayer, It's all up to You. As many weeks as You want. Or none. Thanks for sending Lawrence.

And Tommy.

And Monsignor Ryan. Blackie.

He leaves again, returns, renews all the torches, removes one from its holder on the wall, picks up one of the mysterious cans near the altar of preparation, and advances toward her, his face gleaming like that of an emaciated Santa Claus, in the wavering torchlight.

"The time has come, my child," he says softly. "Be brave."

Dear God, I love You. I'm sorry.

49

BLACKIE

I placed the evidence in my briefcase. What I would do with it, if anything, remained to be seen.

I could imagine showing up at Richie Daley's office and trying to explain how I had come to possess it. Mystery reader or not, Rich would not give me time to explain how I had solved the locked-room puzzle.

LaPorte? Another matter perhaps.

I made the round of rooms to be certain that I had left no trace of my, ah, explorations. In the study I hefted Baldwin back into his position, with some little difficulty, and shoved his sword back into the upright position. Outside the window the sky was cloudless and the lake placid, the horizon a line between two blue patches in a warm and reassuring quilt.

The best summer I can remember, I told myself as, briefcase in hand, I prepared to beat a strategic retreat and figure out what to do next. Even the Cubs were winning.

On the first step of the stairway I heard a resounding thump from the study, like someone pounding the floor with a sledgehammer.

Calmly I told myself that there ought to be no such noise. It was not there. I hadn't heard it.

I descended to the next step.

Another thump.

And a powerful chill—not in the environment but in my veins.

Blackie Ryan, priest detective and gray eminence to the Cardinal, scared?

You bet your life.

50

ARMANDE

He considered the woman carefully, sumptuous little body tensed bravely. So appealing. Her hard brown nipples reminded him of his first woman, a mother of one of the black schoolchildren at his first assignment. She had undressed in the sacristy while he—never having seen a naked woman before—watched in spellbound fascination. Somehow she had known that he wanted to experiment with her.

But not go that far. Not have intercourse.

He could not stop, could not help himself.

It was unbearably sweet. And sweeter still was punishing her afterward, an action as spontaneous as his initial pleasure. She seemed to want that too.

But later she complained to the bishop. It was the beginning of his fall from grace. Life might have been very different if she had not seduced him.

Admittedly he had kissed her rather forcefully, the first woman he had ever kissed. But that was merely a sign of affection. She should not have promptly taken off her blouse, under which, shameless savage, she was wearing nothing.

He had often dreamed of completing her punishment.

Now was his chance.

He tilted the kerosene tin.

51

BLACKIE

Curiosity triumphed over fear. Cautiously and, I freely admit it, with madly pounding heart, I crept back into the room.

The offending video camera lay peacefully on the work table.

"Okay," I said, trying to sound like a registered exorcist. "What next?"

One of the cabinets began to thump, as it had been advertised it would. Being blessed with more curiosity than common sense, I explored the doors and shelves of the cabinet. The rumbling stopped.

I continued to explore.

There was one space in the cabinet, about eye height (my eye, probably not yours), in which there should have been a drawer but wasn't.

I pushed and fiddled, pounded and jabbed, twisted and pulled.

Niente, as they say in Rome when you ask how much power American Catholicism has in the curia.

Then, on instinct, I twisted the knob on the next drawer.

Again nothing. Dummy. Larry Burke would have tried that.

Okay, she's his woman and that's proper, but a little competition in ingenuity never hurt. What would he not think of that a kinky character like Wolfe Quinlan might have?

Perhaps the same knob on the opposite cabinet.

I twisted it confidently.

Nothing, damn it.

Aha. I pushed it and the hidden compartment blew open. Try to outsmart Blackie Ryan, will you?

Inside?

Sure enough a VHS tape and a half-sized, unsealed envelope. Inside the envelope were two documents, folded in such a way that the signature, Wolfe Tone Quinlan, could be witnessed and notarized without the contents being read. Both signatures were dated July 3.

Both were duly stamped with the seal of a notary public.

I opened the first.

It read, "I hereby revoke my will of June 1 totally and completely. I wish to leave nothing to the Church of the Angels of Light. My previous will is now in force."

The other read, "I hereby revoke any and all gifts I may have made to the Church of the Angels of Light for reasons explained on the accompanying tape."

I considered the material. It would be much safer for the moment in my possession than anywhere else. I dropped the envelope into my briefcase and looked around for a video player. There was one on a shelf against the far wall. I popped the cassette in, flicked the switch, and prepared to turn on the TV.

The player didn't work.

I sighed and dropped the cassette into my briefcase too.

Not all that bad for an afternoon of burglary.

With no sense of urgency I ambled back down the steps to my father's antique gull-wing Mercedes, with a brand-new engine, and drove back to Grand Beach.

The leisurely way along the lakeshore.

52

SUE

He grins apologetically over her. "A thousand pardons, child. One of your great beauty ought not to be confused with a coarse woman who accompanies us only because there are no others. You will be transformed last of the three, after the Virgin whose handmaiden you are."

He strolls over to Sister Hilaire and lovingly pours the contents of the bucket over the woman's body. Its smell reminds her of her mother making blueberry jam long ago.

Kerosene!

There is still time. She begins to saw feverishly against her wrist, paying no attention to her own wounds. Better to bleed to death than to burn to death.

Laurel before me! Dear God, no. Not the only one I have left.

Armande holds the torch in one hand, the sword in the other. He stands above the woman like some mad Aztec priest and chants a long and unintelligible song.

She tears wildly at the binding. She's almost free.

Armande gently touches the torch to the woman's feet. A slow fire begins and moves gradually up her body. Hilaire cries in terrible pain.

Momentarily fascinated, Sue pauses in her work. Dear God in heaven, help her!

Then she goes back to her work. Soon, but not too soon, the woman is a mass of flames. The gassy smell of the burning kerosene blends with the terrible sweet smell of burning human flesh.

234

Armande continues to chant. The flames grow higher. The smell is asphyxiating her. His chant reaches a high pitch. He plunges the sword into the burning woman's body. A fountain of blood leaps out with the flames.
Sue loses consciousness.

53

BLACKIE

My first action upon return to my father and step-mother's house—those worthies having departed for the Glenlord Restaurant to consume the best pasta in our part of the world—was to call Kiernan O'Rourke's home.

He was there.

"Sure, Monsignor. Always glad to help the Church. Well, I don't remember everything. It's been a few weeks, of course. Yes, that's right; I made the call for the police from my bedroom—routine nine-one-one.

"Could I see the entrance to poor Wolfe's study? Yes, as a matter of fact, I could. Nope. No one came out. Burke had sent the punk next door to tell the Fosters. Shrewd way of getting the kid out of the house, huh?

"Anyone in the corridor? No one except Burke, standing all the while at the head of the stairs like he was some goddamn watchdog, if you know what I mean. Excuse the language, Father.

"Anytime, Father. Anytime. Give my best to His Eminence."

So.

Then the videocassette on my father's large-frame TV screen, described universally as "gross" by his grandchildren, who nonetheless did not disdain to use it.

I knew what I would see, but I was still shocked: Wolfe Quinlan, unshaven, bleary-eyed, red-faced, in his crimson dressing gown. His message was short.

"I'm confused and not feeling very well, so this will be short. I've found out that Father Armande is a fraud and a murderer. He killed Mrs. Carson Long because she knew too much. Never mind how I found out, I found out. I'm revoking all my gifts to him. He might try to kill me so I'm putting these documents together with this tape so he won't get away with it.

"He's a lousy son of a bitch. Took me in completely. I had great faith in him. Thought he'd straightened out my life.

"I'm sorry. I fucked up again."

Tears streamed down his cheeks as his face was replaced by TV snow.

Enough to merit Christian burial, I thought. Elmhurst is in another diocese but Mount Carmel is in Chicago. Burial and a requiem Mass in the cemetery chapel.

The phone rang. Larry Burke. Did I know where Sue was? He hadn't heard from her all day. About to drive out to the house, kind of worried. Couldn't find Laurel either.

I knew all right, damn fool that I was.

I told him I would call right back.

Mike the Cop answered at their apartment in the Hancock. I told him what needed to be done. In a brilliant afterthought that redeems some of my stupidity I suggested the fire department. Because I didn't believe in a hell with literal flames it did not follow that poor, crazy Louis Connery didn't.

Then I called the Coast Guard in Michigan City. PO/3d C.S. McLeod, beloved of Mary Kate's first son Pete, answered. I told her what I needed and why.

"Shunuff, priest," Cindasoo replied.

I had hardly finished my call back to Larry when the big white Coast Guard Sikorsky with its defiant red stripe settled on the front lawn and PO/3d McLeod herself—looking like a thirteen-year-old playing Coast

Guard person—threw open the door. I was whisked away at 180 miles an hour above the frothy white caps of Lake Michigan toward the setting sun and Hyde park. I prayed all the way to God, Mary, and all the saints and angels of whose existence I was aware. Barely avoiding the spire of the Laura Spelman Rockefeller Memorial Chapel, we arrived with the fire engines. With Cindasoo racing after me, I rushed toward the house, which was obscured by a shroud of dirty orange flame.

54

SUE

Her eyes flutter open. The old man is peacefully cleaning away the remains of his first "oblation." The charred body of Sister Hilaire is dumped unceremoniously down the basement stairs. He begins to scrub the altar, whistling cheerfully.

At first she thinks it is a dream. The terrible stench of human flesh is real enough. She remembers opening her eyes before. He was spraying the burning corpse with a fire extinguisher.

He uses the hose to clean the altar. Then he sprays a room deodorant can around the sanctuary. The calming smell of the deodorant struggles with the awful stink of burnt flesh, and loses.

Then she remembers that Laurel is next. She gropes for the knife and cannot find it.

The old man puts on his white gown and his scarlet cape.

"For the Virgin I must be in full dress. She is the message the Messenger sends."

Her fingernails, now bent and broken, find the thin slice of steel. With cool fury she cuts away at the bandage. There is still time. There has to be time. Dear God, grant me enough time.

The old man brings the second bucket of kerosene and lovingly paints Laurel's body with it. In the wavering light of the torches, she sees bafflement in her daughter's eyes and the beginning of fear.

Hang on, honey, mother's coming.

"Know, O Virgin," he croons, "that it was I, the High Priest, who through the power of Lucifer the Light Bearer freed you from the oppression of your father. I ordered that he die and he died."

She cuts through the last bit of bandage and rips her arm free. He shuffles by her and she lies immobile. She must now be crafty. She must not strike until she is free to fight him.

He shuffles back, torch in one hand, sword in the other.

"Know, O Sacred Virgin, that you will be my bride, my queen, my consort, for countless millennia as we journey the realms of light. There will be peace and contentment and pleasure for countless ages. World without end. Amen. We will then finally return in fire and light for the fullness of time. You must now suffer a little, in preparation for your voyage. In a few hours it will be as nothing. In the actual moments it will be painful. Moreover, I cannot end your little torment as I did the torment of the slave woman. The sword will pierce your virgin flesh only after you are on the journey. Tarry a little and I will be with you."

He bends down to kiss Laurel, holding both weapons high above her head. The child's eyes are now wild with terror.

His back is to Sue. With two fiendish jabs she slices away the bandage on her other arm, drawing blood from her wrist. Watching his torch-holding hand with one eye, she slashes at the bond on her right foot. She is stiff and awkward and cold. The knife drops out of her hand as she moves it toward her left foot. It clatters to the floor.

The old man, chanting his Babylonian hymn, does not hear the sound of the falling knife. With elaborate ceremony he blesses Laurel with the torch, shaping over the child a grotesque sign of the cross.

Jesus, help me, she prays. She leans over the side of the altar on which she has been bound and searches frantically for the knife in the darkness of the sanctuary floor.

Carefully, like a mother bringing a bottle to a baby's lips, he moves the torch toward Laurel's feet.

She finds the knife, pulls herself back on the altar and, oblivious of her still bound left leg, lunges toward the High Priest of Lucifer.

Her nerves are as firm as the shaft of the blade, her hand as cool. Her eyes are hard, her aim is deadly.

Savagely she pushes the blade into the side of his neck, shoving with all her strength against the resistance of skin and muscle and gristle. Then she tugs it toward his throat, as if she is carving a tough slice of leftover roast beef.

He squeals like a stuck pig. His rapier crashes to the floor. The torch in his other hand wavers, dangerously close to Laurel.

She continues to slice. Blood bubbles out of the side of his neck in a rush of dark red foam. She releases the dagger.

I'll smother the fire with my body if I have to, she thinks, clawing frantically with bloody hands at the remaining bond. Finally she pulls her leg free and looks up. The High Priest is tottering toward her, his face glowing ecstatically. The dagger juts at a grotesque angle beneath his ear like some monstrous tumor.

He is pointing his blazing torch at her.

She rolls off the marble slab in the opposite direction. She crashes to the hard stone floor in a jarring fall. Momentarily she is dazed. Then she sees the old man, staggering dangerously above her, flaming torch jabbing awkwardly in her direction.

She rolls over again and scampers away, thinking irrelevantly of the little Olympic gymnast who won the gold medal. He lurches after her, his life slipping away but his face bathed in a glorious smile.

She is still stiff and awkward. Her muscles ache, her wrists are bleeding. She tumbles into a corner. He totters above her.

Better me than Laurel, she thinks as, gasping for breath and beaten, she waits for the fire. He'll never live to get back to her.

Then she remembers Lawrence and with a burst of effort shoves the old man's legs. He falls back against the wall, the torch hand slips, the flame is at half-mast.

She struggles up the wall to her feet and drags another torch out of its holder. Fight fire with fire.

She gestures with her own flame at him. He backs away toward the basement steps. She follows him, now confident that she is the winner.

In a last dying effort he leaps toward her. The flame passes inches from her face. She smells the smoke, feels the heat, cringes from the pain.

He misses.

She counters with a thrust of her own. His white robe flares like tissue paper. Screaming, he falls back toward the basement stairs, sways momentarily, and then, a mass of fire, tumbles down the stairs. His voice fades like a dying factory whistle.

She rushes to the door and locks it. He will not come back from the dead like the monster in Halloween.

Moving with unexamined instinct, she dashes into the sacristy, turns on the faucet to which the hose is connected, and then rushes back to the sanctuary. The hose is leaping like an angry snake. She tames it and drenches Laurel's body, washing off the kerosene. Her little girl is now unconscious.

She drops the hose, ignoring the water spraying on the floor. She begins to tear at Laurel's bonds. Only a few more seconds and they'll be out of this place. Stark-naked on 57th Street. Hyde Park freaks.

Then she feels herself being lifted over the altar and slammed down on Laurel. She hears a roar, first like a waterfall, then like an exploding cannon. The room fills with heat.

Gasoline, she thinks, blowing up in the basement. The house is on fire. It will be a tinderbox in seconds.

Fear possesses her, consumes her, overwhelms her. She struggles off her daughter's body and runs in terror to the door of the sanctuary. There is a hallway and an exit at the side of the house.

She throws open the door. The hallway is clear, only a few wisps of smoke. Freedom and life are only ten yards away. She takes the first frantic step.

Then she remembers the face of the little girl a few moments after she emerged from the womb. Pretty even then once all the blood had been cleaned off her.

No. I will not permit her to die.

The sanctuary is filling with smoke. The stone floor, once so cold, is now unbearably hot, like sand on the beach on a ninety-degree day.

She gropes in the darkness and smoke for Laurel, finds her, and tears savagely at the bandages that bind the unconscious child. Three of them come away quickly. The fourth, tying her right hand to the metal ring set in the altar, refuses to budge.

She is now so tired, a humiliated and degraded mass of aches and pain, her muscles stiff and awkward, her leg cramped, her hand wet with her own blood. The smoke is thick around her. The door to the basement is alive with fire. When it goes, everything in the room will be consumed.

Armande will win.

No way.

She rips away the last bandage from Laurel's hands and pulls her unconscious and heavy daughter by her shoulders off the altar and on to the floor.

Laurel lands with a heavy thud.

Sorry, kid.

With strength she does not believe she has, she grasps Laurel underneath her shoulders and drags her toward the hallway.

In the distance she hears the sound of fire engines. They've come to it early, she thinks, but I'll never make

it to the door. I'm too tired, too weak, too beat.

She pulls Laurel's body halfway into the hallway. The door from the basement explodes and fire and thick smoke race into the sanctuary like a herd of hungry scarlet wolves.

With a mighty heave she drags Laurel out of the room and slams the door shut, a temporary barrier to the spreading fire.

It is only ten yards to the exit, but Laurel is so heavy, the fire so hot, the smoke so thick, and Sue so tired that it seems like ten miles.

She despairs a thousand times but never quits. She is only a foot or two from the exit when the door from the sanctuary blows up and the wolf pack of fire races toward her again.

She lunges against the exit; the big oak door does not budge. She lunges again and it spins open grudgingly. She pulls Laurel to her feet and with one final burst of energy and hope stumbles onto the little porch and topples toward the two stairs to the sidewalk. Firemen in black and yellow suits drench them instantly with water. It feels cold and clean and good. Like Lake Michigan in the morning. A child in a sailor's suit and three men wait at the stairs, anxious and astonished. One is Lawrence. She hands him Laurel, a charge to be protected. The second is a thin handsome man with silver hair and a warm smile. The third is a round little priest.

Her vision is blurred. Perhaps she is going to die. A new videotape is put on in the back of her brain. Black and white, not color. Old film.

No, not a priest at all. An elfin boy child at 93rd and Glenwood, looking up in admiration at the sixth-grade crossing guard. She is probably dying, maybe even dead. But she is a sixth-grader again.

"Oh, hi, Blackie."

She collapses at their feet.

55

BLACKIE

The three of them sat around my coffee table, a quiet little network of tenuous meekness. I might destroy that network in a few moments or provide it with more strength. There was, however, no choice. They all needed truth.

Lawrence and Sue were sipping, very cautiously, from glasses of Jameson's (twelve-year special reserve, greater love than this. . .). Laurel was playing with a Diet Pepsi.

At first I was constrained to recommend courses for Sue to take in Loyola's philosophy department. She clung to the catalog the way a little girl would cling to her dolly. Her tan suit and thin beige sweater, mannish in their style and cut as the fashion section of the *New York Times* had demanded a week ago, said "college professional." Labor Day sun and makeup obscured her pallor.

"Who's Whitehead?" she asked. Suzie lingered, helpless and confused in the face of public acclaim for heroism and the horrors of registration day. But Sue she was at night, doubtless the first night out of the hospital, and Sue she was determined to be in the day.

"Process philosopher. God is process. Fellow pilgrim who suffers."

"Neat!"

"Would you listen to Betty Coed?" Laurel snickered. "Getting ready for her sophomore slump. Well, you won't have to worry about your freshmen fifteen anyway."

243

"Freshmen fifteen?" Her mother removed her glasses to consider this threat.

"Sure, freshmen always put on fifteen pounds. Maybe since it's been so long"—Laurel considered the possibility with wicked delight—"you'll put on fifteen even if you're not a freshman anymore."

"Gross," Larry murmured.

"If that happens, it will be Lent all year round." Sue's jaw jutted confidently. "Forty and more I may be, but I'll never be fat and forty."

"It'd be funny for a week or two," Laurel giggled, not wishing to give up her joke. Sue, preoccupied by registration-day anxiety, ignored her daughter's good-natured taunt and returned to the catalog. The freshmen fifteen was a distant problem. Registration was an immediate difficulty.

Laurel's smoky eyes rarely left her mother, on whom she now gazed always with fascinated adoration. She too was clad in the professional garb, in light blue. Walking down Michigan Avenue in the week-after-Labor-Day golden glow, they might have passed from a distance for sisters in their middle twenties—when Laurel was not slouching.

Larry watched these two women, currently very much in his custody, with amused admiration. He was more relaxed and more cheerful than he had been in his early visits to the Cathedral Rectory. Clearly the joys of physical sex in his life had not diminished. More likely increased.

Laurel was out of Billings Hospital in a day. Tom Burke, Biddy Murphy, O'Connor The Cat, and their band of Merry Persons had appeared that night at "Flavs'" (as she was now called) bedside, as if they had heard Robin sounding his horn from the middle of Sherwood Forest. They frustrated all attempts by the hospital administration and security force to eject them.

The doctors decided to get rid of Flavs partly because she was unharmed and partly because they wanted to send her horde of Irish Catholic adolescents as far from the hospital as they possibly could.

The University of Chicago Hospitals, admirable institutions that they are, have no experience dealing with a
faerie horde, the Tuatha Dé Danann trooping out of an-
tiquity.

Sue was released five days later, pronounced both
physically and mentally well by the doctors. Larry kept
her there a few extra days till the media publicity abat-
ed. I gave him the tape and the documents, which both
the women saw at once. We had a private Mass in the
chapel at Mount Carmel as Wolfe Quinlan's casket was
reinterred in the family burial plot. Somewhat surpris-
ingly, Kevin attended.

I gave them a week to relax before risking the moment of truth.

"There are a few things we still have to clear up." I
refilled my glass and gave myself a number of points for
not saying "one or two questions" like they do in the
English mystery stories. "First of all, the poltergeist
phenomena that involved me in the first place."

Silence.

Then a sheepish smile from the now slouching Laurel,
who in such a posture looked too young for her clothes.

"You know I did that, Uncle Blackie."

"Laurel!" her mother exclaimed.

"I mean, I couldn't help it. The last night I did it in my
sleep. That's why I left. I didn't want to set the house on
fire like the chick in *Carrie* or something like that."

Not quite the whole truth. The literature says that the
adolescent (usually but not always female) who pro-
duces poltergeist manifestations has some control over
them. But enough of the truth.

"Well, like, I knew I did a few things like that when I
was a real little girl. They scared me. Then I saw *Carrie*
and it really freaked me out. I read a book on it and it
said that this power faded away, like, when you were
fifteen or so. I was kinda mad at you, Mom, because
Daddy died and I thought it was your fault, but I didn't
want to hurt you bad or anything like that. So I split. I
hope it won't happen again. I'll try real hard...."

Sue rose to the occasion with impressive meekness.

"Oh, honey"—she embraced her daughter—"I think it's neat to have a little girl that's psychic."

"Bigger than you are." Larry laughed.

"Only taller," Sue countered and then blushed.

They all laughed heartily. Laurel murmured "Betty Coed" again as her mother released her.

I refrained from all comment on the subject of comparative chest measurements.

First test passed with flying colors. Now the hard one.

"There is, finally, the matter of the murder of Wolfe Quinlan."

Silence as deep as in Mount Carmel Cemetery at midnight.

"But, Father Armande... I mean, the papers all said..." Suzie put in a brief, helpless appearance.

"Father Armande was out of his mind." Larry rubbed his face with his hands, as though he saw the joy vanishing from his life.

"May I proceed with a scenario of what happened?" I removed Larry's chart from my briefcase, which was leaning against a leg of the coffee table (Sue had promised she would redo my parlor, giving it a much more Dickensian atmosphere).

They all nodded sadly.

"First of all, I am not an officer of either the police or the court. I see no need to raise any questions with law enforcement agencies in Indiana. We still need the truth, both as a basis for further living and as a protection from anyone else stumbling on the same scenario. Understood?"

They nodded again, no more happily.

"Sometime after you left the study, Sue, and your late husband elected not to follow you—though he could have because as far as is on the record, you had no way to lock the door from the connecting bathroom and he did—there was a final visitor to the study, one who had been there before, because everyone had been there before. The visitor may have come at an invitation from Wolfe or *sua sponte,* as we say in the mother tongue.

"There was a discussion. It became at some point an

altercation. The visitor for reasons we may postpone shoved Tancredi from his pedestal on the person of Wolfe Quinlan, who, at the moment, was either prone on the work table or rising from it.

"Wolfe Quinlan bled to death. The killer—I use the term without implying moral or legal guilt, nor dispensing as yet from either—is terrified. The threat of public exposure and explanation is intolerable. The killer makes the first of two ingenious improvised decisions. The keys to the closet are on the work table, in their usual position. The killer wants to hide. Since the earth does not open, the only other thing is to grab the keys, snatch up certain evidence, and run to the closet. Perhaps the closet is already unlocked. Perhaps the keys are brought in case it is locked. Perhaps already the killer has seen the wisdom of locking the closet from the inside. Or perhaps the killer merely wants to escape forever. These matters are unimportant.

"The door is battered down. The horrible sight is observed. Various parties are sent on their assignments. The killer now has a second and even more brilliant inspiration, one that requires the cool courage that comes from despair.

"The closet door is gingerly unlocked and opened. The killer peers out. The horrid embrace on the work table is still there. But no one is in the room. Moreover, no one can be seen from the closet in the doorway or the corridor. The killer decides to risk it.

"First, it is necessary to slip along the wall, holding the evidence—see how I trace it here on the chart, and into the bathroom. The killer, perhaps with the plan unrolling a fraction of a step ahead of the killer's movement, unlocks the door to the master bedroom—always presuming it was locked. . . ."

"I tried it." Larry Burke looked up at me with hard eyes.

"Indeed. In any case the killer opens the door to the master bedroom, sets the bolt so it will lock when it is closed, props the door open with a convenient maroon wastebasket that waits under the sink, and scurries back into the study, still out of sight and still undiscovered.

"Is the closet locked now or has it been locked already? My guess is that the killer is running on overdrive, fueled by horror and panic, and is elaborating the plan with each passing step. The closet therefore is unlocked until the killer returns from the bathroom.

"What next? The killer cannot keep the keys. Put them on the table? Then someone else may figure out the plan. No. It takes great courage to creep near the dead body and slide the keys into the pocket of the dead man's gown. The killer pauses perhaps, sick with horror at the sight of the corpse, and frightened of capture. Nonetheless, the deed is done. The keys are deposited. Still carrying the terribly incriminating evidence, the killer hurries into the bathroom, kicks aside the wastebasket and plunges into the master bedroom. The door closes. The locked-room illusion is maintained. The killer then disposes of the evidence and joins the converging group at the head of the stairs. An extraordinary performance, don't you think, Sue?"

"It wasn't me." She was slumped over, playing nervously with her Loyola catalog. "It really wasn't. I was in the kitchen phoning for a priest."

"You know it wasn't her, Uncle Blackie." Laurel was sitting up straight now, a woman again. "You're just giving me a chance to admit that I killed him. You know I did it, but thanks for permitting me to say it first. Yes, I loved him more than anyone else, and I killed him."

"You dashed through your mother's room. She didn't see you because, as she says, she was on the phone downstairs. Then you went through the bathroom that connects her room to yours. Next you disposed of the evidence, took a certain action, and permitted yourself to be roused from your feigned sleep and to be led into the corridor. A heavy sleeper you were said to be, but you were awakened by the noises in your mother's room during the poltergeist phenomenon."

"I was, like, causing those. But it doesn't matter."

"As to the evidence"—I reached into my briefcase

and removed a dark green Dartmouth College woman's sleep T-shirt, torn from top to bottom—"I knew this had to be somewhere because you were wearing it when you and Tom were talking on the balcony. Yet you reappeared after you were awakened in a short blue T-shirt, University of Michigan doubtless, which was much less modest. In your rush, you grabbed for whatever was available and pulled it over your head, not noticing until it was too late that it was a regular shirt and not a sleep shirt."

She nodded her calm agreement. "I knew I should have burned that one, but I, like, tried to forget the whole thing, even to pretend I didn't do it."

"To have destroyed it would have been a terrible mistake, Laurel," I said as gently as I could. "One of the main reasons for this meeting today is so that I can apologize for searching through your personal belongings. Incidentally, may I congratulate you on a standard of neatness that is rare among your generation. Even this garment was neatly folded. Indeed, it was your reputation for fastidiousness, doubtless inherited from your mother, that led me to both hope and fear you would retain the torn shirt in its appropriate place. I justify my intolerable behavior on the grounds that I feared that if the evidence was of the sort I had expected it to be, you might have destroyed it or might eventually destroy it. That would have been a tragic mistake. This bit of fabric and our interpretation of it is your best defense should anyone else figure out your astonishing puzzle." I passed the torn green cotton to Sue. "Indeed, so effective would it be that the matter would quickly be dropped."

I did not say what great relief I experienced when I discovered the T-shirt was torn.

"Honey." Sue had removed her glasses from her purse and was examining the sleep shirt. "Why is it torn?"

Laurel looked at me questioningly. I nodded.

"He tried to rape me," she said dully. "I mean he knocked at the door of my room about a quarter to two, woke me out of a very deep sleep, Uncle Blackie"—she managed a quick grin—"and asked me to help him finish up with the stones. I was so cashed that I hardly realized what I was doing. So I rubbed my eyes and went after him. When we were inside the museum, I realized that he'd been drinking again and was really cashed out of it. I was like scared, but he wouldn't open the door.

"Then, well, he pulled off my shirt and began to play with me. I. . . I didn't stop him at first because I was so afraid of him and because I loved him so much. Then I said to myself this has gotta stop. So I kicked him and ran around the work table. He came after me, grinning and laughing, and grabbed me again. I pushed him away as hard as I could and he fell back on the table. I jumped up on the stand with Tancredi, trying to hide behind him, I guess—by then I was out of my mind. He jumped up from the table and I, well, you know what I did, Uncle Blackie. I pushed Tancredi down on him. I didn't think it would, like, kill him. It was an accident. I panicked because I knew I'd have to explain what he was doing. I wanted to protect him from that. Everything else was the way you said, Uncle Blackie."

"Did not such protection of your father put you in grave danger, both legally and emotionally?" I asked as softly as I could.

She shrugged her huddled shoulders. "What difference did that make? I had to protect him from what people would say, didn't I?"

"But not protect yourself?"

"I'm not worth that much." Her face was stony, her eyes dry.

"That's a pretty geeky thing to say, young woman."

She smiled thinly. "I guess it is, Uncle Blackie. Kathleen O'Connor would tell me that I was a total dork." She took a deep breath. "It's not true. I am worth something. Maybe even a lot."

So the child's name was Kathleen? Spaced-out Laurel would know that and no one else would. Perhaps. . .

Missing the nuances completely, Sue leaped to her feet, ramrod stiff, eyes blazing. "How did you know he was trying to rape you, you bloody little bitch?"

Now the moment of truth.

Laurel slouched into her chair, as if she were wishing once again the earth would consume her. She glanced at me, implying, "See, it's always this way."

"Because he had done it before. I can't remember a time when he didn't paw me a lot. He loved me more than anyone else and I guess things were confused in his head. I knew it wasn't quite right, but I didn't understand. Then... do I have to, Uncle Blackie?..."

"Yes."

"All right... Well, when I was like in sixth grade and had started to wear a bra, you know, Mom, younger than most of the kids, he... Oh, God... he made love to me. Maybe five or six times. When he was cashed. I don't know even if he remembered the next day. I didn't... I didn't understand it much, but I was scared and I felt, well, used. Then when he stopped drinking, it never happened again. I told myself it was all a dream. Kind of funny, isn't it? Father Armande didn't have a virgin to immolate after all."

"Why didn't you tell me?" Suzie—for it was totally her now—thundered. "Why in God's name didn't you tell me?"

"I tried to, you stupid bitch!" Laurel exploded from her chair, screaming with rage. "I tried every way I could. You wouldn't listen. You didn't want to hear me. You were afraid of what I might be trying to say. You didn't know how to control him. It's all your fault."

"I don't remember." Suzie was sobbing, searching in her purse for a tissue. "I don't remember."

"Of course not." Laurel was pitiless. "You tuned me out completely, so there was nothing to remember."

Suzie pressed her hands against her temples, trying to recapture a conversation that would have been meaningless to her even if she could recall it.

"Your mother had a lot on her mind," Larry said very quietly.

"I don't care. I don't care!" One more touch of emotion and Laurel would be so hysterical we would have to take her to a hospital. Dear God, help them. Response:

It's in your court, Blackie Ryan.

"You don't care what?" I demanded.

She hesitated. The whole world, their whole world, hung in dread suspense. Say something, Blackie, you geek.

"Don't dork out, Flavs," I shouted at her, "and blow it."

"Oh, Uncle Blackie." The air went out of her balloon. "I mean, I don't care what happened, I still think my mother is like totally awesome."

Then the two women were in each other's arms, laughing and crying and hugging and kissing. "I'm sorry, honey, so terribly sorry," Sue murmured into her daughter's shoulder.

"I love you, Mommy." Laurel's long arms lifted her mother off the ground. "I love you."

Larry Burke watched as though he were at the most solemn moment of the old Benediction of the Blessed Sacrament ceremony.

Meekness had won by a hair's breadth, which is about all it can ever expect.

Larry put his arms around both of them. Two arms, one blue coated, the other tan, emerged to include him in their embrace.

Laurel and Sue would continue to fight. That's the way God designed mothers and daughters because, I suspect, She enjoys watching a good fight now and again. Nonetheless, their love would endure and flourish.

"He said, 'Sorry, kid,' when Tancredi hit him," Laurel murmured through her tears. "I think he looked relieved just before he died."

There were many ironies in the fire. Wolfe Tone Quinlan had died at the hands of the two women he loved most in the world. When Sue threatened to leave him and rejected his advances, hurt and angry, he turned to the bottle. Then, more mellow and still wanting affection, he summoned Laurel, probably with no conscious intention of forcing sex upon her. Lonely and frustrated and not realizing completely what he was about, he tried to satisfy his sexual needs and his human pain with her.

He had matured sufficiently to break with Father Armande at his wife's instigation, yet that break had set in motion a series of circumstances that led to his death. Sue's incipient maturity saved her husband from Armande but later killed him.

I trusted that the two women would not reflect in any great detail on these ironies. I certainly was not about to mention them.

"I'm sorry. I fucked up again." A fitting epitaph for Wolfe Tone Quinlan, but also perhaps sentiments that won him salvation.

He was not the first nor would he be the last father to do so. God help us all, we must protect young women not only from rapists on the street and random religious nuts like Father Armande but many of them from their own parents. Laurel would spend the rest of her life fighting with ugly memories.

For Laurel our hopes would be necessarily cautious. She had been badly scarred. The scars would remain with her for the rest of her life. She would suffer under enormous and permanent psychological handicaps.

She would not be cured of them. Perhaps she could transcend them.

We had another drink, Laurel asking for an "Uncle Blackie chocolate sundae," and came down gently from our emotional high. There was much pain lurking behind the smiling, tear-stained faces. Mary Kate would soon, I was sure, be asked for help. I was hugged and kissed fittingly and the promise to refurnish my room raised to solemn status. I required that Lawrence F. X. Burke keep his promise about returning to Mass on Sunday.

"I may not be alone at the rail." He looked at me questioningly.

"I leave judgments in these matters to God."

It would be worked out in due course. That the Holy Spirit wanted me to separate them or forbid them the Eucharist seemed, on the face of it, absurd. The Holy

Spirit is neither a canon lawyer nor a bureaucrat in a curial dicastery. For which we all must be profoundly grateful.

As I showed them to the door of the rectory, he hung back for a brief word with me.

"What caused the rappings in the cabinet and the movements of the video camera?" he asked. "Laurel wasn't there then, was she?"

"Ah."

The temperature in the dark hallway seemed to drop about twenty degrees.

"We cannot explain it as a poltergeist phenomenon, can we?"

"I don't see how."

"That sends a chill through me." He shivered in support of his words.

"Tell me about it."

We walked in silence, each with our own thoughts, to the rectory door. I was kissed again and promised that, God willing, I would see them soon.

"I'll be all right, Uncle Blackie," Laurel promised me with a fierce hug. "You just watch."

She hugged her mother and Larry again for good measure.

"Of course you will," Sue said with grim determination. "Totally."

The three of them, Sue in the middle, guarded by her two protectors as she approached her fabled sophomore slump twenty-four years late, walked happily north on Wabash, toward Chicago Avenue, in the balmy warmth of their love and the warmth of the September sun. For the moment no dark and evil bird lurked behind them.

In the memorable words of O'Connor The Cat, "Summer is over but life goes on."

FROM <u>WHO'S WHO</u>

Ryan, John Blackwood. Priest, philosopher; born Evergreen Park, Il., September 17, 1945; s.R.Ad. Edward Patrick Ryan, USNR (ret.) and Kate Collins; A.B., St. Mary of the Lake Seminary, 1966; STL, St. Mary of the Lake Seminary, 1970; Ph.D., Seabury Western Theological Seminary, 1980. Ordained priest, Roman Catholic Church, 1970; Ass't. Pator, St. Fintan's Church, Chicago, 1970-1978; Instructor, classics, Quigley Seminary 1970-1978; Rector, Holy Name Cathedral 1978- ;created Domestic Prelate (Monsignor) 1983. Author: *Salvation in Process: Catholicism and the Philosophy of Alfred North Whitehead, 1980; Truth in William James: An Irishman's Best Guess*, 1985. Mem. Am. Philos. Asc.,- Soc. Sci. Stud. Rel., Chicago Yacht Club. Address: Holy Name Cathedral Rectory, 732 North Wabash, Chicago, IL 60611.

SPECIAL BONUS

The Prologue to
Andrew M. Greeley's
Next Blackie Ryan Mystery

HAPPY ARE THE CLEAN OF HEART

to be published
in September 1986
by WARNER BOOKS

PROLOGUE

Murder, I thought with a wry smile, is as delicious as the taste of white chocolate mousse.

Mentally I savored the picture of the lovely face collapsing under the impact of savage blows, coming apart like the face of a statue being devastated by a hammer and chisel. Or the mound of delectable white chocolate mousse being sliced up with a spoon. Human bones cracked more easily than did marble statues. The fog, rolling in rapidly from the dark, grim-faced lake, became bloodred in my mind's eye. Tonight was the final chance, the last opportunity to discharge the hatred of so many years. I turned away from the lake and walked slowly up Delaware Street. The fog drifted ahead, leading the way.

Many times had the image of the face shattering under savage blows brought cleansing peace at the end of a bitter and anxious day. It had been a fantasy at first, harmless if hateful daydreaming. As my sense of outraged injustice grew and festered, the fantasy became richer and more demanding. In dreams, often, I did destroy that offensively lovely face, having first brutally beaten and tormented the victim's body. In the morning, before full consciousness, I was often not certain whether it had only been a dream.

What had been a pleasant fantasy gradually became an emotional and physical necessity. Lisa must die if I were to survive. That ought to have been clear long ago. Now it was so obvious that I wondered how there could ever have been any doubt.

Moreover, tonight murder was absolutely safe. They would never know. The door would open, a quick blow of the cosh to her jaw to stun, a jab with a hypodermic syringe would render her silent but not unconscious, then a leisurely but savage beating and sexual violation and, even more pleasurable, the final destruction of that hated face. A few quick blows to the head and all would be finished. I could slip out of the hotel room, ride down in the elevator, dispose of the disguise, and walk freely away in the fog-shrouded streets of the city.

It was all so easy, once you had the courage and the imagination.

God, I thought, licking saliva, how sweet revenge would be.

Most of the John Hancock Center was hiding in the fog, neither seeing nor seen. Across the street, in front of the white brick Westin Hotel, tongues of fog licking at its cream logo and gray awnings, long lines of travelers waited patiently for taxis and buses to take them to O'Hare, like concentration camp victims waiting for the gas chambers. Still encased in the fog, I avoided the main entrance of the hotel and entered at the door across from the entrance to the Hancock apartments. How like Lisa to try to hide incognito in an inexpensive hotel instead of staying at the Whitehall down the street, where she belonged. Or the Mayfair Regent over on the lake. In either she would have been as safe as a cloistered Carmelite behind her double grill.

I crossed Michigan Avenue and walked a half a block toward Rush Street before turning around and strolling along the construction site where the 900 North Michigan building used to be. Typical of the city to destroy such a landmark. Whore city.

Should anyone see the dark-clad figure slipping through the fog, it would be thought that perhaps I was some pervert drifting over from Old Town. My disguise, easy and simple, would confirm such a suspicion.

I hesitated at the Michigan Avenue entrance of the hotel. Stupid fool, don't go in that way. Why walk the whole length of the lobby? Walk by the main entrance and go to the second entrance on Delaware, across from the door to the Hancock condos. How dumb can you get?

Shaken by the near mistake, I breathed deeply before entering the revolving door. Take it easy, relax. This is fun, not work.

Lots of fun.

Inside, the hotel was a mix of chandeliers, mirrors, and marble—fake Versailles—with a curved, free-standing staircase to the second floor. A long line of exhausted travelers were waiting, like kids in a rock concert ticket line, to check in.

I ducked into a washroom and quickly adjusted the final details of a disguise, no longer a pervert, now a person of mystery but completely respectable. Male or female? Those who saw me would hesitate, not quite sure. Before leaving the security provided by the door of the stall, I caressed the cosh lovingly, solid oak covered with hand-tooled leather. It would do its savage and brutal work efficiently—first the nose, then the cheekbones, then the jaw, then the eyes, and then the final crushing blows into the temples and the forehead.

The excitement of vengeance and execution heightened my sensations, particularly the sense of smell— liquor in the bar, human sweat crowded around the registration desk, cigarette smoke hanging in the lobby, the indefinable aroma of illicit sex that seemed to flourish in all hotels.

Often I had imagined slashing her face with a razor-sharp little knife, but crushing it seemed somehow more satisfactory, although the knife was still available underneath the belt of my black trousers. Obliterate it, wipe it out, crush forever her offensively piquant eyes, her marvelous cheekbones, her pert nose, her lightly smiling mouth, her cute little chin; eliminate Lisa's hateful beauty forever from the face of the earth with savage, brutal, pitiless blows.

Thinking about it was like imagining sex a few moments before you met your lover.

Lisa finally had gone too far. All else might have been forgiven. What she had done now deserved death, clamored for death, insisted on death.

My mouth jammed shut, fingers clenched, teeth gritted. No, I must not lose control now. Save the pleasure for afterward, when the job is done. Orgasm should occur at the end of sex, not at the start of foreplay.

In the lobby, I looked around and smiled. Anonymity was easy in the busy rush of the middle-range executive and convention hotel. I picked up the phone and softly whispered Lisa's room number. There was no answer. Where could she be? She had not gone out, of that I was sure. Why was she taking so long? Typical of the woman's stupidity and incompetence.

"Ms. Malone," said the bright, cheerful voice, loved by tens of millions of Americans.

I spoke softly.

"Oh, sorry to have kept you waiting." A giggle. "I was in the shower, singing in the shower, if you can imagine that. Come on up. I'll mix you a drink."

That would be useful, I thought, permitting myself a faint smile. Sip the drink slowly and luxuriously, describing to the temporarily paralyzed woman exactly what you were going to do to her, amusing yourself sexually and inflicting delicious pain as a prelude to even more terrible agony.

Again I fought to regain self-control.

I boarded the elevator as quietly as a cat slips into a kitchen and lightly touched the button. Two fat, tipsy businessmen shoved the doors open just as they were closing, raucous Willy Lomans, caricatures from a *New Yorker* cartoon. At first I paid them no attention. Then with dismay I realized they had not pressed a button. They were going to the same floor. It did not matter, of course, it did not matter. No one would know what happened until tomorrow morning, and the businessmen would perhaps be on planes flying home before the news reached the papers. They were sufficiently inebriated that they would not remember their companion on the ride to the fourth floor. Even if they did, my disguise was brilliantly effective for all its simplicity.

Yet, nevertheless, I hesitated, an airline pilot inspecting a dubious weather report. The risks were higher now, not very high, but still higher than they had been. The probability that others would get off on the fourth floor had been considered, weighed, evaluated, and then dismissed as not important; theoretical probabilities, I was discovering, were not as disturbing as actual dangers.

The businessmen turned in the direction of Lisa's room. I turned in the opposite direction, walking the full length of the corridor until the sound of their noisy laughter was shut out abruptly by the harsh clang of a slamming door. I hesitated, facing the wall at the end of the corridor, heart beating rapidly, mouth now parched, nerves as tense as the strings on a harp. To the left were the exit stairs. I need only follow the carefully conceived escape plan. Step out into the stairwell, quickly shed the unisexual disguise, stuff it in the small carrying bag, walk down the stairs to the third floor, board the elevator, descend to the lobby. Perhaps it would be satisfaction enough to dream tonight once again of what might have happened, revel again in the fantasies of make-believe pleasure, pretend for a few hours, at any rate, that Lisa had been destroyed.

If they ever found out . . .

Most journalists hated Lisa so much that they wanted to do to her what I intended to do. They were merely less honest with themselves about their feelings. But if Lisa were killed, brutally, savagely, mercilessly, the media would have no pity on her murderer, no bail, no psychiatric excuses from standing trial, no favorable coverage of last-minute vigils at Cook County Jail before the switch was thrown on the electric chair. Lisa

Malone's killer would be hounded into the grave, even if they secretly felt that the destruction of that evil woman was utterly appropriate.

I considered very carefully. The chances of exposure had only been increased minimally by the two businessmen on the elevator. Indeed, that possibility had already been considered, had it not, and been discounted? Why hesitate now when it might be weeks or months or even years before there was another similar opportunity?

Finally, so what? A world in which Lisa Malone continued to exist was by no means to be preferred to death. It was intolerable that Lisa should live. If her death meant my death, then so be it.

I turned and walked calmly, confidently, down the empty corridor to Room 403 and knocked on the door, the smooth feel of the cosh providing strength and vigor to the knock.

There was a wait, almost as long as in the lobby. The fool had gone back into the shower.

Finally, the door opened slightly and Lisa's eyes and nose appeared, freckled with drops of water.

"Well, hello." She threw the door open. "What are you doing dressed up like that? Come in, come in!" She threw her arms around me. "It's wonderful to see you!"

I was filled with love for my victim, the same sweet, soft, mellow affection that Lisa always produced in me, melting away anger and tension and frustration. Destroying Lisa would be an act of hatred, but also an act of love.

She was wearing a white terry-cloth robe, hastily thrown around her slim, elegant body. Her midnight-black hair was pasted against her head, framing her ethereally delicate face. She smelled of soap and shampoo. I worshiped her, adored her, loved her.

Lisa, sensing the passion of the embrace, tried to ease gracefully away. My love would not be denied. Ever so gently and delicately the cosh banged into the side of Lisa's head.

Her eyes widened in surprise and then in stunned

disorientation. I lowered her carefully to the floor, gently peeled back the shoulder of her robe, removed the hypodermic syringe from the bag while Lisa shook her head as though to clear her vision and struggled for consciousness and articulation.

I jabbed the needle into her arm and pushed the plunger.

Lisa cried out, not loudly, but enough to frighten me. I stifled her scream with a firm gloved hand.

The drug took effect quickly, as it was supposed to. Lisa's body relaxed. Her eyes became glazed. She lay on the floor confused, tranquil, and helpless.

I picked up the drink that had been prepared on the coffee table. Yes, of course, Lisa would remember what kind of drink it would be at this hour of the day. I was exhilarated, sky-high. Murder was the most powerful aphrodisiac. Slowly, for now there was all the time in the world, I sipped the drink and then placed it on the coffee table.

"Don't go away," I said to Lisa with a giggle and went into the bathroom and turned on the shower, adjusting the temperature so the water was the hottest possible.

"Scalding water." I returned to the parlor of Lisa's suite and picked up the drink again. "That comes later."

I drained the glass and then filled it up again with the materials that Lisa had thoughtfully prepared. Then I sat down on the sofa, beside which Lisa was lying, passive, beautiful, powerless. Slowly, gently, tenderly, I removed her terry-cloth robe, loving preparation by a pagan pirate for the ravishing of a frightened Christian matron.

Such a lovely body, slim, lithe, yet intensely erotic. Marvelous breasts, full yet neatly sculpted. Perhaps eventually the knife should be used. All in good time.

I lit a cigarette, puffed on it leisurely, and then delicately pressed the glowing tip to the smooth skin on Lisa's belly, savoring the sweet swell of burning human flesh.

Lisa tried to scream. All that emerged from her lips was a soft whimper.

Her eyes dulled with pain and then looked at me with a mute plea for mercy, a plea that faded into resignation. Almost as though she had expected her death sentence and was resigned to it. A single tear appeared in each eye.

I willed hardness of heart. Now was no time for pity.

"Timelessly beautiful"—I laughed—"just as they say in the papers. You and I are going to have ourselves a very interesting evening, Lisa Malone."

Drink in one hand, I began to fondle Lisa with the other, caressing and hurting at the same time. "Do I see a touch of fear in those lovely, if glazed, blue eyes of yours?" I kissed her lightly on the lips. "Well, there's nothing to be afraid about, Lisa dear, not for a while, anyway. Let me go through the agenda and tell you exactly what I'm going to do to you."

I twisted one of her beautiful breasts viciously. Lisa's attempt to shriek with pain was only a faint whimper.

"And let me tell you the ending first. After everything else is over, and after I've had all the fun I possibly can with you"—I held up the cosh—"I'm going to smash your brains out!"